MOUNTAIN

A NOVEL BY

ROBERT KUNCIO-RALEIGH

"Mountain," by Robert Kuncio-Raleigh. ISBN 978-1-949756-78-4 (softcover); 978-1-949756-79-1 (eBook).

Published 2019 by Virtualbookworm.com Publishing Inc., P.O. Box 9949, College Station, TX 77842, US. ©2019, Robert Kuncio-Raleigh.

All rights reserved. No part of this publication may be reproduced, stored in a retrieval system, or transmitted in any form or by any means, electronic, mechanical, recording or otherwise, without the prior written permission of Robert Kuncio-Raleigh.

For Sara

My love, my helpmate, my friend,

and the kindest person I know

> Somebody must show that the Afro-American race
> is more sinned against than sinning,
> and it seems to have fallen upon me to do so.
> *Ida B. Wells*

🍂 🍂 🍂

> The wind was a torrent of darkness
> among the gusty trees,
> The moon was a ghostly galleon
> tossed upon cloudy seas,
> The road was a ribbon of moonlight
> over the purple moor,
> And the highwayman came riding— riding—riding—
> The highwayman came riding, up to the old inn-door.
> *Alfred Noyes*

Contents

Money and Value
In the Eighteenth Century VII

The Plain and Compleyte Life of Joseph Mountain 1758-1789

Chapter 1 1
Chapter 2 11
Chapter 3 33
Chapter 4 57
Chapter 5 75
Chapter 6 99
Chapter 7 115
Chapter 8 129
Chapter 9 153
Chapter 10 173
Chapter 11 193
Chapter 12 213
Chapter 13 235
Chapter 14 255
Chapter 15 267

Author's Note 283
Acknowledgements 286

Money and Value
In the Eighteenth Century

Some notes on British money and valuation between the eighteenth century and the present are necessary to understand the subjects of robberies, slavery, and day-to-day living in this story. This is a generalized guide meant to give you a rough idea for those contexts; nothing more. If you desire a more in-depth discussion, almost any search on the web will provide you with the detail. Use the terms *"18th Century British Money and Value"* in your search.

British money has been digitized, but the various denominations referred to (and colonial denominations) stem from Roman tradition and are the same as in previous times.

One pound (£) = 20 shillings
One crown = ¼ pound (5 s.)
One shilling = 12 pence
One guinea = 21 s.

A guinea was considered a more gentlemanly amount than a pound for payment in services, being more conveniently portable. It was a gold coin, not a note, and amounted to one shilling more than a pound. If one paid a workman, it was in shillings or notes; if one paid off a bet or another gentleman, it was in guineas. Pennies were coppers and the smallest denomination. Pennies were abbreviated *d.*; shillings *s.*; and pounds £. *Quid* is slang for a pound. *Bob* is slang for a shilling.

Valuation

A middle-class person, it is estimated, could live a no-frills existence on £1,10 s. a week, or keep a household, exclusive of lodging. Some say one should multiply the money then by approximately 75 to 100 times to get today's value, so £ 100 would equal £7500 to £10000.

At the time of this writing, the English pound was worth $1.40 = £1. 1 shilling = $.07. Some estimate 1 shilling in 1760 would be worth 20 of today's pounds, or $28.00. Because value is so difficult to assess accurately over time, just choose one of the methods above, or make the equivalence of $1 in the eighteenth century approximately equal to $30 today.

That means Thomas Mifflin gave a stipend to Joseph of £65 x 100 x 1.40, or $9100, for his trip abroad.

A wealthy plantation owner might make £1000 a year. A pair of fancy shoe buckles would cost £1; silk handkerchief 8 s.; playing cards 7 1/2d.; a pair of plain pistols £3, 15d. A supper of bread, cheese, and beer 3d.; dinner of meat, bread, and a pint of porter 6-7d.; a fine dinner 1 s. Chicken at Vauxhall 2s. 6d.; beef cold at Vauxhall 1 s.; enough gin to get drunk 1d.; to get totally besotted 2 to 3d.; a bottle of wine 5s. A pound of coffee 4 to 6s.; a pound of tea 7 to 16s.; Champagne at Vauxhall 8s.

A working woman's gown 6s. 6d.; petticoat 4s. 6d.; stays 6s.; a clerk's suit of clothes £4 10s.; a man's plain suit of clothes £6 to £8. One could get a silver watch for £5 5s.

Suffice it to say, Joseph's occupation yielded plenty to live on very well—if one had few vices.

The Plain and Compleyte Life of Joseph Mountain 1758-1789

Chapter 1

It is 1787.
Joseph Mountain crews on the Lethe,
a slave ship bound for Jamaica.
On watch early evening, he has an epiphany,
and begins to write this journal.

The second dog watch. Almost silence. Only the wind and sinking darkness surround me as I keep my eyes on the sea. We are four days out of Ghana bound for Jamaica and Ste. Dominqué, where I intend to leave this loathsome ship and search for home. It was a year ago that I visited Jamaica, working as a mechanic and part time cook on another schooner—the *Fanny*—captained by Mister Sinclair. She was a pretty ship, like her name, fitted with new sails white as clouds and painted a green as dense as a deep forest. Tea, woolens, scotch whiskey, and rice, as well as small goods from British crafters, was our cargo. Jamaican planters would be enjoying those musky spirits now. The cloth would be comforting babies. We returned to Liverpool with rum, sugar, molasses, cotton, tobacco, and eight passengers, and not a woman among them. Their absence made me think on Mistress Sarah, Essie, and Nancy. It was strange to miss them.

All around me at Jelly Houses and card parlours, in the parks and on the streets of London, were a rainbow of women, once. But I missed Sarah's scolds, Molly's fritters, Essie's teasing, and Nancy's and Jenny's delicate young love.

The wind has changed; with it, its odor. This ship is a larger schooner than most—fleet, carrying three masts instead of two and able to run in good wind past some of the more belligerent brigs that roam the coasts of Africa and the Caribbean. And we carry a more valuable, though troublesome, cargo. At speed it sounds like a great cat, hissing through the water as the waves, white mice, flee in its wake. We are the *Lethe*, captained by a Portuguee called São Malno, who has nine years traveling to Cartagena, the Caribbean and Bahia, with a crew of eight. She is old, her wood lined and bored with the tracks of worms that have lived here for some ten years. Her brass is dull and pitted; her sails a patchwork of canvas and waxed threads. She has a gun just aft of the foremast, should we encounter the Barbarys. That is unlikely now that we are well into Atlantic waters south of the Cape Verdes. The *Lethe* is yare, but I shall not return on her.

I am sick of ocean adventures, piracy, my boyhood fantasies. There has been too much of them. They have filled and thieved my youth. Once, some ten years ago, the sea was an enticing adventure. Then I felt luck had bowed to me when I met Tom Wilson and Francis Hyde my first week abroad. When I joined them, I became a pirate of sorts, as I had dreamt; I had good friends and money; every day was a new exploration. I had been lucky enough to enjoy the trust of my associates and true freedom. And though, I'm certain, those men took me for a callow colonial—a true naïf—I soon proved my mettle and earned their respect. I slid into my profession as easily as this red sun now sinks into the sea.

It took me a time to learn and to be wary. All men are the same creature, civilized above, but feral under the skin. Whites were no better than others, though when I landed in London in 1775, I had lived my whole life with them. I was one of them except for my color. I had grown up in Philadelphia, which was an active mixed community. By then neither Pennsylvanians nor the British supported slavery, so when I walked the street in that town or in London, other than the color of my skin, there was no difference in the way I was treated. Only a few dared call me blackie, darky, Negro, or nigra boy. I knew them to be calumnies, but I had been taught by my adopted Quaker parents to disregard them and be a better person by doing so.

My 'parents', Thomas and Sarah, were eminent Quakers, well-respected, modestly well-off, learned, popular, and godly. They fostered this discarded Negro boy as their own and raised me to be a man who would be an asset in Philadelphia. I had even managed to be in the company of men who now are famous in the new country—Messers Jefferson, Franklin, Dickinson—when they visited Mister Mifflin at home the year before I left. I knew so little then about the world, nations, cities, the daily intercourse of men, or even true friendship.

When I landed in England, I soon learned. In London, Francis Hyde told me after that first robbery that I was a quick study. He had expected less, I'm certain, but I took his compliment as a goad to do my very best. Indeed, that night I made the first of a fortune that has grown and sustained me these years. I might have been a value to the community once, since I looked and comported myself as a gentleman, but I was more—the pirate of my dreams, a highwayman of some renown, an educated gambler, a burglar, sailor, and now, a slaver. A black slaver? Is there any logic in that? Yes, I am on the *Lethe,* and the *Lethe* is a slave ship. Now, surely my life has become a cat's paw knot, tied so tightly as to need some sharp device to cut it.

What have I learned? When I got on the ship *Chalkley* in May of '75, I was seventeen. I had been nicely attired and had been given a substantial stipend of £65 to start me on my tour of Europe, which Mister and Missus Mifflin had said would broaden my knowledge, especially of worldly manners. I had received tutoring in sciences, classics, French, Spanish, and knew how to play the fiddle and pipe, had been taught to ride and shoot a pistol, though being a Quaker I was warned that I might only use it for food or protection, but not against any man. I could fairly write and read, and indite a gracious letter. Having served in the family for many years as I was raised, I learned how the gentle class lives, and I learned too well. I had almost forgotten that Fling Mountain and Belle Lee, my true birth parents, were slaves, now free, but still living in Pennsylvania.

The wind has changed again. Last night it howled so mightily that the frequent crashes of thunder, lightning, and even St. Elmo's fire at the main masthead had some of the crew praying. I was. Yards and masts creaked with tiny screams as the great sails flailed and slammed against the wind. The stays thrummed like giant stringed instruments. Our cargo below my feet moaned and would have been moved to terror, had they seen the spectacle. Even still, they cried out in darkness. Those on deck were frozen in dread from the storm and waves washing over them. Fickle as the world is, tonight the breeze is fair, from the east, but it wavers. We still make good speed to the Carib. There is no comfort for the cargo when we run and heel, but 'tis a faster sail and closer to home. I have heard the old colonies, my old home, are now a brave new nation.

Our 'cargo' consists of 571 men, women, and children stored directly wherever there is space below the deck in two compartments, a space with barely room to move, like stuffed rags to fill the spaces. Those under the grates have some respite from the effluvium of odors. The smell is worse than any sty or London gutter I have ever known. New crew, as I am, gagged at first at its severity and retched, adding to the smell. On one side of the barricado on deck aft are some of the women; on the other, children and young men. These are shackled and watched closely for fear we will lose some to the sea, where many unfettered have been known to cast themselves. I sleep in a hammock on the after deck. I kept a cold eye on them at the beginning. Now my spirit has softened by their discomfort. Their suffering is always with me.

In the afternoons, we bring those below topside and feed them all an afternoon meal of salt pork or fish and horse beans. Any dead are thrown to the sharks. They also get their meal. Those who are very ill are sometimes treated, and then shackled and towed in a lifeboat, since we must quarantine any who may have the pox or plague. We clean as much as we can, but sea lice cover some of them like powder, so thick their skin appears to move twice when they are disturbed—humanly first, then with vermin. Our surgeon is a simple crew man who has medicines, but I would never seek his curative powers. Like a child, he imagines how to mix the colored powders and how much to dose, and gives the same for flea bites as for tumors. I expect with seasickness, bloody flux, pox, dehydration, malaria, and suffocation, we will have perhaps 320 nearly healthy slaves at voyage's end. Some, like Lazarus, will have to recover before the market. No crew man goes below except Jeb Burkin—a willful man—whose duty is to slop them out. Do that or he'd spend time in the brig for six days for his past sins. Cap'n is a smart one. When our weather is good, as it was fair today, we bring those who can stand up on deck without their shackles—albeit, well-guarded with pistols and cutlasses–to exercise, and of course, we include the prettiest of the women to dance for the crew. Some of the children who are stored aft or on the sides of the foredeck are also left free at these times to play, but we keep a lively eye on them, since two of our crew show a peculiar liking to the youngest boys and girls. Cap'n is hesitant to use the cat on any of the cargo. Only those especially ordered before the voyage have been branded with their owner's marks.

This is a desperate venture, though countless have taken the same voyage. The temperature below is hellish. Today, it was as bad topside. I drip sweat into the breeze. After tomorrow's assembly, we will wash the deck and use tobacco smoke to remove some of the stink. Yesterday, some who had fallen sick had thrown themselves into the sea to be eaten by the sharks that follow the ship for their dinner. One foretop man who is particularly cruel laughs hysterically when this happens. Olaudah, an able slave I have purchased, says that some believe their souls will return home if they perish this way, to wend their ways to Ghana. He also tells me that two of the slaves below slew another one between them by suffocating him, so to breathe better. I have known one to brain another with a loose nail to the same purpose. The guards who are responsible for any loss lose one week's rum ration and will join Burkin and the slops for a week's penance. Cap'n angered at the 'escape' slaves make this way, as he calls it.

Now I must admit, Captain and I examined all of the cargo and passed over or deemed not fit for shipment those who had wens, worms, swollen limbs or private parts, were crippled, aged, had falling disease, or were weakened by their trip with the Ouagadougou traders from the interior. We have been fortunate in our losses. Only eight have been thrown to the sea from dying so far, and two of those would fetch little, for they were diseased. We will see. Two who had been brought from below today refused to eat. If we must, Captain says, we will force them to eat with the funnels and mouth priers. If they do not, we will lose them also. Pity. They could fetch £30 or more and could provide good labour for their owners.

Oh, this stench is satanic. It is not enough we provide barrels for their waste, or smoke the decks with tobacco, but not every needy slave can reach the slops, so the deck below is soaked—not by the sea, but by vomit, blood, shit and urine, and every foul emanation of a human body one could imagine. Today a child fell into one of the slop barrels and died this day, drowned in humiliation. I had just spoken to her this morning. She was only four and took delight in the whirligig I had shown her how to play with.

I have decided I will write all this down in my chap book. I am moved to do this and record it as a testament of my life, my errant ways. I am not without feeling as I write. I must control my wrath and anguish. I do it now because I bear such guilt and shame for what I do and have done, that I must confess before I return home. Yes, I am a black man. I was a child born of slaves, who was freed, as they, and had an advantage of the riches whites have and which I squandered in my youthful freedom. I am now a mate aboard a notorious slave ship, having by fortune put here, and see the horrors of my heritage enacted every day. So, I shall start when this watch is over. I will tell this story as truly as it happened from my days in Philadelphia until I can no more. Perhaps some young woman or man in Boston, Philadelphia, New York, or elsewhere may read it, or like those who once told me stories, relate my adventure to them as a lesson of life.

I have contracted with Captain that five of the young men in cargo—Olaudah and four others—are mine to 'own'. I intend to free them as soon as we make port. Nathan—my London broker—has instructions to send my small wealth to New Orleans; I have enough with me for the time. When we make port in Kingston, I intend to travel with them to Ste. Dominiqué, when they are fit, for there is a man there who is gathering freed men to liberate that island. I have also contacted former associates who are now in New Orleans to meet with them. After that, I intend to see the new country. I will find the Mifflins, who unfortunately have not heard from me in so long they must think me dead—that, or the worst reprobate—and Fling Mountain and Belle Lee, my birth parents. I intend to travel to Philadelphia to try to rebuild my prodigal life. Thence, I hope, to New York and Boston, where the war and revolution began a month before I left--thus to immerse myself in the spring waters of freedom.

My watch is nearly over. At twilight, a ship begins to come alive: Every sound is magnified and distorted by the wind and sea. Shadows creep out on deck from the thwarts and stays; sheets and halyards hum with the wind, howling in storms. Every flap of the jib, every creak of a shroud adds to the macabre aura of this ship. Then one must add the clink of chains, the wails and moans of the women and men and the mewling of the children. My heart is nearly still with suffering. I feel enrobed by the humid darkness of this starless and moonless night by the black of Africa which I carry with me, below decks, and the black and empty universe above and behind me.

Chapter 2

Philadelphia 1775.
In which Joseph spends his seventeenth year,
meets some soon-to-be-very-famous men,
desires to sow some wild oats and harvests nettles,
visits his birth father,
and sets out for the Grand Tour on the Chalkley.

Mistress Sarah called me a polite boy; a bright young man who had learned his manners well enough to be an asset in Philadelphia society. She especially said this to her friends when I served from the kitchen during various 'entertainments'. She called me unusually sprightly in my activities and was pleased that Mister Thomas had adopted me from his father Samuel when I was still in swaddling clothes. They treated me as their own and taught me the Quaker religion, writing, reading, and various sentiments of virtue.

I was free born in Samuel Mifflin's house in Fairmount, a free child, in a large house surrounded by forest and close to the Schuylkill River, but I was raised by Mister Thomas and Mistress Sarah Mifflin, his wife, who I learned later had wanted a child but could not have one. Unlike my real mother, Belle Lee, Mistress Sarah treated me better, I suspect, than a child from her herself. Molly, our cook, says she coddled me and protected me like a mother bear, always nearby lest I meet some mishap. I can remember the lilt of her voice as she spoke to Molly, "My, isn't Joseph the best little gentleman. He's all I could have wished in a son." This was when I was only six years old. This lilt was well loved music to me. Of course, this made me secretly very proud, since I had been born to a slave mother.

Belle Lee was my birth mother. She had been freed in 1756, and in 1758—the year I was born—she had married Fling Mountain. Both were still living in Reading and in Philadelphia, in my last year there, and I believe they still have homes there, though Fling has moved to the Northern Liberties section of Philadelphia, up along the Delaware. Since 1775 when I left Penn's 'greene country towne' I have lost touch with them, as with my adopted family, Mister and Mistress Mifflin. The Mifflins were the ones that taught me, nourished me, comforted me, and sent me out into the world. The war is now over. The United States is a new country with freedom as a touchstone. I intend after this voyage to travel to Philadelphia, and to visit all of them if they are still alive.

Let me tell you more. Mistress Mifflin was a good mother. A diminutive woman, both I and Mister Thomas were a head taller. She was slight and often reminded me of a fledgling in her own nest. She was quiet and thoughtful, but she had a nettlesome streak, ruffling her feathers when Mister Thomas or I angered her. She encouraged me with pride, and when it swelled me up, I was urged to apply myself so that Mister Thomas could easily teach me those skills I used so well when I arrived in England; namely, riding, shooting, skill at cards, playing the fiddle and pipe, and guile. Mistress and Mister Mifflin taught these as life skills, not as I now used them. Now cards and guile are not Quaker virtues, nor would I ever accuse Mistress Sarah or Mister Thomas of teaching me those skills, but they showed me a cleverness in their sundry efforts in debating, diplomacy, and negotiations that I used after I met Francis Hyde.

I recall the day I learned to load and shoot a pistol. I came home with Mister Thomas, puffed with pride from learning to hit all my targets. He had smiled broadly while he praised my learning. He had shown me how to load and prime the powder, set the flint and aim it. We had set three targets near his office on the Delaware and paced off a distance. It took me several times, preparing the pistols we had, so that my hands had nearly tired, but on the last two shots I had deftly hit the marks. Mister Thomas told me I only needed practice.

As he told his wife of my accomplishment, her countenance and body tensed in anger. "Thomas, thou art a fine teacher, but thy lessons are wrong. We are Quakers." Mister Thomas held her and said, "it might 'haps be valuable in the coming years to have those skills." He kissed her, but she pushed him aside. Then she turned to me, her face serious, like a judge. "And you, Joseph, should know that your pride, showing like some rooster, like every virtue, can be a bad thing also. You will not use guns again. Now, wash for dinner." It was a brief scold that made me pause the next time I held a pistol.

Mistress Sarah taught me my manners at the table, where I silently sat at times and met sundry folks; she also taught me some dancing steps for the reel, minuet, contradance, and allemande. Molly was my happy partner during these lessons. Both Mister Thomas and Mistress Sarah guided my dress and comportment as a gentleman. Being Friends, we dressed more plainly than other folks, but I admired small things like buttons, ribbons, buckles, and embroidery; a plain habit makes one hunger for fancy. In short, my family raised me as a white person of quality and not as the dark son of some former slave.

Molly, our cook and housekeeper, also taught me enough kitchen skills and recipes to stand me in good stead later when I went to sea, it turns out, though I'm certain she intended me not to be a sailor cook—as I had been—but a good husband. Other than my color—which was (as Mistress Sarah called it) 'cinnamon', only slightly darker than a weathered white sea-captain—there was little way to make me feel different. I was her son, loved and happy.

I was strong, though my build might be called slim, taller than my foster father, who was just under six foot, agile, and Molly said handsome. I lacked fullness in my nose and lips, sharing the features of last generation's white blood, and my hair was brown and straight, so I could wear it like a wig. My manner defined me, not my color.

My father taught me some English and maritime law and some natural and physical science, geometry, and a little astronomy. He said all boys should know these things. He argued with me, so I could debate with him whether one tax was good for the colony or the king, or whether the king's army should be billeted at our neighbors near the river or whether their navy should be allowed to press crew men. I was learning of events surrounding us, of history—of the wars that seemed to thrive among the colonies while I was growing—mostly between natives and colonists, and then the French and Indians, and then the British and the French, and then of British troops shooting people in the Boston streets. Mister Mifflin told me that the spectacled man who frequently visited was a Mister Franklin, who played with electricity, the substance of lightening, invented eyeglasses, printed an almanac and newspaper, started a library and college, and I forget how many things. A very smart man. He made me read Mister Franklin's paper and would question me afterward. He was proud he adopted me almost 17 years before when I was abandoned by a Mulatto mother and left with a man named Fling, who without dispute said he was my real father. I am not a full-blooded African, but a quadroon. I love Belle Lee, who bore me, but I love Mistress Sarah, who raised me as her own. Fling Mountain, who sired me, took no interest in my life, was a drunk, having more interest in a dram of spirits or a cone of opium than his flesh and blood. It was Mister Mifflin whom I owe my skills and learning and manner to. He never made me feel small or useless. He encouraged me in everything. I love him also.

Both Mistress Sarah and Mister Thomas, being Quakers by faith and of an anti-slave sentiment, thought it a blessing fate had cast me their way and arranged with Fling Mountain, who had no dispute, to have them adopt me. He could not raise me, nor had the inclination except to be fettered in the thrall of spirits, opium, and idleness. I did not know until that last year that Fling expected some monies for the 'trade', with which he expected to raise his spirits. The Mifflins thought the act of slavery was against the Lord's law. I was raised by them in their gentle religion. I have followed little of it since I left them, but I, betimes, remember its precepts. One's early learning is hard to shed. I can remember

Mistress Sarah reciting, and I after her: "God's spirit is in everyone. He can access us immediately and we, him. We do not need priests or churches or special rituals to minister or worship. Our worship comes in silence and being moved by God to speak." "And," she would say, "we should follow a religion of love, Joseph, as Jesus taught, in every moment of our life and in all we do."

I will not argue its value, but I have done much that would redden Mistress Sarah's and Molly's cheeks and anger Mister Thomas. As I write this, I must say the world, it seems, believes otherwise than those simple teachings. What I have seen and done is past. I now intend to correct my wrongs to others if I can. I do want to believe in something higher than men, but like my blood, my thoughts about whites and blacks and human differences are mixed. We are wilder than Monsieur Rousseau's *creatures sauvage* and may never be tamed.

Mistress Sarah was a cousin of Mister Thomas. They adopted me shortly after they were married. Belle Lee as a wet-nurse raised me until I was weaned and started to crawl, and then abandoned me when she left Grandfather Samuel's house, so, I guess, I was like Moses in the bulrushes. After I was adopted by Mistress Sarah and Mister Thomas, Mistress Sarah had come under some malady that left her weak for several months—so Molly had told me. So, it was left to Molly to change, comfort and feed me. After Mistress Sarah's restoration, she became my real mother, succored me when I ached, played with me, joined me in my laughter, lullabied me to sleep, and chastised me when I was naughty. After my first robbery, I remember thinking she would have surely used her 'switch', a feeble branch of ash that she threatened my backside with when she thought I had erred.

I remember Mister Mifflin watching her carefully, since she was often ill—as people said, delicate. I thought not as I was growing, but when I saw her dockside the day I left, I saw that she was slight, a frail woman who had worked, as her husband had, to withstand the hard colonial life. Mistress Sarah was still like some nesting bird, but she had a fierce temper about those who were cruel and sinners.

I notice as I write I am sometimes redundant. Please forgive and bear with me, dear reader. I write, as we all remember, like a chalk mark on a children's hoop, spinning my tale over and over.

Being of Quaker temperament, our house showed no riches and was simply furnished. Mistress Sarah did not spend money on rich meals or finery. She would find an old pot and fill it with various oddly shaped sticks and grasses to decorate our kitchen; she would harvest Mister Wister's purple blooming fronds in the spring to brighten the dining room. At the hearth there was always a toasty fire on cold winter's nights. She did loving things for the whole family. She was a woman who spent her free time helping others in our community, telling me once "Jo, the Lord put you here not just to enjoy this world's riches, but to help those with less to enjoy also." In fact, the April before I left, she started knitting me and Molly stockings to keep our feet warm for the 'coming conflict.' Simple, humble stockings were like brocaded finery to her. She was also Scotch-like with how often we had tea, saying, "The British feel we should pay unnatural prices for tea and tax us, Joseph, so they will only get a few pennies from this household. Joseph, we will be patriots. We'll save on parties, also. You can play your fiddle for Mister Mifflin and Molly and me. That will be much more fun.

I know you are bashful playing for guests." It was much more fun, since when I played for "company", I often felt like a servant. I loved Mistress Sarah as if her blood ran through me.

And it was the same love for my foster father, Mister Thomas Mifflin. He was a robust man who had little time for foolishness, idleness, and wasteful living. He was active in the early politics of the colony. I now have learned that he later served as Quartermaster for General Washington during the war. That was stroke of good fortune since, Mister Thomas had been in the import-export business and Philadelphia's Port Warden while I was growing up. That I would often visit him on the Delaware and at the port also contributed to my interest in the sea and pirates. Being warden, he had charge of all docks and safety on the water, buoys, pennants, reckless behavior on the water, and such. He used a small skiff to patrol the river at times and would often take me with him when I asked. He collected duties, a job that angered him, saying, "The Brits will take everything they can squeeze out of the colonies. Someday, they'll be the ones to pay." His responsibilities also involved preventing privateers from using the port, so I heard many stories about those 'legalized pirates'. He accordingly was a careful, very bright man who served as a good teacher. He would let me man the tiller when I was older, nodding toward our destination, and he let me secure the boat when we arrived, carefully eyeing my anchor and cleat hitches, and how I prepared for the next trip. He taught me how to ride a horse and treat the animal with kindness. More so, he taught me most of what he had learned as a boy, so to all intents I was like him as I matured. I owe him all my wise learning and the 'white's' knowledge that I have. I hope he is well.

In my teens, I began to hear more and more of the British king's rule of the colonies. First, it was so often spoken of in our household that I'd be deaf to avoid it. Mister Thomas and Mistress Sarah came back from New England in 1774, the year before I left, where they had been on vacation. Thereafter, he often spoke of Samuel Adams, Josiah Quincey, John Hancock, William Dawes, and other patriot men he had met there. When he told me the story of Crispus Attucks, he emphasized that he was the first hero of the 'coming storm' and that I should remember him with pride because he was of my race. These men had fanned his hatred of the British rule. He angrily spoke of it more and more the year before I left. There were nights Mistress Sarah, Molly, and I sat by the hearth that year because Mister Thomas was demonstrating with other Philadelphians of like mind to protest Parliament's Coercive Acts. Against the rule, he spoke for a united front among all the colonies, Molly had told me. That summer was when I met Mister Dickinson, Mister Franklin, and Mister Jefferson, from Virginia colony, at one of Mister Mifflin's dinners. From the little I heard, I understood there was to be a war. Mister Franklin was a printer and had put some of Mister Paine's writing in his newspaper. Mister Jefferson had memorized some of it and was saying those politick words at the table, until Mistress Sarah asked him how his apple crop was and whether he would remember to bring some apples and some of his delightful sweet cider for them the next time he visited. The politicks stopped when the red-headed man smiled and said "Miss Sarah, I would be delighted. They are a fine crop. You speak like a diplomat. Perhaps you can join us at congress when we men are arguing a subject too long. Yours would be a welcome voice." Both Mister Franklin and Mister Thomas laughed. Mistress Sarah blushed. We had a nice, simple dinner that night. That was in September. Then Mister Thomas was elected to the first Congress. He was also made a Major in the city's 3rd Battalion.

That preferment caused a large discussion at home. The first week of his promotion, Mistress Sarah was silent when he was present. His appointment caused him to be ejected from the Quakers. Miss Sarah continued for a few days more, but later relented. She said the freedom of the colonies from the king was a treasure that would be difficult to attain. I hope that I may return to them and hear of those years, tell my stories, and not be judged too harshly. I have all but disappeared from their lives; I do not know where they live now, since their former house was used when the British occupied the city. I'll find them. They can't have moved far. I would hope they welcome their prodigal son home now, once this voyage is passed. I have heard Philadelphia is larger than the few squares it was when I left. In the year before the conflict, I was sent to London for my education, on Grand Tour. Now I wonder if those kind people who raised me, sent me there to keep me from harm's way. I also wonder now how the new country follows Mister Jefferson's words about 'all men are created equal' and having 'certain inalienable rights' when I see the slave trade continues and hear stories about the poor and forgotten.

Philadelphia was good to me. On my days off I'd explore, as young boys do, imagining being an adventurer, from Bainbridge south to Vine north, and sometimes to the farms beyond. I loved the idea of wandering, betimes riding in caravans on land and sailing by brigantine as a pirate by sea.

Grandfather Samuel lived in lands to the west along the quieter, more sedate Schuylkill River in a large mansion made of the local stone called schist. Friends of mine and I would often range into the forested land there, setting playful ambuscades for each other and laughing about them all the way back down the river to the city proper. There was a beautiful, deep wooded wilderness near a stream called the Wissahickon where Bill Upton, Cam Toler, and I would ramble. We had a secret fort near Devil's Pool, and at times, when the heat was too much, we would strip to swim in the creek's deep waters and then lie on the flat granite rocks, baking like drying fish. There were cliffs there. Trouts in the brook, and quiet, like some of the places in England where Hyde, Wilson, and I waited to 'touch' someone. Sometimes we would see deer, rabbits, a stoat or mink, may haps a badger. After a day, the walk home was unsettling betimes, if we chose a way that passed the outskirts of the town, for the middens there were so unlike the woodland, filled by men's waste. Those woods, though, hung on with everything to please my senses, soon erasing anything less wholesome.

Mister Thomas lived near the Delaware—a fortunate location for a port warden and for me, who loved to visit the wharfs along High Street and watch the ships enter the port to unload their cargos, smell the pitchy craft, gawk at strange fishes and sea-drift. I would imagine lateen-rigged feluccas cruising up the Nile as I lay on the shore, crocodiles lying in wait for a wing-maimed ibis, exotic women in naught but colored scarves, 'gyptian men transferring smuggled contraband slyly from ship to ship and winking at me as they secretly moved their opium and gold. There were no more pirates I knew of, save for those on the Barbary Coast, and those were 'slavers'. It took me some years before I knew what that word really meant.

Between the voices on the street and those at the port, I did learn much of 'the coming storm'—words that often confused me until I was old enough for Mister Thomas to explain about taxes and the crown and its imposition on Pennsylvanians and the other colonies. I often asked too many questions, I think, since Mister Thomas would often quiet me and tell me to ask Mistress Sarah. Mister Thomas often went to the state house with other men, especially in the year I left, when there were meetings of the 'congress' and the representatives who attended it from other colonies. If I was near Carpenter's Hall or the area near Third and Chestnut, I would sit on a stump or tarry to see some of them arguing in the street. I heard that Mister Mifflin had visited the City Tavern with them to sometimes have a cider or some stronger drink after their negotiations. Again, it was up to Mistress Sarah to explain. She said spirits, beer and cider were now allowed, since Mister Thomas was no longer a Quaker. Red-headed Mister Jefferson had brought a basket of apples and four large jugs of cider. He and rotund Benjamin Franklin were often there in the evening. I had heard from Molly that the two of them were always pinching her and staring at her bosom when she bent to fetch some firewood or pour tea. I did not know that Messers Jefferson, Dickinson, and Franklin were rebellious, illegally fomenting revolution, and in fact, never imagined that I might hold in my heart the same passion until later during the riots in London and in my hatred of slavery. An uneven time it was. One day, there would be news that seemed to stir the whole city like angry bees; on others, all was as quiet as creatures foraging in the wood. A fire was smoldering.

When my family duties were over, I often would walk the length of Pine Street west to the Schuylkill River. I found it amusing, since I was tall and thin, sometimes dwarfing those I passed on the street, some who shied away as I passed. I was strong enough to heft the barrels from the basement and beat some older men at arm wrestling, but still lanky enough to be unimposing. Women still were attracted to me—Molly said because of my quiet demeanor and refined face, that when I spoke, I was the gentleman Mistress Sarah had hoped for. In short, by my seventeenth birthday, Mister Thomas said I had a future in the growing city.

Living near the port on the Delaware, I could fish the water from the western bank, especially in the spring for the shad runs, and proudly bring home fat female shad full of roe to give to Mistress Sarah for dinner. I'd watch the slaves across the river in New Jersey colony, who worked in the iron works and warehouses, take their rest. I bravely approached seamen from both the Camden and Philadelphia sides. I often spoke with sailors and watched the ships: barks, sloops, an occasional huge galleon carrying cargo from Europe, ketches that colonial sailors preferred. The older and my favorite—the brigantine—was the ship pirates liked to use, since it had speed and maneuvered more quickly, and like sleight of hand could rob other ships.

There were ships from Europe and the Caribbean, many of which I was certain had escaped pirates and, from some of the tales sailors on shore had told me and my friends, tempted me to great adventure—I ached for the chance to try. Unlike the Schuylkill, which had small boat traffic, the Delaware fed my dreams. Once I had met a man who said he had been a sailor aboard such ship and told me several tales of piracy. He talked of the Barbary Coast and African buccaneers. He said that years earlier, Philadelphia had been a favorite city for pirates to take leave in and spend part of their booty, and he also said that at times Philadelphia ships were often prey on the way to London and south to the other colonies. He often spied on them to tell his mates that intelligence—"Intelligence, mate, was always valuable."

But much of that had been done before I'd been born. It only fueled my interest. My father said that when he was growing up, the lieutenant governor had put out a warrant on Blackbeard because many of the city's merchants, and some residents, themselves were even in league with that captain. He told me some south Northern Liberties' natives had even been pirates themselves—I guess an appropriate place for my birth father, Fling Mountain, to live.

I also loved the forests along the rivers, especially north along the Schuylkill where there were many kinds of trees. Mister Thomas, and Grandfather Samuel—when he chose to walk with me—would name them and have me pick a leaf from each to remember. They are still there: Black Birch, Black Oak, Black Walnut, Cedar, Cypress, Chestnut, Poplar, Gumwood, Hickory, Sassafras, Ash, Beech; and Oaks of divers' sorts, as Red, White, Spanish, Chestnut, and Swamp. I once made a book with leaves I had gathered pasted on the pages. Once, when he wasn't busy, Mister Wister took time to look at the book and tell me about some of the trees I had written down. I remember he had a very inviting garden next to his house on the next street from ours. I carefully wrote what he told me into my book. This interest of mine was something Francis Hyde was happy that I knew, for we would often rendezvous before robberies near trees he knew by name, the gibbet walnut or the hanging beech. I learned to love the forest.

Mister Mifflin told me I had William Penn to thank for them, as well as for the square in the city near our house where I met Essie Dickinson. Indeed, I did feel strongly about her. She and I would often sit in the shade of trees in William Penn's "greene country town" and talk of our dreams. I knew she was fond of me by her pout when I said I wanted to sail the seas and see the world, and to have her there along with me.

For Mistress Sarah and Mister Thomas, I also served to be an economical addition, especially in their young household. Philadelphia was an exciting, growing city—some say the second largest in the British Empire. In April of 1775, there was an unseen energy in the air. Mister Thomas was a rich merchant and, very active in local politics, was active in the congress formed there that year, and was actively helping realize the excitement those men at the City Tavern or the colonies were about to experience. I learned only little of this. As a teenage boy, my thoughts turned to young lasses, although none had singularly caught my eye—save for Essie Dickinson; I was otherwise distracted by some studies which Mister Mifflin caused me to pursue, and stories, which I devoured like an old reminiscing sailor. I often dreamt with Essie, lying on grass and gazing at the clouds. I imagined I was a ship's captain, with a hold full of coin and riches—that was the dream. Alas, the reality was that I became a mechanic and cook aboard several, but never commanded my own ship.

This was a high-spirited time in Philadelphia, for the First Continental Congress was meeting at Carpenter's Hall that humid summer, and there was the constant hum of both mystery and gossip influencing daily affairs. Wherever I walked, there was gossip, which I attended carefully and was as curious as the next to hear the stories at dinner, in the kitchen and on the street. Mister Thomas interpreted the gossip for me and filled my thoughts with stories of the rebels' actions and the dangers awaiting them from the crown. The April before I left. some dissenters in Boston had been shot by the British soldiers.

At night after dinner, Mister Thomas, sitting under the chestnut in the back yard, would tell some stories at my pleading about pirates who lighted their beards with fuses to frighten captives, and exotic tales of sailors being marooned on islands with one-eyed giants and voluptuous women. I especially liked these—I know I must have irritated Mister Thomas, for I urged him for more beyond patience.

During time from my chores in my rambles, I might seek out Essie Dickinson for a visit. She could be sweet, inviting, and tempting. She was like an aspen; lithe, strong, and now maturing with full womanly features. More than once I experienced an urging that I know now to be sexual heat. She had rosy cheeks, black hair, and sun-burnt skin, matching me. She tempted me. And teased me. Just as quickly as she showed a leg or her thigh, she would stop, smile, and ask me about something mundane. 'What's that bird's name, Jo?' When I cooled, she would say 'Want to see something secret, Joseph?' and then she would often show me a hint of 'sundry' things about her. A trace of pink nipple. A wisp of secret curls. Though I would be brought to a blush, she never allowed me more than a peek. This tickled her but was a source of great confusion to me, knowing no other behavior. I often left her place with an intense private ache as I walked.

Mister Thomas and Mistress Sarah would only infrequently hold dinners. For most of these, I was asked to dine privately with Molly, since they were mostly politicking discussions. From time to time the last year before I left, I was invited to dine more often with the family and sundry guests. Since I had some small talent with the fiddle, I was often asked to play.

I do recall that some of the rich friends of my parents would refer to me as a colored or Negro boy, angering Mistress Sarah when she heard such. Only then would I feel less myself than when I was solely in the company of the Mifflins. Few in Philadelphia believed in slavery, and fewer would believe that once had they served on such a ship as I sail now. There were, I remember, many free blacks there, but many were also no better than indentured servants. I am certain that some of those feelings stayed with me and helped my attitude once I met Thomas Wilson and Francis Hyde and set about my career. Even at Quaker meeting, no one spoke of slavery.

Some things did embarrass the Mifflins, and I realize now that it was my thoughtlessness. Though I knew better, an inside voice urged me. I used a borrowed pistol and won a turkey for our Christmas by shooting well at a contest the year before. A friend of father's—Mister Franklin—had writ a notice of it in his paper that week, so the attention I received from my fellows had raised my sway among them earlier in the year, but when Mistress Sarah heard I had won it by using a firearm, I was sorely chastened by Mister Mifflin and her. I also am guilty, though they never heard of it, of dicing and playing Ombre with Topher Norris, Camber, and some others. With Essie, I once gambled with cards, playing 'war'. Our rules were if I lost a play, she told me to take a piece of clothing off. If she lost, I was to tell her to select. I laugh now about how one day we played that way but never finished. Her mother came home from market and immediately started to climb the stairs. She was fortunately slow enough that we were able to dress up with what little we'd lost. Her mother asked what we were doing; we said 'playing cards'; our disarray and mien probably said otherwise; Mistress Dickinson said that was nice and left us to rearrange ourselves. I have often though about Essie and try to imagine her bare body beside me. Those sins aside, to my credit, I was well behaved and had even won a footrace in which I ran from square to square and to the docks and back during one of the harvest celebrations.

Then my life was to change. On a day in early April of my seventeenth year, I had been along the Delaware at 5th and High just north of Society Hill and walked toward home with Essie. That morning, Mister Thomas had promised me a surprise. He'd said it would make me a full man and prepare me to be a gentleman. Essie and I guessed. Was it to be a trip to Boston? Was I go to the university across the river? Would I be asked to join the militia? I could only guess it was some sort of travel, but it was important not to be late for dinner. It had filled my brain all day so totally that I had scarcely any other thoughts. I said goodbye to Essie, nearing my house. She kissed me on the cheek. I went straight home.

Mister Thomas's surprise was this: He said he had great plans for me. He was sending me to England, there to meet with a legal counsel who would manage my money, that I was to travel to various European countries to learn their customs, languages, and manners. Some called it the Grand Tour, or *Tour Complet*. I was stunned by Mister Thomas' offer, with much subdued excitement. I willingly accepted it and promised to return at Christmas tide to Philadelphia. I was warned to stay unpolitick, especially about the current fervor in the colonies, and to follow the words of Polonius in the *Hamlet* play which he read to me after dinner. I somewhat remember part of it:

> Neither borrow nor lend;
>
> For loan oft loses both itself and friend,
>
> And borrowing dulls husbandry.
>
> This above all: to thyself be true,
>
> And it must follow, as the night the day,
>
> Thou canst not then be false to any man.

Mister Dickinson and Mister Franklin were there as guests. They applauded the words and adventure. The latter added after the Shakespeare that I should be careful not to spend "as much as tuppence for a penny's worth". Mistress Sarah wept, as well as Molly, and I was invited to have a small sip of Port after dinner was cleared to celebrate the occasion. I did see Mister Franklin pinch Molly thrice on the buttocks and whisper to her several times but hid my blush when hers showed. I was distracted. Sleepless that night, I stared at the ceiling and the shadows of trees outside with endless thoughts.

On the next day, Mister Thomas and I visited several merchants near High and Chestnut on Third for a small portmanteau, large enough to carry a few books in, which Messers Franklin and Norris had donated—for my welfare. (These were Dryden's translation of *The Aeneid,* and a fine quattro bound in red Morocco of Shakespeare's *Tragedies.* I also received a fine duodecimo of Juvenal's *Satires* from Mister Jefferson.) That day, Mister Mifflin also purchased sets of clothes, shoes and sundries, as he made great words about the necessity to be carefully groomed and shaven. Frankly, I had simple outfits, but carefully made, and it was certain that they would last many months. I was a Friend and should dress plainly. I gladly thanked him for his generosity. His only caution was to follow fashion only after it was no longer fashion, to avoid coxcomb's feathers and such, so that I was not perceived as too forward, frivolous, or well-to-do. He also gave me a list of addresses to which I was to communicate once I arrived in London—particularly the solicitor who had charge of the stipend which Mister Thomas had provided for me.

Most importantly, he warned me of footpads, highwaymen, and other rapscallions who might try to steal from me or take some advantage. He warned me to always keep my identity, as well as my papers, secure—particularly those manumission papers which proved me a free man. I carried two sets separate. Mister Thomas showed me how to secrete one in the lining of my waistcoat, so it would be safe. It is with irony I remember his cautions after the life I have lived since. I ignored many, to my peril.

The ship I was to take was the *Chalkley,* owned by Messers Drinker and James and captained by Joseph Spain. Thus prepared, I made certain to take time to inform and celebrate with several friends: Bill Upton, Margaritte Norris and Essie Dickinson, and Camber Toler, with whom I had had social and learned intercourse with from time to time. All of them shared my happiness without jealousy. Essie secretly told me she hoped I would return, that she liked me very much, and I should stay safe from harm. They expected letters so often that I laughed; for I could do nothing else but write letters, had I kept the promise to write them as often as they wished. Near week's end I thanked Mistress and Mister Mifflin for their generosity, especially for the 17 years they had raised me, and for the many gifts they allowed me to share. I told them I loved them. And I told Molly. It was a teary time. I visited my step-grandfather Samuel and walked with him for an hour or so while he railed against the crown. I kept my silence and left with his blessing and a blue cravat, and a fine small sword and hanger. We laughed about the badger living under his house. He embraced when we parted.

I then visited my birth father, Fling Mountain, who was living nearby in the Northern Liberties near Fishtown. It was then he told me of my birth mother, Belle Lee, who now lived in Reading and who I, with little time, would not be able to visit before my journey. He cursed her habits, which he said would kill her, things like bathing and eating too many fish and vegetables, smoking tobacco and drinking chocolate. I smiled and endured his rants. Having no address for her, I resigned myself unable to visit now. I scorned him, for he was besotted and drunk at the time, a shameful human being. I would have to contact Belle Lee by letter and on my return at Christmas. I will also seek him out once again when I return.

As I write this, I am moist-eyed, for it was a time like none other I had since. I was leaving my young history and starting another, without the ones I loved. The next day was also teary. I said my farewells at dockside. It was such a flurry. Hardly able to leave, I boarded the *Chalkley*. Mister Thomas and I met with Mister Drinker and Captain Spain (who shared my forename). High tide is when we sailed, which was at three that afternoon. It was April 17th the Year of our Lord, 1775. I prayed for safety for my family, friends, and myself on my journey. It was to be a month at sea.

Chapter 3

Finds Joseph learning to be a sailor;
he receives a useful gift, finds quarters in London,
and meets Messers Wilson and Hyde
who persuade him to join their band of entertainers.
Joseph fires a pistol and makes some money.

I was 17 when I said my farewells to Thomas and Sarah Mifflin and Molly and my friends and the nurturing streets and port of Philadelphia and climbed aboard the brig *Chalkley* to begin my life's adventure. I had hugged Mistress Sarah as long as I could, wept as I kissed her, and still was tearful as I turned to hug Mister Mifflin and shake his hand. Mister Mifflin had finished his business aboard. I thanked him once again for the opportunity he'd given me. He put his arm around my shoulder, proudly telling the captain to "keep his son safe." I remember the word 'son' hung in the air like an Italian putti. He looked at me with a smile; then said, "Be safe, be smart, be a good man; make us proud of you."

It is sometimes difficult to remember the details as I write. I may repeat myself. When you sew years of experience on your coat in writing an account, you find it difficult to reach your undergarments, close to your heart, so be patient with my tale. I am rendering it as true as I can bethink myself. I find myself pausing to limn the pictures in my mind, so when I harken back, it is as true as it was at the moment.

As I watched my family fade into the distance when the Chalkley left the pier, I soon was distracted by the work of the crew and the sea's sound and smell and the limitless waves. I was so entranced that I awoke with a start when Captain Spain called to me, "Joseph, please follow me to my quarters." I remember stumbling and ungallantly making my way, for I had not "sea legs" yet. But I did feel a kinship that we shared the same name.

When I arrived at his cabin, he told me that Mister Thomas had told him of my interest in sailing and such, and he introduced me to a crewman only a few years older than I. "Joseph, meet Mister Cutty. Cutty is a hand of the foretop and is a seaman. He is assigned to school you in sailing, learning this ship, and to answer any questions you may ask. It is as your father wanted. I hope you find it acceptable." I nodded, and we shook hands. "Now, Joseph, Cutty will show you your berth and help you stow your gear. Welcome aboard." As we left, Cutty spoke. "Hae ye any experience with ships, Jo, if I may call ye that?"

"Yes, you may, sir, and no, only pirate tales and talking with seamen in port."

"Call me, 'Sails'; 'never 'Sir'; 'Sir's' for Cap'n. When we arrive in Dover, you'll know at least how to shoot a line."

With that we went to a small cabin I was to share with a muttering white-haired man who complained of my color. At that, he was quickly moved by Sails. I saw naught of him for the rest of my voyage; I had the cabin to myself. My excitement at being at sea helped me to ignore the man's bluster and insults.

Sails had indeed been at sea since he had been 8 years old. At 16 he was rated a seaman and was among those special crewmen who were topmen, roosting in the masts like flocks of birds and, save for the officers, the elite of the ship's skilled crew. He was a gruff boy but had a bright demeanor and a smile that beamed when he was amused. Fit and tan, Sails had a long shock of blond hair tied at the nape with a piece of a red bandana.

I wondered how I would learn so much in three or four weeks, but I applied myself as I had in my past studies. Sails immediately started with his descriptions, setting time to the tempo of the waves and pointing to a thing as he spoke and we walked: 'Luff, leach, clew, tack, larboard, lee, roach, sprog, starboard, binnacle, afterdeck, midships, bilge, bowline, cathead, capstan, crosstrees, gangways, helm, jib, stay, windlass." He did it with such speed, I thought it impossible to keep pace, but in two weeks I had learned what he taught and more, and soon was at ease.

One day I was tardy coming on deck. He called on me. I remember being chastened, for I had thrown some clothing together with books on top of my locker.

Sails looked at the mess and waggled his finger. "Jo, a seaman keeps his belongings like his thoughts, neat and orderly, not everything on top and nothing handy," he said, pointing at the jumble. I was embarrassed and quickly put things in order.

Sails answered my hundreds of questions with the patience and humor of a new father to his inquisitive child. I and Sails had quickly become friends. I had shared some of my life stories with the him. He returned the favor and warned me of dangers, especially along the Barbary Coast, the Caribbean, and simply in British ports. With those tales and stories of slavers, I began to forget the romance of the pirates. Though midshipmen and 'waisters' at first referred to me as 'blackie', the foretopman never once called me any name but 'Jo'. It reminded me of Essie.

England was especially a danger. I had heard of 'press' gangs, but only in Mister Thomas's politick arguments in the colony. Sails sarcastically smiled and told me if I wanted to work on his majesty's ships, I only needed to look like a vagrant hanging around the docks. If I wanted to work, as he, for a merchantman, then I'd better apply, have a skill, and look honest. I told him all I had was my strength, and I knew some cooking. He stopped me with a shout, "Aye, a cook is the best crew 'sides Cap'n, if you are good. Good for you, Jo. Jes' stay off the docks and look 'espectable." It was a happy moment for me, and I remembered it well. I was never pressed.

It was the adventure I had dreamed of. I had made another friend in Sails. We had both done each other favors, certain to strengthen our friendship. We often would fish aft, especially after the third day when we crossed the warm stream that ran from the Caribbean. He called it the 'Gulf.' I noted the change of color and could see the difference in current. It was there we caught large fish, a Mako shark—whose teeth I saved—and several Dorado, which some of the crew called Dolphin. Shining gold and blue, they were different than the larger dolphins who swam athwart the ship like clowns escorting us. At night, I watched the moon light on the water which stayed at the ship's side; even tho' we made much haste, the sea held it like a captured creature. There were nights, while we were in the warmer water, that the water appeared to glow with a myriad of jewels, giving off its life. I remember seeing this often after it was the dark of the moon in the Caribbean.

I liked to fish, and when the water was not the cold Atlantic, would do so early in the morning and early evening. During the dog watch around 4 o'clock, no one was aft, so I would settle there and watch the water change color and think of friends at home—the Mifflins, Essie, Molly, and that city—and hope that all was well. On one day I caught a clump of seaweed and within it found a large, angry blue crab; mad, I suppose, for he waved his claws seriously at me until I returned him and his weedy ship he was traveling on back to the sea.

The next day was a bad day for those atop, like Sails and most of the passengers, unused to the ocean and below decks, for there was high wind, thick weather, and cold rain. Sails was serious all day. We did not meet. Although I had not experienced it before, my stomach rumbled, and for a short time I felt a little close. This malady passed, and I was able to return from the gunwale to continue reading about London and Europe and things to see.

A week later, there were always sea birds astern, and as we finally crossed the stream, flying fish landed on deck. Blue skies. Clouds so high I could not see the tops. At night, either a bright moon or countless stars. Heaven.

The ship was not as comfortable as home. Because of my one-time cabin mate's dislike for my color, I was fortunate to have a snug and simple cabin alone, but others were not so fortunate, as I learned from their complaints on deck and at meals. They were thick with sea lice, and heat, and cold, and seasickness and smells, and damp, moanings during weather, foul water, and bad food. Somehow, I had no complaint, for I worked at what Sails taught and the chores he assigned, kept clean, and slept soundly nights.

Cap'n Spain kept a scoured and strict ship, and I grew to appreciate the crew scrubbing and skilled at sailing. Mister Mifflin must have known from his own experience that I would arrive safely. I never felt in danger or was beset by sea lice or very ill. Thanks to Sails, I was busy all day learning skills I used most often a few years thence.

Sails told me story that frightened me one night when I sat with him on watch. I think he wanted to be certain of my safety. There is a town in England before we land, he told me, called Newport. "Never go there, Jo," and he stared at me hard, "there's a constable there will throw you in the prison for a tuppence, and it's said he leaves men in gaol long enough so they starve to death. And for sumfin minor." He stifled a small laugh, almost as if he'd had the experience, and looked to sea. "We will pass it near to port."

When he chose not to walk about and teach, we often played at draughts, and that's where I learned the most. Sails and I enjoyed playing, though he often won. He told me so much betimes that my days raced. It was then he warned me to be careful of gamblers and of spending my time at games; "for you can make much wealth in the moment, but you can lose much wealth at length." He showed me how to palm a draught and use it to later play an extra one. He seemed to worry much about my safety, but I know now it was his good soul that worried for mine. A friend I do miss.

He also warned me during our games about footpads, pick-a-pockets, and such. Mister Thomas had warned of the same before I left, so I listened carefully. I said nothing to Sails, but I wondered silently that these thieves must be a plague, that I had to hear so many warnings. "They are everywhere at your elbow, waiting for swag they can get." And for once he said of my color, "your color will make them see ye better, mark ye, and set ye as a target. Think you are weak and easy. I'm sorry, Jo, but mos' folk think Africans are simple, stupid animals. I don' know why. Ye are God's creatures, same as me." He looked seaward, and I, at the deck silently. Then he'd smile and win the game and turn to me and wink, point somewhere on board and ask me to name something. Fo'c'sle and cockboat. Mizzen and poop. Orlop and stem. I was happy.

We were making good speed in the third week. I learned to play the shanties the crew sang as it worked. I would play the pipe and fiddle, and the cabin boy would hammer a bucket like a tabor; another might rattle a block while he played as the crew sailed our ship. Captain Spain showed his pleasure by clapping as he watched us, and Sails would often wave to me far aloft, one hand on a sheet. So, it was: "Fathom the Bowl," "The Drunken Sailor," and "Fare Thee Well My Dearest Nancy" to lighten the work. It was a merry time for me and the rest, and it moved the clock.

By the fourth week I was at home aboard. One morning, with the breeze luffing the sails and the crew cleaning, they met a ship—the *Dover*—and Captain hailed to it. We slowed and anchored abreast. An hour later I was invited to dinner with two guests and the *Dover's* captain and mate. Sails indicated that this was an honor to eat with the Captain, so I dressed in one of my newest outfits. I had my newest wainscot, britches, and a starched shirt. I wore my grandfather's blue cravat. I was to meet my first Londoners. They were bound for Boston and spoke freely of the troubles they had heard the colonies were giving the King. It was obvious after a time that their loyalty and mine were different; one could spoil the social if I spoke, so I listened to them quietly. The Captain also steered the discussion carefully away from the politick shoals.

At dinner we ate lamb and pudding—I understand it was a treat the cook was saving—and the guests all had wine, as did I, though being from a Quaker household I was not used to it and felt a little unsteady. I listened. When they heard I was starting a Grand Tour, they all started speaking at once, making recommendations. One man recommended an inn called the *Black Horse* near Charing Cross, where I might stay when I arrived in London by coach. He generously wrote down careful directions to it from the coach stop in port. I thanked him. At the Captain's request, I played a song on the fiddle. I only missed a few notes; I suspect from the wine. It was a favorite of my mother's, "Miss Hedge's Minuet." The visitor's applause embarrassed me. I became homesick and thought I should write the Mifflins.

There were two passengers bound for London who dined with us. One, a thin and swarthy man whose disposition moved everyone to a dark humor, and the other, a man Sails had spoken of, who seemed full of subterfuges and plots. He didn't—nor 'seems did anyone—trust him. I remember him well because he praised my table manners and dress, saying that I would easily find my way in London society. After dinner we had a portion of Sherry and rum. Oh, I slept very soundly that night. I always slept comfortably at sea, in tune with the cadence of the ship and waves rocking me after my labors and study. The sea suited me, I felt. Only once during that short storm did I feel mildly ill. I loved the breeze when they were making good headway, the birds, the creatures like the grampus and seals I saw, the tales of the sailors, and the Captain, albeit a kind one. The journey had fed my dreams. Had Thomas or Molly or Sarah seen me after three weeks, they would have remarked on my high complexion, my new strength, and my agility, for the work I did with Sails and in helping on some daily tasks had by haps prepared me for my life at sea in those years that followed.

The day after the dinner, I sat down and wrote to Mistress Sarah and Mister Mifflin. I wished them and all they spoke to good fortune and God's protection. I told them of the Captain's kindness, of Sail's help and friendship, of the fish and creatures I had seen, the wonder of the sea, the dinner, and my fears when I disembarked. I wished they could be there and thanked them again. And I asked them to write to the *Black Horse* in Charing Cross, or to the solicitor wherein I would get my funds with their news. I gave the letter and an enclosed sealed private note for Essie to the Captain, who said he would see that the Mifflins got them on his return.

The end of the voyage passed quickly and with almost perfect weather, or so Sails had said. When at last we passed the Downs, you could smell the land, greet the birds, and see the dotted horizon, gray and green awaiting us. Sails was true and pointed out Newport, with a shout and a nod to our lee. A spit of land in our last hour signaled the anchorage, with a great blue heron fishing in the shallows. Captain had cargo for the British fleet, sugar and rum, and told us that we had one stop at Folkestone to discharge it, so we sailed on with the chalk cliffs to larboard and in short time came upon the ships of the greatest navy in the world—his Majesty's—like an armada of geese, the white sails as wings in what seemed an endless flock.

At anchor, while the crew worked, I took my leave of Sails and he, me. We had no tears, but we were serious. I gave him my address at the *Black Horse*. Captain Spain requested my presence. I thanked him for all his kindnesses. In return, he presented me with a brace of pistols, finely worked in mahogany and silver. He said he would have been proud to have me as a son, that I would make a fine sailor—should I choose to be one—that my parents would be proud and that he would tell them so, and finally warned me that I should be careful as a black man—that I would be a target to some. The pistols would be fine protection, especially on the highway. "I know you are a Quaker, Joseph, but use these for protecting your life and others." We quitted each other with many thanks. I waved to Sails, who was at work high in the foremast. He descended to the deck, clapped me on the shoulder, and said I'd make a fine sailor.

Goodbyes were something I had not had many of, and my eyes teared again as we said our words. I was surprised at myself for having so tender a heart. I left the ship to make my way to London. It was the 17th of May, my 17th birthday, in 1775. I felt the heavens were shining down on me. I also felt that day that 17 was my lucky number.

As I disembarked, there were several men calling out the names of destinations and soliciting fares for their coaches. I took the advice of the Londoner I had met at dinner and went directly with my portmanteau and fiddle to the *Four Kings*, a scurrilous inn near the foot of the pier, enquired of, and paid for a coach, and in an hour was bound via the Dover Road for London. It had started to rain.

The ride was long owing to the weather, a mud-clotted road, and knee-deep ruts. At one point, near Ashford, it took 5 hours to go 4 miles. This was not my idea of adventure. Though I was young and ready for anything, even if it was the mire and swearing of the coachman, the downpour and complaints of the passengers, I kept a smile. Life is exciting, especially with newness, and everything was new. The accents, the flora, the rain, the countryside, the wise-cracking, the curses.

My coach was a rackety box, clattering all the way to Maidstone, where I left it and stayed at a post house for several hours and had dinner. It was my first meal in England, and the cook at *The Ship and Compass* served up pudding much as Molly had made, and roast beef. I had tea afterward as I waited for a post coach. We left for London during a violent storm. I thanked God that we were now on land. I and my two fellow riders had much to talk about. We often found ourselves speaking so loudly that when a rut stopped the ride, we looked at each other embarrassed by our shouts above the silence. One was the tall, gangly, dour one from the ship, who suggested that I buy a horse to avoid such an experience once more. It was from the others that I learned about Charing Cross and nearby Pall Mall and St. James Park.

When I finally arrived early the next day in Charing Cross at the *Black Horse*, I met the innkeeper—one William Humphreys—who upon seeing my fatigue and distress, immediately had my luggage removed to a room on the second floor, offered me a toddy and assured me that I would be called for dinner, seeing as I "had endured some hardships on the trip and was a young colonist, welcome to London". I undressed and fell to bed for several hours.

When I awoke and dressed in late afternoon, I played my fiddle for an hour in my room, enjoying the window view of trees, promenade, and people. I then sought out Mister Humphreys. He was a rubicund man, white-whiskered, who had the habit of laughing frequently and reminded me of John Dickinson, Essie's father, save for the beard. He might have been Father Christmas, had he been dressed in a red or motley suit.

I thanked him for his amity and paid him 1s.2d. for a week's lodging. My room was clean and convenient and had a view of a small pond and promenade on the side of the public house. The inn itself radiated warmth, not only from its hearth, but from its old, worn cedar timbers, its comfortable furnishings, and the beauty of the paintings that hung on its walls. It made me feel as if I were in the Mifflins' parlour on a cozy winter's day.

I told Humphreys I wanted to purchase a good horse. He promised me one, young and fast and dark like me. A brusque man when he wasn't laughing, Humphreys showed me sympathy. Humphreys looked me up and down that day, as if assessing my worth. I suppose my demeanor betrayed my anxiety in some way, for he immediately spoke. "Don't worry, lad, you are in good hands here." He said he was an abolitionist and sympathized with men like me who had been stolen from their home in Africa. He promised me some fine entertainment on the weekend when two of his friends would be playing. He had heard me practicing on my fiddle, complimenting my skill.

He intimated that I might be able to get some revenge on rich whites who had enslaved my kin. I had to speak, "Sir, I was born free and never knew slavery. My foster parents are white and have given me a life like theirs. I have no bone to pick with any race."

Afterward, when we had concluded our business, he introduced me to the men who changed my life. While we had been talking, I had noticed them setting a stage with instruments and a fabric scene that could have been the woods at Wissahickon. It was, as I was to find out later, supposed to be bucolic, an arcadian woodland to put the audience at ease. At dinner in the coffee room, Mister Humphreys seated me with them, introducing one as Mister Francis Hyde—dark and blue-eyed with a limp and about the age of Sails, though he was much shorter—and t'other, as Thomas Wilson—tall, reedy, and whiter than snow—white hair, pink skin, and the lightest eyes I had ever seen. I had heard of albinos but had never met one. He seemed older than both Hyde and me. I, without reason, distrusted him.

After we were settled at our repast, I inquired whereof the scene on stage, and I was told that they were going to act out a short woodland scene from the Bard's "A Midsummer's Night Dream" to whet the audience's taste for an evening of pleasure. Then they would play some music, Hyde on the bagpipes and concertina, and Thomas Wilson on drums; then Wilson would juggle some plates and tankards and spoons—he was quite adept—and Hyde would change the scene and wander in the audience.

We had had several glasses of ale when Humphreys joined us. I spoke a little about the voyage and quite a bit about Philadelphia. The three of them would ask about the rebellious feeling in the colony, the richer planters, and small things like how we dressed, entertained, our sport, and the more we drank, the more I answered. Humphreys had several suggestions; for one, Hyde and Wilson should offer me a chance to join them in their endeavors as travelling entertainers. He nodded at Francis Hyde. They seemed to share some silent message. "You'll see after dinner some London entertainment, courtesy of them, Jo." Thomas Wilson looked at me with a smile that made my neck hairs prickle and invited me to play something on the fiddle, which I did for one or two songs. "We need a fiddler, don't we, Francis?" Hyde agreed, and we drank a bit more. Humphreys said the horse I rented was ready.

He then invited us all out to the courtyard, where he had the groom bring out a horse. 'Rogue' was as black as pitch and spirited. When I mounted him with the groom holding the bridle, he bucked once, twice, then settled. The others shouted 'huzzah.' It was then that Humphreys compared me on my horse to the statue of Charles I outside on the square, blackened with age, embarrassing me. It was how his inn was named. Both Hyde and Wilson remarked that it seemed like fortune had led me there. They suggested that I change to riding clothes, and that we try Rogue and see the sights nearby at the same time, being as they weren't going to entertain 'til after dinner.

I was in thrall by the circumstances. I had barely arrived, and I had rented a horse, purchased lodgings, met several nice gentlemen, and was offered a means of earning doing what I liked—playing the fiddle and pipe. So much was I subject to Hyde's, Humphreys' and Wilson's encouragement, and my own callow and innocent temper, that when I joined them in their adventures, it was a kind of enslavement. I learned from them over the course of several years where they came from and what their habits were.

Let me start with Bill Humphreys—I wish him well, for he always treated me fairly. He was the equivalent of a bawd who had a string of whores supporting him, save that he employed highwaymen, pocket-filchers, and footpads. These had been supplying from his headquarters at the *Black Horse*, and now, I warrant, the gentleman who recommended this place on the *Chalkley* had pointed me in this direction as a lamb to the wolf. Now I know he kept a stable for my sort, and surely had a horse for me.

Thomas Wilson had been an orphan from the Cotswolds and had spent several years in the circus as a geek in the sideshows, where he would tear the heads from rats and for a coin afterward offer to lick his fingers. He attracted a crowd merely because he was an albino with red-stained hands, dying them with beet juice aforehand. His real skill was that he was an adept juggler and very quick with his hands—so fast that he could lift my watch on horseback and return it to me later. He was equally talented as a pickpocket, having learned it from his childhood.

Francis Hyde was always my favorite. He had a cheerful nature—one that allowed him to inveigle himself into your confidence. He was the one who sealed my initial decision to join them. Francis was also a talented footpad and pickpocket when he was a lad, but he found himself in Newgate when he was six, had been molested by a murderer, and had gained a limp when he'd killed the man to escape. His gimp never healed. He was one of Bill Humphreys' first and most dependable highwaymen. It was him, like Sails aboard the *Chalkley,* who taught me all I knew about being a gentleman of the pike.

After their invitation, I was primed. I left them in conversation with Bill Humphreys, repaired to my room, changed and wore my pistols as a precaution. When I returned, Francis Hyde eyed the pistols and remarked that they wouldn't be necessary, but that we might stop and try them since I had them. Humphreys was quick to provide him and Wilson with a brace of pistols each and, eyeing mine, pointed out a shop far across the square, saying if I ever need a repair or tinder or powder, the shop of John Knubley there was a reputable one —"one of the king's armorers". He then examined Captain Spain's gift to me carefully, showing the engraving and the newly designed pan that prevented misfires to Francis and Thomas.

Once mounted, we passed through the great arch through which the coach travelled into the courtyard and were on our way, with me on Rogue in line. In St. James Park we saw some of the King's Guard, Buckingham, and another palace, and then rode to the river. Francis seemed pleased that I was there, told me that Humphreys was an old and valuable friend and one to be trusted, and he had said that he'd heard I played the fiddle very well. "And pipe," I interjected. Thomas talked about how they acted different parts in small dramas and played music, and that he was a juggler. "We do other things to supplement our income, Jo. Perhaps we'll show you."

When I suggested we find my solicitor's address and told them more of myself, we were so close that we barely had left the river, stopping at Barrow Lane. The office was closed, so we rode on to a field across the bridge. Hyde dismounted; we followed. He paced off a distance, pinned a handkerchief to a tree, and returned.

Looking at Thomas, he smiled. "Let's try your pistols out, Jo, and wager a crown on the outcome. Two shots only. I and Tom will shoot first." They primed the ones Humphreys had supplied.

I primed mine, breathed deeply, remembering Mister Mifflin's instructions. I was excited but breathed carefully and waited. Tom took his time and clearly missed his first, striking a tree further in the distance. He showed some mirth but muttered as he stepped aside. When he limped to the line, Francis seemed bemused, as if he were going to pick an apple a bin, and quickly drew his pistol, turned, and shot. He hit the cloth and made it puff. With a droll smile, he blew the pan off and reloaded, looking at me. Regardless of the breathing and Mister Mifflin's quiet voice in my ear, I raised my fine Knubley pistol, wrought in mahogany and silver, and shot. Short, puffing the dirt and missing as well. Nervous.

"Shall we double the bet?" Hyde laughed. Tom looked at me and winked, the first real expression of amity he had made.

"No," said I and fired my second shot, hitting the cloth spot on. Tom shot and hit, the handkerchief puffing on impact. Hyde missed to the ground. "We're square", Hyde said and clapped us both on our backs. "We must practice, boys. But first, let's have dinner." We rode back along Pall Mall and returned to the *Black Horse* via Piccadilly, so I could see more of the city. I lost all fear and was with new companions in London.

We drank and ate with gusto that evening. Our pistol match was a focal point of our conversation. It also seemed that Bill Humphreys and my new friends had talked of our day, and he regaled us with what seemed was his best wine and victuals. Duck and beef, fish pie, and pudding and turnips, carrots, and pease. After dinner, I stayed a short time to hear the entertainment.

Francis and Thomas played on bagpipes and drums and danced and juggled. They dressed as women and danced and preened and made light of some visitor in the audience, causing us all to laugh. Afterward they walked among us and asked for donations. (I learned later that while one of them proffered a hat for coins, the other might unclasp a bracelet or filch a watch from the contributor.) I enjoyed the performance. The long day had worn me, so I took my leave, thanked them and planned to meet them in the morning. Returning to my room, I fell into my feather bed and did not stir to dawn.

The next day, Humphreys had laid the table well again. I had my first sausage—a banger, he called it—and English Cheshire cheese, soda bread, and a pint of stout. I arranged with Bill to buy my horse and a saddle and tack, and I sat with Francis and Tom. They asked if I was brave and if I would like to make an income. "What would I have to do?" I joked that with my color, I stood out, "if they hadn't noticed." Tom said he had the same problem with no color, but he had found stratagems to compensate.

This was their business: They invited me to travel the countryside with them, with music and tricks to entertain travelers at inns. I would see the country, meet people, and I could increase the funds which Mister Mifflin had provided. So, a'night they were involved—they said—in sundry ventures that availed them of their money, for the entertainments brought them little, a few farthings, some watches and trinkets. Since I could ride and had a horse, could shoot and was game, would I like to join them? They made the case that I could fiddle, play the penny whistle, and being a black, could dance.

Even though it offered adventure, friendship, and some wealth, I hesitated. I had heard and been warned about men like these. If I should refuse, would I be in danger? I wanted to consider it. They were good company. I missed my home. I didn't know. It didn't strike me as crime. Humphreys added that it was a gentlemen's sport, where comportment, behavior and manner was as much as the encounter itself. Francis had said it was a small way of taking from those who supported the crown's cause against the colonies. "Look at it as helping your folk at home," Wilson added. They only urged me a mite, for I had shown by my manner, I was unsettled. I said I would think on't. And think I did. For much that day and the next and several after. It was against all I'd been taught, but how was I to know adventure unless I dove into it, swam, and tired myself? I didn't know. Then, imp-like, a small voice said to try, see if you like or not, then decide.

It was suggested, since I was new to London, I should take the week and explore for myself. I did. They would return from engagements to the south for the next five or six days. I saw a cock fight, shops for new clothes, and a great many gin houses, some doxies, and places I could easily spend my money. I returned to Barrow Street, where I introduced myself to the agent Mister Mifflin had contracted for me, one Mister Josiah Rouster, received my money and told him where I lodged. He gave me the full stipend, saying I was mature enough to spend it frugally. That business being over, I returned to my quarters. On several days I visited parks and rode, took my pistols to some farmland and practiced, and read with interest articles in the news about highway robberies. I took coffee at several houses and importuned some visitors about crime in the city. When Francis and Thomas arrived back at Humphreys', I had made my decision.

I told Hyde I could not long remain an idle spectator. Hyde said we could pretend to great art, for with juggling which Thomas was expert at, and music and dance, we could espy those we might rob at night when they made their way to their next destinations. I saw this as adventure and agreed, with the reservation that I would hurt no one, would rob only the 'fattest' targets, and would quit if I felt too much the sting of conscience. At that we clasped hands, and I set to fiddling that night with "Stony Point," "Trip to Bath," and "Highland Laddie" while they entertained. We were set to be highwaymen. A still voice told me it was wrong, and yet another told me I was a pirate on land.

Humphreys joined us at the table and revealed that he knew from the moment he saw me and heard me play that I might be the man Hyde and Wilson were searching for in their adventures on the road. "Lad, you'll be a fine one," he told me. "Francis has forgotten more than I ever knew. He'll make you a good 'un." He, after all, was keen at noting a visitor's value, and having the wherewithal we needed, could abet our plans.

Francis Hyde told me what he had planned and what I should do. He repeated his instructions thrice. That evening we set out east from London about 8 o'clock. We were each armed with a hanger and a brace of pistols. We had also suitable 'mistery' dresses and a dark lanthorn, which Bill had supplied. The plan this evening was to attack the mail-coach, which would start at 12 o'clock at night from the *Ship and Horse* tavern, between Woolwich and Graves-end, about 9 miles from London.

We were on the spot at the hour agreed upon and disguised ourselves for the adventure. As we waited, I remarked that the huge tree we were under was a Copper Beech. Francis said it was a famous tree in the area and had served as a gallows for men such as we. Hyde and Wilson chortled. They were dressed in white frocks and boots, with their faces painted yellowish to resemble Mulattoes. Since I was darker, I dressed in black, wore a large tail wig, black gloves, and a black mask over my face. Anxious though I was, when the stage arrived, I started, and caught the leading horses by their bridles, while Hyde and Wilson each presented a brace of pistols in at the coach window and demanded of the passengers their money. There were four gentlemen and one lady in the coach. They denied having any money. Wilson said, "Deliver, or death." I was sweating. I cocked my pistol, not knowing why, trembling. I shot once into the air. Too anxious. This frightened those in the coach, I guess, for the noise was enough to have them give us a bank note of £50, one other of £20, and about 60 guineas in cash. Rogue also started, but I calmed him quickly. With that over, Hyde startled the coach horses with his quirt. As they galloped away, we retired to a wooded and unfrequented place, shifted our dresses, discarding them, and made our way to Chatham in the county of Kent to divide our spoils. My anxiety abated, and when we pulled up, I smiled at Francis, though I wondered if he had noticed my state. I had been shaking the whole time. For the first time, Thomas Wilson smiled broadly. He complimented my skill in shooting a warning into the air, enough to frighten the passengers. I silently nodded in assent, but I knew it was a beginner's nerves, Quaker guilt. I still wonder if he knew.

That night, by a careful route we returned to the *Black Horse*. Humphreys took our horses and his share. I was full of the thrill of the highway, my new friends, London, and a new occupation. Why not pursue it a'time? I felt only the slightest guilt.

Chapter 4

*In which Jo writes to the Mifflins again,
plies his new trade, is tested as a footpad,
and meets Sybil Gaye, who reads his Tarot.
He attends a badger-baiting, learns he likes blood sports,
and pursues some of London's vulgar pleasures.
For a moment he confuses lust and love.*

Francis, Thomas, and I congratulated ourselves on our success together. With Bill Humphreys we celebrated at the *Black Horse* eating and drinking with no thought for cost. We spent days resting and shopping for new clothes, books and other frivolities. It was nice to have money like this, and the new experience. The danger of being apprehended added salt to my new ventures. Here are some typical news items which I add from the *Courant* present day that I had seen similarly then

🌿 🌿 🌿

On Tuesday 8 women went, all in white, to the King, to beg the life of a condemned highway-man; but his Majesty was pleased to tell them, that he had resolved not to pardon such.

🌿 🌿 🌿

Letters from Exeter say, That the highway men continue to be very audacious in that country, that by night they attack houses where they expect any booty, in great numbers; and among others did lately assault the house of Madam Fulford, a rich widow gentlewoman, within 7 miles of Exeter; and notwithstanding she has a great family of servants, and that several gentlemen her friends who were there accidentally, fir'd upon them from the house: they had the Impudence to continue the attack for several hours before they could be beat off.

They say that 40 of that gang are since come towards London, where they hope those concern'd will be carful in looking after suspicious persons.

❦ ❦ ❦

Yesterday at the night Session at Old Bailey, two highway men received a sentence of death by hanging at Tyburn; one young foot-pad was sentenced to be burnt on the cheek; and one pocket-thief was sentenced to be burnt on his hand.

❦ ❦ ❦

At Wednesday Sessions two highway men were sentenced to Transportation to the American colonies for repeated Menacing and robbery near Ashford. One had been previously gibbeted and branded and t'other had been three times before the Sessions for similar Complaints.

❦ ❦ ❦

These notices I read with great interest, but my youthful vigor made me take few of them as a warning that I might similarly appear as a 'news' item. So, I plied my new trade, learning from Bill and Thomas—but mostly from Francis—the finer methods to 'touch' my victims.

Bill Humphreys' share of our take bought new disguises for future adventure, though when he offered, I demurred, for I fancied my black waistcoat, gloves, and britches—the whole like night—and felt it was in keeping with myself as the 'dark one'. My mother had thought me lighter complexioned, and that was so, but not in the perceptions of the British I had met. I only chose to cover my face, wear gloves, and don a periwig to cover the parts of me that made me stand out. There was no reason to risk being identified as a darky. I had become a highwayman, a nearly gentlemanly profession, or so the public did station my occupation. I intended, if I sinned, that I would sin with style and grace and good manners. I would not have the public think I was some street ruffian on horseback, with pistols.

Strange, the Brits' perception. Like their insistence on Lordships and Countesses to separate the poor from the rich, they also ranked their thieves into classes. Pickpockets, who stole small things and harmed no one, were high in their rank, as were highwaymen who rarely even loaded their pistols and showed good manners to their prey, often returning a crown or two or kissing a lady's hand. I suppose the pickpockets, usually being young children, were forgiven for filching a handkerchief or small purse. But footpads, who ran in gangs, were often armed with clubs or knives or hooks and swords—and used them. Physical violence was the dividing line. They were the lowest of the low. Men and women of this profession would often maim or even kill during a walking theft of a hat or handkerchief, desperate to sate their impoverished tastes with a hunger for bloodshed and pain.

It was my desire for adventure that had led me, and the persuasiveness of Bill, Francis, and Thomas who had taken me 'under their wings', as Sails had, and helped me lead myself away from what I had learned at home. In those days, I must blame the foolhardiness of youth. Though I knew I was doing wrong, I thanked them all. Their tutelage made me adapt more quickly, and their tales fed my hunger for the day-dreams I had had.

It was at Hyde's urging that I contacted Mister Rouster on Barrow Street and told him that I would be travelling abroad, needed any funds left for me, and I would no longer need his services. Hyde said, 'Jo, you can save your pelf at one of our agents and not have to worry about inquiries, legal or otherwise,' and I took his advice. Mifflin's solicitor had received no letter from the Mifflins—he suspecting the vagaries of shipping and conflict in the colonies to be the reason—and anxious to leave him quickly, in my guilt I lied, telling him I would stay in touch. "Mister Rouster, my new venture in maritime trade forces me to travel, which I think a blessing, but it leaves me scant time to be at home. I will contact you, no doubt, when I have legal matters to settle." With that I asked that letters be forwarded to the *Black Horse.* By that visit, I had also nearly severed my connection to my past, of which I spoke little.

That was one of many ways in which I began to corrupt my life. I could not let Philadelphia and the Mifflins go, however. Some say one's home is printed on one like a book, and I still have yearnings as I write this. They never left me. I would be reminded at strange times of Essie and Molly, and Mistress Sarah, and wonder what straits Mister Mifflin or Messers Franklin and Jefferson were in during their conflict with the crown. Despite my reveries, I began to sever my ties to home. I am certain all those who wanted me to write every day might know I was lost to them.

As I write, I remember how dreary London was betimes. When the three of us returned from the highway after one venture, I remarked how one could smell the city from miles away, how a sooty air hung over it in the distance as we approached, and how Philadelphia seemed like a tiny country town, fresh and clean by comparison. There, one could walk on the street without being besmirched by foul water from the gutter and by chamber pots emptied out the windows and passing coaches engulfing people on foot in waves of horse manure and fetid water. The rivers didn't stink in Philadelphia. Both the Schuylkill and the Delaware supported myriads of fish and wildlife. With the Thames, one could only imagine what denizens roamed it waters. It was an enormously long sink for the folk that lived near it. Even Parliament had heavy draperies installed to help keep out the odor, being as the swamp flowed past their windows. But Philadelphia—the whole city, not just small gardens—was pleasing. Wilson remarked that when I lived there, I didn't have 20 crowns in my pocket, and Hyde added "nor your fancy waistcoat." Nevertheless, I believe I was homesick and vowed to write a letter home that night.

That night I did indite a letter to Mistress and Mister Mifflin. I told them about the shops and parks in London, the politick talk that I'd read news about Lexington and Concord and the skirmish there, and Bunker Hill and the rest of the news I had read of the colonies, of having met the solicitor on Barrow Street, getting my generous stipend (for which I thanked them heartily), some things about my new friends and my horse, and said I had gone into the import business, and had made my first money. Since I had not then heard from them, I promised to write again and wished them safety, health, and God's protection. I sent my love. One of you might say I lied and was a dissembler, but I loved them and did not want to shock them by my lawlessness, so torn by my past and enticed by my future. I had become part of the better class—though not of the peerage—nor did I act how they paraded their extravagant riches in front of others almost as an insult betimes to the poverty of the lowly. I had new riches without qualms—in that time I had heard £50 per year was the average income—and the accompanying extravagant vices filled my leisure time. Some nights I made twice that average income on one short ride. I still retained the sense of my parents, and was as good a person as I could be to the poor and bereft.

I applied myself to learn my new profession. In my soul, I felt only a twinge of guilt and no regret, and my past slipped rapidly away. The people I robbed were gentry. Being Quaker, I planned with Nathan to save money in Lloyds Bank. I rented new quarters from Bill near the *Black Horse*, purchased new clothes, and learned to gamble. Cards were a specialty of Francis. He set out a special project to teach as much as he knew to me; feeling as keenly of me as I had of him, I became an apprentice of sorts. Once I had learned his ruses and feints, we especially sought out those gambling haunts with rich clientele.

We dressed accordingly, and if necessary, to paint the correct picture, we hired a carriage for the evening. This sojourn from robberies pleased me, for diversion; kept horseback at late night from becoming a pall. Wilson, whose ghostly demeanor was singular, only took part in the robberies. He was too memorable. For my gentleman's manner, I was a novelty. It was never my color that was notable. London had many freed and indentured black men and women, so to see a black of means everywhere was not a rarity. Albinos were rare. Wilson was rare.

Our cheat was simple: since we could not mark the cards, we developed unobtrusive signals. We never arrived together. The last rule we followed was such that one or the other might be chosen as a chance on-looker to join in the game, after the other had been playing. Thus, one of us was persuaded by a group to become a partner in foursomes.

An observer, I often heard Francis say to me, "Sir, do you know this game?" and I would answer "Yes, sir. In the colonies, it is played by many. I learned it from my mother. I'm afraid I'm not very expert. You all seem to be very adept. Is it played for money?" The latter usually set the hook—to use an angler's term. Francis would allow the others to invite me to play a few hands, saying, "We only venture less than a guinea or so. Would that be acceptable?" I would pause, as if counting what I had in my pocket, and would then assent and introduce myself to all at the table with an alias name like "Robert Cherokee from Atlanta" or "Desmond Brown from Maryland" and continue to paint a picture of myself in some wild setting or on a plantation, for the guests who inevitably thought me exotic.

We played Put and Whist, but preferred Ombre. That was where the money was. Now, Ombre became extremely famous in our time, since it was the game described in Alexander Pope's "Rape of the Lock," and could be played as defensively among associates or offensively by a single player naming trumps. Women made the game faddish, emulating Belinda in Pope's famous poem. We had an added asset to take advantage when women played, because we both were considered 'handsome' gentlemen. So, we flirted to gain some advantage. Of course, I was always Francis's partner.

Taking snuff, adjusting one's wig, pouting, scratching parts of one's body, clearing one's throat, laughing or chuckling, or flirting—all could be part of the signals that we would work out ahead of an evening's cards; and we would change them each night, so as not to be discovered. We also were careful never to go to the same place on the same night twice. We would select from inns, parlours, bawdy houses or Jelly houses, to never encounter the same gamblers twice. At table, as much as several hundred guineas might change hands; and should we lose, there was always the highway on another night. Rarely did we lose. We were careful to assess the value of each fellow gambler. Often one of us would appear at a location only to assess a mark's worth.

Although it was below us among thieves, it was not so far below to temporarily work as footpads on the street. I had already assumed the air of a gentleman highwayman, occasionally wearing wigs of high fashion and lace at my cuffs, affecting snuff, kidskin gloves, and hat and garter ribbons in these street side incidents. When I worked as a footpad, it troubled me and my reputation. I felt it beneath me. I followed Mister Mifflin's advice. I was not a fop, but until

Francis reminded of me of my background, I could have become one. I favored quality clothes. Embroidered waistcoats with gold thread on black satin. Silver shoe buckles. Shirts of fine linen and ruffled cuffs. Soft kid gloves. Wigs were expensive, so I often wore a tricorn and plaited my hair at the nape. On my garters I added a small ribbon for each success by horse. I did not forget Rogue; his mane was braided and intertwined with black ribbon. All of this changed on days. And on many nights, I wore workman's clothes. When I played at cards, I dressed plainly. Like a Friend.

Some days after the former robbery, Hyde and Wilson and I met a Captain Hill at the foot of Rochester bridge near Chatham. It was late at night on our return from Richmond Park. We had doubled our money at cards, with Francis and I making close to £350 between us; were in very high spirits from drink, had met Wilson at the *Shovel and Spade* and were returning to my new quarters to plan for the Cheswick stage the following night. It was an evening that one savors, I remember, with a light breeze that smelled of new flowers. We rode our horses at a trot, for our mood was high from the night's venture. We were buoyed by the work of the spirits we had drunk.

Hill was a captain of the marines. We had seen him in the daytime mounting his horse at Brumpton barracks, which was about half a mile from the bridge. He was known to stop at *Black Horse* a' times, so we quickly disguised our faces and hands, dismounted, and walked directly before his horse. Wilson asked him the time—a common ploy to stop a new touch. "Whoa. Sir, do you have the time o' night?" Hill made no reply. Hyde then caught the bridle, I, his left hand,

and Wilson presented a pistol to his breast and said, "Deliver, or death."

"Gentlemen, I assure you I have naught but a few shillings." Then Thomas demanded his watch, by again threatening "Deliver, or death." The watch was gold and valued at 50 guineas. We left him his shillings but took his watch. Bill Moses would fence that, post haste. I wished him 'safe travel' after Francis hobbled his horse. We then walked towards Graves-end, but out of sight changed our tack for Rochester, where we lodged at the *Mariner's Inn*. Captain Hill put up a great hue and cry for us, but the pursuers—thinking us bound the opposite way—entirely mistook our route and left us to a quiet dinner. The next morning, after breakfast, we took the post-chaise to London, where we arrived about six o'clock in the evening.

Our booty—such things as we acquired that were not money, viz. watches, buckles, rings, fancy hangers—were delivered to a broker whom we constantly employed. Such brokers knew the value of the swag and redeemed it for cash or notes. Ours was a Jew and lived in St. Katherine's Row, near Tower-Hill. His name was William Moses. I myself used another, Nathan Wryowicz, a Polish broker—this to keep my winnings more secure, for I had thought Wilson as a likely cheat. I must admit, I was as biased as someone who disliked me and my color—only because he was so pale. So like others of similar attitude, I also thought him capable of treachery, dishonesty, and menace. As I write, I realize now how prejudice arises from the most trivial differences a'times. We are not made by the Creator to tolerate any variation from what we perceive as common.

There were also other brokers in different parts of England, with whom we had constant communication, and who were perfectly acquainted with our modes of acquiring property. But after such a jaunt, with naught but a watch, as with Captain Hill we thought it advisable to replenish our wealth instead of rioting on our spoils.

After a few days back in London, it was concluded that I should go alone and attempt to "touch" some gentlemen who frequented the plays at Covent Garden; this, considering my age and inexperience, was thought rather a bold stroke by Wilson. But Francis set this as a test for me, and I agreed, for my confidence had grown. Being villain enough to attempt anything, I did not hesitate; but posted myself agreeably to that direction. Overconfidence is the vanity of youth. It was a frustrating night, for my efforts were wholly unsuccessful, and I returned empty. Wilson cast a cold eye at me. Francis, on the other hand, laughed at it, saying, "Sometimes a fisherman only wets his hooks, and sometimes he catches a school."

I was not yet the top of my class in skill, though I had the wherewithal and the affect. Criminals had their own hierarchy; footpad and pickpockets, and housebreakers were considered far below highwaymen—the elite of their class. A 'Gentlemen of the Pad' or highway man would not dishonor himself by stooping to pick a pocket or snatch a purse, for a fine coach deserved to be robbed; a poor man, not. Highwaymen would often return a shilling or two to one who had to continue a journey, and would address ladies and gentler folk appropriately with the best manners. I did many a time. Many would wish their victims "Good Night" or "Good Day" as they courteously took their leave. There were one or two ladies I kissed good night, and several men who were not nobility who I excused without payment.

It was footpads who were usually more dangerous. It was not unusual that Hyde and Wilson and I worked as a gang. There were other gangs of seven or more members who often ran houses of ill-repute, and these residences often served as warrens for fences and whores. It was early in the century that the more famous highwaymen were active. These, like Jack Hawkins, Sixteen-String Jack, and Gentleman James Maclean, were held to be legends. I wanted to imitate them. They, like most others, were hanged before they were thirty. I did not want to mimic them in that regard. They were careless. I would be different. All used disguises and masks. All planned their locations and targets. But murder and robbing the Mail were the only capital crimes, the gibbet being reserved for the latter. Oftentimes arrested highwaymen were whipped, stocked, burnt, branded, or released unless they were deemed nuisances and thus sentenced to transportation. I laughed: that would be a free trip home to the colonies.

I suspected Wilson, I don't know why, to be in league with a thief catcher, one of those informants who leaked to the constabulary. Snitches were sometimes paid to bring their pigeons to the gallows. I had picked a gentleman's business, with great benefits for a young man and few disadvantages. I could rove in the sinks of the city to pursue wine, women, song, and games of chance with the wherewithal to enjoy it to my heart's content. Even though I sought youthful pleasure, I was not dissolute. I would keep a close eye on Mister Wilson, the whitest of whites.

The next night I took my place, again being tested, much to my displeasure, at London Bridge, while Hyde stood at Black-friars, and Wilson at Westminster. At half past 11 o'clock, I met a Captain Duffield and asked him the time of night. He responded, and I showed my pistol, responding: "You know my profession; deliver or death." He stepped back to strike me with his cane, and I moved to the side. I cocked my pistol and told him to deliver instantly, or death should be his portion. He then threw me his purse, which contained about 10 guineas, and a silver watch, which was valued by our broker at a paltry £6. Francis told me later that he had probably thrown me his 'robbers' purse', for many travelers and persons on the street carried a second purse with less for the thieves and secreted a first for themselves. This practice, the news said, was because of the larger numbers in my profession—especially as footpads. I and Francis and Tom are of that better class—not scum, refuse collectors, rag pickers, footpads, tinkers, or vagabonds, the offal of flash houses or other thieves' dens. I despised this change. I wanted to be on horse again, away from the smell of the gutter.

We may have frequented places of disrepute and disorder, but I insisted we remain sworn to be gentlemen. It seems strange, but it was the money that drew me. The reputation, I abhorred. I made certain Hyde, Wilson, and Humphreys take oaths that they would not noise my name about. They did. Now I know Quakers do not take oaths, and I had not. I and Hyde, the same night, obtained about 40 guineas of Sir John Griffing; Wilson about £30 of a Mister Burke; and each a watch, one gold, the other pinchbeck. The next day we saw advertisements in the news, describing the robberies and offering rewards for the perpetrators. The catchers would be alert. I thought it wise to lie low. Francis and Tom urged me on for one more.

The next night, with no or little difficulty, I robbed Hugh Lindsley of 16 guineas, 30 gold crowns, and a gold ring. Hyde, on the same evening, took from Lord John Cavendish about 20 guineas, and Wilson robbed William Burke of 11 guineas. We now concluded to remain in London for a while, as *gentlemen of pleasure.*

Francis said that it was time I learned some of the pleasures my work's rewards would provide. Distrusting Wilson, I told Hyde that I wanted to pursue them on my own, secretly hoping to widen my horizons. I did not want to end up at the end of a rope or on a gibbet to assuage an obvious jealousy an associate might have had of my successes. Francis wished me well, telling me of locations in London where I could find leisure entertainments.

It was the day before I left on my own that Francis Hyde introduced me to Sybil Gaye. I had seen her at both the *Shovel and Spade* and the *Black Horse*. At both places, she seemed to attract a small gathering, not only by her beauty. She was a gypsy who read Tarot cards and told fortunes. She was also a doxy who was skilled at picking pockets, and shortly after I was introduced to her, she laughingly returned my watch, which she had just lifted. I thanked her, had laughed hard at her joke, and we talked for a short time. She was tall, thin, and blue-eyed with a complexion that could have made her my sister; she had a melodic laugh and was spirited. Her smell was like cinnamon and vanilla mixed, and it lured me as well as the tinkle of her laugh. I was having fun and for the first time away, almost forgot Essie. "If you want the company, Jo, Sybil can show you around," Francis offered with a wink. I was embarrassed but asked her, and she agreed. So off we went arm in arm, two cinnamon 'darkies' to explore the city.

Now that I try to put my story down, I remember her well. I discovered what luxury women could provide: blood sport, how to lose at cards, and some loss of innocence. When Francis Hyde met me a few weeks later, I was a different man. I learned to like gambling at blood sport, the first of which was a night I spent at the pit at *The Plow and Sickle,* where I saw my first badger-baiting. Now, I was partially drawn to the contest because I remembered that a badger had lived under Grandfather Samuel's house on his rambling estate on the Schuylkill River. Grandfather had warned me not to crawl under the veranda or go near the badger's lair, because I might get bitten or clawed. Mister Samuel had said they had incredibly dangerous vise-like bites and very powerful claws from digging so much. "And once they got you, they won't ever let go." So, when Sybil told me that one could bet on a dog or a badger, I was interested.

We entered the basement of the inn among a boisterous crowd of men, watched the contest for a few minutes, and then decided to wager. A badger rested in an artificial den at one end of the pit. A competing dog was released, and almost immediately the two animals scrapped, slashing, biting and tearing at each other until the dog's owner separated the two. If the dog is faster at capturing the badger, he wins, and the reverse. On the last match I observed the crowd, trying to prise what intelligence I could from it, but all I saw was the unlaced bodices of the women screaming for their favorites, ample pink mounds tumbling almost out, and the red-eyed men with blood in their mouths yelling at the badger to kill the fucker while they salivated over the breasts they saw in the galleries.

I lost money. The badger was a big winner. And Sybil lost some of mine. Some £20. But I loved watching one creature vanquish another. The next time, I would seek the place in St. Giles where I could watch dogs kill rats.

Sybil and I spent that day and three others exploring the sights around London and enjoying each other, talking, watching clouds, going to flash houses, eating well, and exploring each other's bodies. My memory of her is like a broken glass, clear and sharp with many fragments. I followed her like a hound on the scent. Pungent, sweet, musky, she was impossible to resist. I learned much with her, for I had no experience like this before, and she had a fearsome hunger for my body and much experience. Pure lust ruled me for those three days and nights. I would approach her bed like a slavering dog hungering for her secret parts, her rouged lips, her powdered lips, her erect nipples, her soft skin, her warmth and smell and luxury. I was nearly crazy thinking I would do anything she wanted; she need only ask. At the time, I thought I was in love.

Fortunately, Mister Humphreys warned me it was only a young lad's juices which had me in their thrall. When we finally decided to part, she said she would read my Tarot. Though it was not permitted to me as a Quaker to believe, I agreed. I was less Quaker since I had arrived, anyway. We sat naked on her bed, and she looked at me with her liquid eyes. 'Shuffle, Jo.' I did. She laid six cards in the shape of a cross before me. She said I was on the right path toward freedom and would share it with others, that I would find riches, lose them, and have a moment in life that would be a transition. I listened like a puppy to his mistress, hoping for something more wonderful to taste. She turned the last card with a snap that focused my attention on't.

I was frighted, because it was a picture of death in all his dark robes, a skeleton holding a scythe to cut men down. She said that both the card before, the man hanging by his foot, and death harkened a change in my life but did not mean what the pictures noted, and that life presented many changes that I should be ready for. These were symbols. They were not literal. I trembled. She calmed me by putting the cards aside and kissing me and kissing me again, and again. My fear was gone. I kissed her again and again and again and again that last night, but the images of the last two cards had etched themselves on my memory.

Chapter 5

It is late 1777 and Joseph continues to ply his livelihood outside London; fearing the law, he signs onto a merchant ship as a cook, and travels to Lisbon. He returns and resumes his profession, visits Jamaica and sees, for the first time, the cruelty of slavery. Troubled, he admits he is tired of robbery.

I missed Sybil's body. I had had such a sensual dalliance those four days. I thanked Hyde and Humphreys for introducing me. Then I forgot that pleasure quickly, for thief catchers were on the prowl, or so it seemed. They had news in the *Courant* of a new man in the gibbet and one hanging set for the weekend. One victim was a footpad we knew slightly; his capital crime was 'a highwayman who had tried to rob the Mail coach'. It was the same coach we had touched in my first robbery. The difference was that it had now been a frequent target, so they carried an armed guard at the ready. Every day a story appeared either in *The Courant* or *The London Gazette* that indicated that one footpad or highwayman had been caught, and had been stocked or transported or hanged. What's more, there were several advertisements seeking reliable thief-catchers to be rewarded substantially at Old Bailey. Francis, Thomas, and I were mostly quiet around each other and now kept close to Humphreys and Charing Cross. One Sunday, while we lunched,

Thomas finally broke the silence, suggesting that we tour some inns in the north, and after some discussion we decided to go to the city of York, about 200 miles from London.

I remember that day we rode out of London via Tyburn and the gallows there in a close drizzle, clouds almost reaching the ground, fogging our way. No one was about as we rode. The lone body still hanging in the rain, sodden and ragged, cast a pall on our trip for several miles. It persisted, so bleak, it was that we only spoke, and all brightened as the day did after the first forty miles. Soon we were planning that evening's touch. After we found lodgings at an inn called the *Pheasant and Crow*, we settled and planned with the owner, who wanted us to entertain guests on weekend nights and immediately said he was aware of our livelihood by Wilson's manner and that he was happy to give us lodgings for free, if we shared our take with him. Such umbrage did Thomas take at his remarks that he reddened enough to look pink. (I secretly laughed.) "What manner? What ho." Francis calmed him and told the innkeeper "Do not say aught of this again, or ye shall be split like a herring." The innkeeper apologized, and after some discussion, we four came to terms.

This made me nervous, for he might turn catcher if we weren't careful, and I told Wilson and Hyde this when we were alone. We made one foray, fetching £130 from a post-coach full of lords and ladies. We left that inn, letting the innkeeper overhear us saying we were going to Scotland to try our luck. We let him have a share of 20 quid. Thence we set out to Liverpool, traveling that night and vigilant should anyone be following. We had gotten away with a simple ploy.

We went on toward Liverpool and stayed at the *Fox and His Lady*. Here we continued several weeks, waiting some favourable opportunities to rob at the plays which were presented nearby, but no one appeared for us to touch. Francis was in a foul mood the entire time, and when I approached him privately, he told me that he suspected both the innkeeper—as I had—and Thomas of peachin' to the authorities. Both of us decided without consulting Wilson to leave for New-Market, to the famous races which took place about the first of June. Our luck changed.

There we found Lord Gore of Richmond and Lord Tufton of Sheffield in Yorkshire. We were much perplexed to invent the most advantageous way of 'touching' them. Since they did not travel at night and remained almost completely proximate to their lodgings, it was at length we concluded to attack them there at the inn, which was very large and greatly frequented by various classes of people. That worked to our advantage. There was always confusion in the air.

About 7 o'clock in the evening, while the attendants of those gentlemen were in the kitchens and stables, new guests were arriving, and children were causing their usual hubbub, we entered the front door of the *Twin Oaks*. Having bribed the porter with a few guineas, we were immediately let into the coffee room. Lords Gore and Tufton were sitting over a table at a dish of coffee, quietly reading newspapers. We instantly presented our pistols and demanded their money, Lord Tufton delivered us one bank note of £1000 and three others of £500 each. Lord Gore delivered us about 100 guineas, and two gold mourning rings. Hyde stared at me, and I at him, for we were stunned by the amount we were taking. Neither protested, but Gore noted aloud, 'I see your

Knubley Pistol, sirrah, and that you have the Turkish taste in its engravature, so I will identify you, sir. I know those Charing Cross armorers.' I clouted him with my open hand for calling me sirrah, silencing him, and left. It was the only time I ever struck a person, except for once defending myself. We left in haste without incident, mounted our horses, and returned to York. When we returned, we described our windfall to Thomas, who was happy to see we had not left him. Sometimes doubts about one's verity leave you without questioning. This is what happened to Hyde and me regarding Thomas as a thief-catcher in training. He had been with Hyde so long that there should have been no doubt about Thomas Wilson's fidelity. As for me? I realized that I was acting on prejudice and no assured evidence.

Indeed, Lord Gore had a good eye for firearms; he had recognized a new, small pistol I had purchased at Charing Cross at John Knubley's, engraved in ivory with fashionable Turkick devices, one I could more handily conceal on horseback or at a walk than the ones Captain Spain had given me. Hyde told me to toss the Knubley lady's pistol in the river, and I did so, though I fancied it. I will get another, less ornate. The 'bloody' laws had been much inflated by the newspapers, but I did not want to be easily recognized.

We quitted New-Market next morning and went by stage to York, where Wilson presented the bank notes at the bank for payment, he saying that there was no risk, since he had not been there. At York we sought an inn on the Foss rather than the Ouse River. We rested that night at *The Three Shepherds.* Unfortunately for us, Lord Tufton, immediately after the robbery, had dispatched his servant to the bank and informed the constabulary with orders to stop those bills, if offered, and to stop anyone with a Knubley pistol. The bills were accordingly stopped, and Wilson arrested when he appeared at the bank to change them. We were fortunate not to accompany him. He had the excuse that he had not attended that robbery, and that the complaint was against two robbers, one dark, the other with a limp. Since he was neither, he pleaded that the justice release him. Nevertheless, they sent him over.

Thomas was sent to New-Market to be examined at next-Sessions before a justice of the peace. Upon his examination, he hole-and-cornered a message to Hyde to swear that he was riding from New-Market to York with Wilson, and that he saw him pick up a pocketbook containing those bills. I saw to it that the coachman was previously bribed and swore to the same fact. Upon this testimony, Wilson was acquitted. I was not sent for as a witness at this examination, as I understood Lord Robert Manners was then in New-Market and would probably attend the trial. The reason why I did not wish to meet his Lordship's eye was that on the night before we left London, I made a most daring attack upon him. He was walking unarmed, near Hounslow Heath, attended by his footman. I met him, presented my pistol, and he gave me 75 guineas, two gold watches, and two gold rings. Hyde and Wilson were near at hand during the robbery, but they did not discover themselves, leaving me "to play the hero alone." A nice coup. I would not have to appear. Fate is often good to us with small gifts. If I had to testify, Lord Manners surely would have recognized me and would have gibbetted me, or at least put me in stocks. What's more, my bias against Thomas might have made me betray him.

During that time, we robbed several travelers but committed no extreme violence. I must say I lost my temper over the pistol and slapped the Lord, but none were treated as footpads would have. Men were maimed and killed regularly with robberies—one had been beaten so badly for a few shillings and a ring that both sides of his mouth were ripped open, his ears cut off, and the tip of his tongue lopped off. That was the extreme; footpads carried cudgels and swords, and used them. Unless there was violence, however, or in the case of the mail or repeat offenders, authorities rarely checked the evidence or 'alibis', and most frequently, a sop or 'witness' freed the accused. The gibbet was reserved for mail robbers; the gallows for capital offenses. We knew that, and so it was easy freeing Wilson. We also resolved never to take bank notes or 'false paper' again, no matter how lucrative it seemed.

At the latter end of June, we again met at the old rendezvous in East London and divided our plunder. The property which I then had on hand enabled me to live very freely for eight months. My time was spent in that round of celebration, which was well supported by the stock of cash in my own possession, and that of my broker. My broker—a Jew, of course, for it is known that they have a distinct talent for handling money and riches, wealth of any kind—protected my earnings. The cliché is true, and that he did. Nathan was his name. Despite his religion, I trusted him and had laid up much, and with his help had grown more wealth, so it was time to try what I had always dreamt about and go to sea. Frankly, I had been spooked by the incident of the justice and the swiftness with which it happened. One small stumble and the pillory or noose could have been my lot. That, with the reminder that I too was different to others, set me to seek employment elsewhere.

Nathan lived in a part of London called Rag Fair but was ne'er in his shop for pawning. There was always someone with a long nose, he told me, who was asking too many questions about the source of his inventory. His eldest son, Billy, had the burden of selling what-nots from the shop. Nathan left the day-to-day business to him who was perceived by the public to be the head of the business, though those who dealt with Nathan clearly knew he was the one who would set the price. For me, because I was a Negro, I think he was particularly generous. It is known among Jews that they share an affinity with my race, perhaps by reason that we share a similar history of suffering, perhaps because we are markedly different than the majority. He knew the circumstance of slavery over the centuries, as the Hebrews of Babylon and Egypt, and therefore lumped himself with Africans who now reminded him of past sins against their ilk. I must say that we never passed a harmful word or business between us, nor his wench, who was named Naomi. She would have, and had, an alibi for him whenever the Newgate constables endeavored to give evidence against him. Many fences also dealt directly with Billy and, though disguised otherwise, the goods in his shop had been gotten through footpads and men in my profession. Nathan was also so clever an engraver that he could change watch engravings so that an E might become an S, and a Y an M. Thus, anyone could testify that thus and so was his watch, but would find the initials changed on examination. Of the ships asea and in port he vouched for and knew in need, I chose a light sloop sailing the Atlantic triangle called the *Sally*.

I had now resolved to quit this course of life which I had hitherto pursued with so much success. Accordingly, I took my leave of London and my fellows, and I entered on board the brig *Sally*, as Cook, and made two voyages in her to Lisbon. Thomas and Francis had the sorry luck to have been pressed by the Admiralty drunk one night near Hound's Ditch, and were now—until they could escape—part of his Majesty's navy, fighting a war against the colonists. I was again lucky, for I had asked Nathan who I should see to become crew on a merchantman.

And Nathan, I must admit, was instrumental in finding me this occupation when I felt the heat of the laws close behind me. You see, I had gained a reputation for being 'different' than those others who robbed the rich on the byways. I was referred to as a large man, fortunately not a Mountain, for that was still my name, and a dark gentleman, for my manners were well remembered from my childhood with the Mifflins, and my complexion was more like a Lascar. My description and color signaled the authorities to look for me when word of a robbery and 'black' or 'negro' was bantered about.

I began my career as a sailor on the brigantine *Sally*, which hauled copper, much treasured by African traders. Copper, being scarce, had been melted down from brass. Some was made into bracelets and became a treasured object of trade, though only for Africans. I never once recovered one copper trinket in my loot. But then, I never had the occasion to rob anyone of African ancestry. Other cargo aboard was glass beads, gunpowder, pans, and molasses.

The *Sally* traveled to Lisbon carrying tobacco from the colonies, firearms, and beads for the trade, especially in Africa; copper, English barrels, and wool goods. I took two voyages for fear of the gaol, the ship being a convenient refuge, and as cook, I was much below decks. It was during that time that I learned to really cook, for cook I certainly was not, though I bluffed that I was when I shipped the first time aboard the *Sally*. I knew the few things Molly had shown me years before, but I recall that was enough to dodge the crew in my prowess. As I write, I find the very act of putting pen to papers goads my memory. Like wisps of fog off a morning stream, people and objects rise. So, I used my Philadelphia kitchen knowledge to master a galley. The crew never complained. Salt Meat was plentiful, and pease from which I made soup. And with water and some rum added a mash. Fish when we caught it. We had ample juice from lemons to keep the scurvy short, and the crew had it daily—some taking the juice mixed with the ration of rum. There was always hard biscuit. I made some simple roasts and breads and soups, and enough victuals as to keep the crew full. They praised me; the previous cook having had a reputation as a miserable provider of rancid foodstuffs, and flinty.

For desserts, one ration of sugar and cheese was ample. The captain and mate had tea, but it was too expensive for the crew unless we dried the leavings and reused it, as I often did for myself. By this time the colonies, I'd heard, were dumping it in rebellion, but I never lost my taste for it. I still sit at tea when I can. I think it English to do so. When I made the bread, I was to use alum, which made the bread whiter and larger. Some say it kept the sexual desires of the crew quiet, but I never found that to be true. I believe that's a different powder. Depending on when we sailed the first few weeks, I gave us squash, which I made with butter and flour and green beans like the French make them. Some soup I made with celery, onions, galley scraps, and rice and beans.

For the first meal of the day, the crew had gruel from oats and butter, dried biscuit, and cider. Occasionally the captain had venison when the owner provided it, and when he did, I saved some and put it in a pudding with marrow.

I became a good cook that first voyage and received a fine bonus. I left the ship after the second voyage and quickly exhausted my pay. Not wanting to draw upon Nathan's bank for me and anxious to experience the environs of pirates in the New World, I embarked upon the *Fanny*, once again as a cook and as a hand to Kingston, Jamaica, with a Captain Sinclair. He seemed an upright master of ship. As a hand, I was to learn more than pots and pans, meats and greens, or for that matter, what Sails had taught me. The voyage also made me understand something of my past, and my real father's and mother's past, that has partly set me to writing this. It was then I began to learn and hate the real story of slavery. That became my object in sailing to Jamaica—to discover my past.

For the nine months spent aboard the *Fanny*, and in Kingston and Spanish Town, Jamaica, I saw how slaves were treated. I did not have to go far into country. It was not a pleasant experience. Everywhere I went aboard ship and land, I was questioned how I could be free with my black skin and did I have proof. This was not new to me, and I carried my manumission documents like the heart of my body, knowing I would die if they were lost. They were simple, with only Samuel Mifflin's (my foster grandfather) signature and the colonial Pennsylvania seal upon it, but once I was deemed a free man, and to boot raised in that blessed town of Philadelphia from which freedom was springing, I was treated kindly. It was also the contrast of this kind behavior set against the treatment of slaves in Jamaica that made me often mutter oaths under my breath, once I was alone. Here is what my manumission said:

> This document signifies that
> Joseph Mountain is a free man of Pennsylvania Colony and was born free at my residence in PHILADELPHIA,
> 7 July 1758.
>
> *SAMueL Mifflin*   SEAL

A simple paper with a man's name and a legal seal. I thank thee, Lord, for being able to own such a trifle. Let me tell you of some of this, for even the treatment of my cargo on the ship at the beginning of this tale was not enough to describe all that God would allow. Though I will not make an oath, as my Quaker teaching prohibits, I would if it would make the reader of this journal believe its words.

I once saw a 13-year-old slave, the son of a cane cutter, beaten to the bone with a stick. When he cried, his arm bone was broken in four places. Then his ears were slit, mutilating him for life. His crime was picking up a piece of sugar cane and eating it.

I saw leg irons rubbing skin raw and neck irons nearly choking women and men. The heat oppressing them as they sought some comfort, flies ate at their bloody limbs.

I saw men castrated for attending the flirtation of their Mistresses who, bored with their husbands, sought some imagined dalliance with a 'black buck'. Masters, too, who mutilated the breasts of their slave paramours if they complained of their conditions.

I saw the cat, knotted with metal studs, used frequently to lash a man or woman for as little as the loss of 5d. of goods not harvested.

I saw both men and women branded like livestock, carrying the disfiguring mark of their masters forever on their faces, second by second reminding the world that they were slaves.

I saw black men smoked with the hams and bacon in smokehouses until they were nearly dead.

I saw men hanged over fires, so their feet burned while they strangled.

I saw them treated worse than dogs or swine, roasted or half-hanged.

Now you wonder why in any of the grotesque treatments I witnessed, I remained silent and did not protest? I was not present at all of them. In many, I had seen the result and been told or imagined the horror. In others, I observed from afar, secret in my station. And in some, I saw but could not protest because I was outnumbered by white men, or because a protest by one of my color might have brought the same to me. Plainly, many times I feared for my life. It could only stoke the smouldering fire in my heart. I weep that I was a frightened witness. I quail in shame before the Lord that I had not had the courage to defend my fellow men and women.

I was in Spanish Town while the *Fanny* was unloading one day that I was allowed two hours freedom from work in the galley, and I took a stroll. I was questioned often and carefully, for there was a market there that day selling foodstuffs and other wares, and there were many slaves selling goods for their masters. My hair and skin were the signals to anyone in authority to stop me. At one point I was drawn up and asked for my papers by an overseer for the local sugar plantation, who questioned me in detail. After he granted my 'freedom', he asked what it was like for a darkie to be free, more so after I admitted being from Philadelphia where the war still waged, for 'freedom' and the colonies were on everyone's lips. I answered curtly, but not impolitely, "Sir, I was free at birth, so I have never experienced what these folk have," as I motioned to the blacks around me. He rejoined. "Share a drink or two with me, then, and I'll tell you some. Ye seem honest and genteel, like m'Lord."

He was drinking a black rum. As we sat at the east end of the market talking of war, he shared it with me—but only after he carefully wiped the finish and lip of the bottle. It was then he told me stories—stories that only deepened my anger at these whites, these owners, these Lords and Ladies, these masters and mistresses, these overseers and bosses. The overseer belittled the slaves he had tortured and went on in a rapture of cruelty, boasting the more he drank, for he had worked outside of New Orleans as a cotton tasker several years before. I questioned him about this. The man had heard of slave revolts, the Maroons and St. Dominiquè where there was growing unrest, and Panama, where they had already gained their freedom. He joked of Panama, saying, "They are in the jungle, dancing around where they belong. Like howlers in the trees. Take no insult, sir, I know you are a gentleman, they's different than you, sir."

I remember it was then I hatched the idea of joining a revolt. He was nearly drunk when he bragged of how he once put a slave who had tried to escape close to a fire and hung a rasher of bacon over him, so the hot grease dripping from the pork constantly dripped on the man. "It was better than the barrel," he said, and when I asked him to explain, he laughed. "You have a barrel that you drive some nails through, y'see, so they are like porcu-spines on the inside. Then you put the rascal inside and roll him around. When he comes out, 'e don't misbehave no more. 'Course then, you still have to wash the barrel." Then he told me I was luckier than I thought. "Y'all draw the lash on ship, that's nuthin' compared to the bull whip. Now that will skin you quick." At that, I thought of killing a man for the first time—grinding my teeth and tensing my body for control—but I held my ire so as not to be put on. I left the enemy, for that was what he had become, and went to the market to buy fresh limes, guava, mango, beans, and ackee for the voyage, using my conversation with some slave women to calm and divert myself as I shopped their wares. How different they were from the animal I had left. It was not until we were out to sea that the breeze could wash me of that man and thoughts of his kind.

We brought London tobacco and sugar, rice, indigo, and cotton for the cargo. I brought fruit and rum. After their engagements with the British fleet, I heard my mates Wilson and Hyde were still pressed aboard their respective ships. I still had decent wealth, so I sought out Humphreys. It was then that I heard news of Philadelphia, that the war was full blown after the colonies had declared independence from the crown, and the British were occupying New York. I followed the news in the *Register, Post,* and *Courant* regularly after that, knowing all my family and friends were now in in harm's and war's way.

At the *Black Horse*, I became acquainted with one Haynes and Jones, both of Yorkshire. Humphreys spoke for them and introduced me to them as 'old hands.' They were partially initiated in the science of *footpads.* When he acquainted them with my history, they soon proposed that I should resume my profession and join them. My former mode of life possessed many charms in my view. I complied with their request; at the same time doubting if they were possessed of enough courage and skill for companions to one who had served under experienced masters, and who considered himself at the head of the profession.

Our first object was to assail the Newcastle stage, which would be in Tottenham-Court road at 8 o'clock that evening. We were on the spot in time, and I urged them thus: "My lads, 'tis a hazardous attempt—for God's sake, make a bold stroke."

Upon the arrival of the coach at half past 7 o'clock, four miles from London, I seized the bridles of the two foremost horses. Jones and Haynes went to the coach door, and said, "Deliver or death." Lord Garnick and several others were passengers. His Lordship said, "Yes, yes, I'll deliver, you bloody bastards," and instantly discharged a pistol at Jones, the contents of which entered his left shoulder; upon which he and Haynes made their escape. I was left alone in the venture. The coachman was then directed to drive on by Garnick, but he replied that I was holding the horses. Lord Garnick then fired at me without damage. At that, I discharged my pistol at the coach without effect. An excited miss, for I rarely indulged in gun play. Once I escaped and rendezvoused with the others, I dismounted. Jones was so badly wounded from the discharged ball—Garnick had loaded lead ball rather the birdshot I used, so the wound was worse than might would have been—that Haynes and I were obliged to carry him into London upon our shoulders.

Being on foot, we were soon overtaken by two highwaymen, who had assaulted Lord Garnick about 15 minutes before we had engaged the coach. He had fired at them, as us, and one of them was also badly wounded in the thigh. It bled so much, I had to tie a knot on't to staunch the blood. The next day we saw an advertisement offering a reward of 60 guineas for the detection of all the robbers—us. The news supposed that three were killed. This specimen of the enterprise of my new associates convinced me that they were not adepts in their *occupation,* and induced me to quit their society. I must say I learned 'tis better to go with experience than youth and brazen attitudes. It made me wonder how long ago it was such that Hyde and Wilson had so quickly chosen me to venture out with them.

The business which now seemed most alluring to me was that of returning to my past. Considering myself at the head of foot-pads, I aspired for a more *honorable* employment, and therefore determined to join myself to the gang of highwaymen whose rendezvous were at Broad St. Giles's, up Holborne, at the sign of the *Hampshire Hog*, and kept by a William Harrison, a native of the Isle of Man. Harrison was the support, the protector, and the landlord of this whole company. Like Bill Humphreys, he was all about the business and making money. He had no tolerance for shirkers or cowards. I assessed him after we met. I knew in an instant he was bad to the bone.

The horses and accoutrements were kept and furnished by Harrison in a large inventory, which he occasionally supplied to adventurers. He enquired my name, and finding that I was Mountain, who was confederate with Hyde and Wilson, he readily admitted me to the fraternity. He asked if I dared take a jaunt alone. Finding me willing for anything, he quickly furnished me with equipment proper for the expedition. I wore none of my finery but dressed plainly like a Friend, and I reckoned a split with him in my favor. He may have been tough, but he knew my reputation. I was also more experienced, having learned not only from past ventures, but also from my voyages.

Mounted on a very fleet horse and prepared with proper disguises, I set out for Coventry, about 90 miles from London. With dispatch in travelling, galloping until the horse tired, I arrived about 10 o'clock that night. I met Richard Watts coming out of a lane about two miles from Coventry. I rode up to him and enquired if he was not afraid of highwaymen? He replied, "No, I have no property of value about me." I then told him that I was a man of the profession, and that he must deliver or abide the consequences. Upon this, he gave me his gold watch. I insisted on his money and cocked my pistol, threatening him with instant death. He threw me his purse containing 13 half guineas and some pocket-pieces.

The gold watch was valued at 40 guineas. I then ordered him back down the lane, where I accompanied him thither. He was a rather poor man, so I chose to return the coins, keeping only the watch, and fled with the greatest haste into an adjacent wood. There I changed my dress and the horse livery, covered them with brush in a bye place, and rode directly to a neighbouring town, where I put up for the night. The next day I took my course for Newcastle in Devonshire, about 270 miles north of London, and thence to Warrington in Lancastershire.

These were long rides, but as a boarder I found comfortable rooms, and thought deeply about doing something different. *Perhaps I could join with Olaudah Equiano or Ottobah Cugoano...they seemed of like mind and seemed to be influential Negros working in the white society, maybe... maybe the path of abolitionists was not the most exigent way. Perhaps uprisings had a place...they certainly caught one's attention...there was an immediacy at their roots...I will read and investigate more...Mister Mifflin always said that education conquered a plenitude of weaknesses. . ..* These also were freed Negroes of some note who chivvied the gentility to contribute to the abolitionist's cause. My thoughts were valuable during these long journeys. I had to pick a direction and follow it.

Outside of Warrington on the King's Highway at 7 o'clock in the evening, I met a gentleman to plunder. I asked him the time of night; he drew his watch and told me the hour. I observed, "You have a very fine watch." He answered, "Fine enough." "Sir, 'tis too fine for you. You know my profession—deliver." He drew back; I caught his bridle with one hand, presented a pistol with the other, and said, "Deliver, or I'll cool your porridge." At this he calmed his mare and himself and handed me a purse of 8 guineas, and a gold watch valued at £30 sterling. To compleat the transaction, I then took a prayerbook from my pocket and ordered him to swear upon the solemnity of God's word that he would make no discovery of this encounter for twelve hours. He took the oath. I quitted him and heard nothing of the matter till the next morning about 10 o'clock, when I saw a detail of the transaction in the newspapers.

Last Evening Crime

Evening last near Lancaster High-Road, Mr. Charles Dunleigh of Warrickhaven was robbed. A highwayman took 50 guineas, a watch, and two rings, and Dunleigh was forced to take an oath on a book of prayer to keep silent until today. He described the robber as tall and swarthy on a fast chestnut horse. He was extremely polite, with the manners of gentlefolk. Charles Dunleigh was not harmed. The robber may be a religious man.

Any notice should be reported to the Lancaster Sheriff.

I sold the horse and purchased a dapple. Thence, Liverpool was my next stage. Here I tarried two days, making observations for evening adventures. I had been aboard in Liverpool on one of my voyages and therefore knew the port. It was there I inured myself whilst I studied persons whom I might touch. There I contacted the owner of the Lancaster coach and offered to be a guard ont' following night, explaining my background as a former constable from Massachusetts colony. He agreed.

On the night of the next day, I robbed Thomas Reeves of 6 guineas and a gold watch worth about £30 sterling while I waited for the coach. To insult him in his distress, after committing the fact, I pulled off my hat, made a low bow, wished him good night, and set out for Lancaster in company with the stage. It occurred to me that riding as a guard to the stage would secure me against suspicion. Accordingly, I accompanied it to Lancaster, and there put up at the *Swan with Two Necks*. Here I rested for three days, waiting for favourable opportunities.

I am writing this all down as I remember it. It has little to do with bias or slavery, but to be truthful is to tell all, not just shaded details, to serve my aim. I was an expert robber by this time. I had learned well, and the reserve I had grew for my travel and liberality later. I have left out minor touches.

On the third evening at 8 o'clock, I stopped a Col. Pritchard, took from him a gold watch valued at 44 guineas, a purse of 30 guineas, 3 gold rings, and a pair of gold knee-buckles worth about £6. The knee-buckles appeared so tempting, I told Pritchard, I could not avoid taking them. I fancied them for my own wardrobe. At 11 o'clock, I left Lancaster and, having ridden about one mile from town, I stopped, pulled off my hat, and bid him "good-bye." I would wear the buckles when I returned to the *Black Horse*.

Finding the area now dangerous, especially by word of my singular gentilness, I set my course for Manchester, where I put up for about 24 hours at the *Bull's-Head*. There I acquainted myself with the proprietor, one Darcy O'Hare, who made signs he knew my profession. I offered him part of the spoils if he would trade my horse and supply me with lanthorn and clothes for a venture.

The evening following, about 11 miles from Manchester, I "touched" a Quaker. It was nearly 9 o'clock when I met him. I enquired if he was not afraid to ride alone. He answered, "No." I asked him his religion; he replied, "I am a Friend." I observed, "You are the very man I was looking for—you must deliver your money. I am also a Friend." He seemed very unwilling, and said, "Thou art very hard with me. Thou art not Godly." I replied, "You must not *thou* me." He then gave me his plain gold watch, 6 guineas, and four bank notes of £20 each. I returned those, remembering Wilson's trouble. I then presented a prayer-book and demanded an oath that he would make no discovery for 8 hours. He refused an oath, alleging that it was contrary to his religion, but he gave his word that my request should be complied with. I then dismissed him and took a circuitous route for London. The guineas which I had obtained in this jaunt, I concealed and carried in the soles of my boots, which were calculated for that purpose, and effectually answered it. Now I am certain of each robbery, just as I have been cock-sure.

The mare which I rode was trained for the business. Her name was Fern, so named by a delicate young lady who had previously owned and trained her. It was obvious that one in my profession had owned and trained her before I purchased her subsequently. Quiet, fast, and responsive, a mahogany bay with a white star on her face. So well trained was she that she would put her head in at a coach window with the utmost ease and stand like a stock against anything. She also would travel with surprising speed. I was so impressed that I posted a bank note for a suitable portion of my plunder to O'Hare and only signed the letter with an alias, inditing it so it appeared to be a bill of sale for the mare.

Upon my arrival at Harrison's (having been gone eleven days), I gave a faithful narrative of my transactions and produced the plunder as undeniable proof. I never shall forget with what joy I was received. The house rang with the praises of "Mountain, Mountain, Mountain, his eminence, huzzah, huzzah!" An elegant supper was provided, and I placed at the head of the table. Notwithstanding the darkness of my complexion, I was complimented as the first of my profession, and qualified for the most daring enterprises. Fatigued with such a jaunt, and fearing my frequent adventures might expose me, I determined on pursuing other entertainments at home. My old dapple horse was given to another highwayman, and he directed to seek for prey. After one month's absence, he returned with only 16 guineas and was treated accordingly by the gang. He was less adept at the business and was therefore ordered to tarry at home, just to visit the playhouses and sharp it among people who might easily be choused of their property. Each took his tour of duty in course; some succeeded; others, from misfortune or want of spirit, were disgraced.

One young fellow of the party was about this time detected swindling and robbing at Guilford in Surry, tried, condemned, and executed at Tyburn. His hanging had drawn a large crowd. Twig effigies of him were sold for a penny. Port and beer, a terribly sweet drink, was sold for a penny. Papers with drawings of the poor lad, hanging with birds pecking his eyes, were sold. Tyburn was a grim market. I would not attend, even whilst the condemned had been 'one of us.' He made no discovery of the rest of us to the court, tho' we all trembled. There were suspicious looks winging their way among all of us. An execution descended like a sooty fog across our band. A plan was now in agitation to dispatch two or three of the gang to Portsmouth, to attack some of the navy officers. Billy Coats, a Londoner, and I were selected as the most suitable for the expedition. We mounted our horses on the next morning, and reached Portsmouth that day, more than 70 miles.

The two who accompanied he and I—Devon Galt and Bill Wheeler—took lodgings at an inn, *The Anchor and Pipe*, kept by a rich old miser. We were soon convinced that he had cash in plenty, and that it "was our duty to get it"; but the difficulty was what plan should be concerted We waited a day while I developed our action. At length, we plundered the old man's house of about 300 guineas, and £50 sterling in shillings and six-pences. This we did while the old man slept, like mice taking his cheese.

There was a very great clamour raised the next morning. E'en tho' the loss was great, the amount given the news was inflated. The house was surrounded with the populace and, Bill said, "thief catchers". The old fellow was raving at a great rate for his loss of money. I stood by as a spectator, and now perfectly remember the chagrin of the old man and his wife. Nevertheless, we remained at Portsmouth two days, and then returned to London richly laden, and received the applause of our companions. The three following months I spent frequenting alehouses and cheating with false dice, as Hyde had taught me. I had a strange feeling that I should set myself to something different. I had tired of robberies. My dreams had turned as stale as week-old stout. I started reading and began to learn.

CHAPTER 6

1779. Jo reads abolition Negro literature for his edification and to stoke his growing 'no bias' philosophy. He rides daily in Vauxhall wherein he rescues Nancy Allingame; encounters her parents, overcomes their hidden racist objections, and courts and marries Nancy in a 'fleet' marriage. He finds it difficult to adjust to wedded bliss.

On days when the weather demanded a warm fire, grog, and a comfortable chair, I stayed at my quarters or went to the *Black Horse* and read Ignatius Sancho's letters, and abolitionist pamphlets by a Mister Wilberforce and Mister Clarkson, and Aphra Benn's *Oroonoko*. I also recall that I was much impressed by the Reverend Laurence Sterne's response to Sancho's letter. Sterne had written a novel which was very popular. I have forgotten the title, but it was faddish and so funny as to make one laugh out loud. Certainly, I disturbed many by my howling when I read it. I carry it in my papers to bolster my desire to do something to change the world and its bigotry.

🦋 🦋 🦋

There is a strange coincidence, Sancho, in the little events (as well as in the great ones) of this world: for I had been writing a tender tale of the sorrows of a friendless poor negro-girl, and my eyes had scarce done smarting with it, when your letter of recommendation in behalf of so many of her brethren and sisters, came to me—but why her brethren? Or yours, Sancho, any more than mine. It is by the finest tints, and most insensible gradations, that nature descends from the fairest face about St. James's, to the sootiest complexion in Africa: at which tint of these, is it, that the ties of blood are to cease? And how many shades must we descend lower to make 'em so.

I also visited a shop of Sancho's in Westminster that he ran as a greengrocer, but he was not there, having been away on a visit to various abolitionist organizations in England to orate on the cause. I might have argued with him 'though, for I sorely missed my family in the colonies, and Ignatius Sancho was an avowed Monarchist in that struggle.

When it was pleasant, the sunlight glazing the trees and buildings and breezes like gossamer cooling the air and freshening its aroma, Fern, my intelligent steed, ached to leave as I saddled her in our stables—especially on Sundays and days while Hyde and Wilson were away—to ride her early, give her an apple treat, and trot to the pleasure gardens at Vauxhall. She would nose me, whinny, and stamp until I was mounted, and we were riding the streets of London. I had found Vauxhall in my wanderings, immediately taking to them, for, like Philadelphia, it was a land full of greenery and near the river, so that for the single shilling of admission, I could ride among the gentry or linger alone by the water. It transported me and my troubled thoughts, clearing them as I trotted among the paths. As in Fairmount, I could recognize the variety of trees, and that with the breezes riffling the ponds and the susurrating leaves, I was relieved of the anxiety I had from so much robbery. I had resolved to enjoy the fruits of my labours, work less, and perhaps travel and sail more. In despite of my resolve, my habits were now too strong. My feelings were like guilt and not guilt. It wasn't so much that I rued and had to atone for committing crimes, but more like exerting the strain of breaking some tethers. These gyves were the principles I had learned all through my years in the Mifflin household, at Meeting, and from my childhood friends. Now that I was reading Sancho's essays and other pamphlets on abolition from the local Friend's Meeting, my reasoning had begun to mature regarding freedom, bigotry, differences, and bias.

My London associates were not bookish, as I had been as a youth. So, I explored places where I might examine politick matters with others. There were a few coffee houses where some authors and students gathered. I would seek them out a' times and listen to small debates while I relaxed with chocolate or coffee. I never took part in these debates, since I was not secure in my knowledge and feared losing the luxury of being a bystander. I never intermixed business with my leisure. I still enjoyed reading and thought it a skill that was the gateway to freedom—freedom from the ignorance that I encountered more and more frequently.

In April I took to Vauxhall Park each morning with Fern and rode the length, noting those who had ridden early and those who were late, some who had tristes and some walking alone. This was a rider's park and a lover's one. Many young couples would sneak off to find seclusion in the woodland

and shrubberies with their pickniks. I would trot or walk Fern to notice new fashion. Cleverly applique'd waistcoats or embroidered ones always caught my attention. Shoe buckles or knee buckles for britches, and decorative hangers, women's perukes, lace camisoles that were worn as outer garments, and beribboned stockings. Early morning, it became my habit to stop and have a coffee, a small cake or pastry and let Fern drink from a fountain.

I believe she enjoyed the park as much as I, observing the people, dogs, and other horses, tasting the grass, and appreciating the odors of that woodland scene. It was so much different than the slopped-up highway, late night sounds, firearms startling her and my nervous body astride.

There was a colonial mixture of all class of people, owing to the cheap admittance and refreshments and sundry attractions. Negros, lascars, whites, china-men, Germans, Italians, French—I would sometimes see a trollope I had seen near Mayfaire, mothers and the infants in prams, other riders—some in formal togs, some not. At twilight many lovers took advantage of the dimly lighted arcades for their sexual liaisons and dalliances. And at night, after the warning at nine to "Take care of your pockets," there were often entertainments of lighted pictures, shadow shows, or clockwork animals to amuse a visitor.

Associate harlots and footpads frequented there, sometimes foiling their own object by their surfeit. I avoided any association with them within the confines of the garden to protect my reputation and my work. Despite the somewhat unsavory reputation of Vauxhall, one could see many lords and ladies taking their ease, and it was there that I met and became acquainted with a Miss Nancy Allingame, a white girl of about 18 years of age. I took the meeting as fateful. But that in a moment. She was different than the doxies and harlots I knew from the by-ways of London, and unlike Essie Dickinson, she was direct and not a tease. She also had a sense of humour and a wit, as well as some sand, which I respect in a woman. I had seen her once before and noted that she rode like a man astride the horse, and was a daring horsewoman, taking some hedge jumps. Her horse was as fleet as Fern. But Fern would easily know when to skip a step and gain a turn, or add one and force t'other into a hitch. I'd bet if I knew her, I could have raced her and won.

Now there were many African women in London, and in the year and a half that I'd been in England, I had met none whom I fancied, so I thought if I had the opportunity to meet any young woman who had good virtues, I would welcome it. It just so happened one day with Nancy. Circumstances were thus: she had dismounted and was enjoying the antics of a clockwork lion as I rode by the bridge, unattending t'others near her. But attending her closely was a footpad I knew bent on snatching her purse. He pushed her down. As he reached for the loot I dismounted and gave him three swift blows with my quirt to the back of his neck, and he fled. He ran with a yelp, dropping his hanger and her bag. As I helped her up, she thanked me, flushed with excitement. I joked that he was like the clockwork lion there, crossing the bridge to eat her. Unflustered, she blushed that her African prince had saved her—what's more, she denied being tasty.

Once she calmed, we walked. Fern nosed her in sympathy. After several minutes of gracious conversation and chatting about horses, my interest was sealed: I telling her my name and that I was the son of a rich merchant in Philadelphia; she, responding that she was the daughter of a privy councilman from a township to the north toward Warwickshire in Islington. She also told me she had seen me before and wondered of who I was. She was thankful for the rescue, kissed me on the cheek, and invited me to visit her home. I said that I would visit either on the morrow, or next day after. As I took my leave, she waved and said, "I know the sorrow of your people," and rode away. When I thought on it, I was not taken in, for I had often heard whites say similar things to inveigle themselves into one's amity, meaning little in truth by such comments. But as I was to learn later, she was sincere, having worked with abolitionists in Islington at her Friends' Meeting and having attended lectures by Olaudah Equiano and James Ramsey, of whom I know only by reputation.

When I met Nancy, as most men whose lives are altered by romance, I began to change. I kept my promise and met her amid the thanks of her parents for the rescue of their daughter, and began to dine with them, frequently visit, and eventually court their daughter.

Her family and she lived in a two-story brick in the latest style with cream trim on the entablature and a red door—was this a symbolic warning? Even on the first day we met, her father, especially, let me know that he knew my race and hoped his daughter would marry well above her station, so "she could, with her connubial wealth, pursue those humanitarian ideas she had and become a contributor to such societies which imparted those ideas. I know, Joseph, you probably wish it also. Now, tell me whence you came to London and how you manage. I'd like to get to know you, since she seems to be taken with her 'hero'." Her mother seemed shy and said little.

We had tea on that visit, and I told them I was from a noted Philadelphia family, describing the town, my upbringing, a nearly complete history; and of my voyage, and Sails, and my two trips to Lisbon. I answered their questions as best I could, leaving out my errant life in the last three years and substituting import-export broker for highwayman, and business proceeds for swag and booty. I was anxious and damp from the visit—sweating, I recall—so that when I took leave, I had to remove coat and waistcoat and open my shirt as I rode.

I had never reacted to white folk before with such disquietude and agitation. Still, I got many an invite from Nancy and began to frequent the Allingames' home. Though they were gracious, I could tell that her parents—particularly her father—were not happy that his daughter was in love with a 'blackamoor'. I overheard one of their squabbles when Nancy and I sat in the garden one day. Her father had mentioned something about 'Mister Othello and his daughter'. Of course, this angered me, but both of us ignored it. When I asked Nancy, 'What of that?', she told me her mother would decide and that she already favored me. Nancy said a mother and daughter share too many stories to ignore.

We continued our rides in Vauxhall Gardens because Nancy had some tender sentiment about it, but we also chose to walk and ride in Chelsea at Ranleigh Gardens, which she considered more fashionable, owing to visits of royalty there. It was more than two shillings to enter, had frequent musick concerts, which we would attend in afternoons with picnick lunches on the grass, and once we attended a masquerade, I dressing as a gallant highwayman and she, as my royal victim. It was a garden for lovers, with lakes, walks, a Chinese pavilion, Handel concerts, and several painted buildings.

On occasion she would meet me, stealing away from her parents on the ruse that she was visiting a friend, and I would buy bread and Cheshire, cold chicken, and a French claret for 5 or 6 s. We would meet in the woods with the rest of the lovers, dine with the breeze and wild creatures. So, I had spent my time robbing—not coin and jewelry, but virtue—by walks and weekly meetings. We soon were betrothed. We wed six months after meeting. Early on, there was much that I told her of footpads and street robbers, but omitted my occupation.

I told her that I took trips to handle the trade accounts of those ships carrying cargo for the companies I represented. I know when she met me, she had been taken by my 'exotic nature' and regaled her friends with some of the tales I had told her. This I learned from some of her friends who fancied me. She had told me of her work with the abolitionists. (One should know that Negroes were considered from a much different point of view in England than in the colonies and had a much freer connection to whites, owing to the prevalent idea there that there are no slaves.) William Wilberforce, forging his reputation as a youthful orator and writer, was largely responsible for this attitude, though as the years moved on, Equiano and other freed slaves contributed to that feeling.

Her father was much against our association—as I have said—being of a conservative and protective nature, threatening at one point to disinherit her, calling me, she said, a damned rebellious colonial and a blackamoor at that. But Nancy was an independent woman with her own fortune of some £500, which had been in trust as a dowry, and her own house in Islington. She was not the chattel that other women were—I liked that. A freed slave's attitude. Beside that, she had an unassailable ally in her mother, who supported her daughter's wishes to marry wholeheartedly. I believe her 'Mum', as she called her mother, genuinely liked and supported me.

In the end, we entered a secret 'Fleet' marriage. These were marriages without carriages, great guest lists, frequently missing the parents, and without all the folderol of banquets, rehearsals, togged-out wedding parties and such. We plainly wanted to be married. And the secret ceremony was appropriately Quaker. The parents objected to the match, we were by the day more and more lusty, and as feisty as Nancy was, she would not give up her virgin's gift until she knew the knot had been tied. Our witnesses were Francis Hyde, Mary Haverhart, Fleet Albemarle, Phoebe Marston, and William Humphreys, attending the ceremony in Nancy's house in Islington. Thomas Wilson was at sea. I dressed all in black, a detail that Francis teased me about as being apropos for work and play. She wore a simple gown of white silk with a small veil. John Dunton was the Quaker pastor. We decided to join the Islington Meeting, for there is where she worked. Nancy had inherited her dowry and the small cottage from her grandfather on her mother's side. Her father was paid a modest salary but would never have been able to supply a dowry of the size required for some gentleman of means to marry her, as he had hoped. So, we felt we were making the whole situation better by our secret vows.

That evening, when we revealed that we were married on a visit to the parents, one might have imagined the walls torn down in Milton's Hell, such a torrent of curses by Nancy's father and such tears and wailing by her mother. We spent many hours talking with them and calming them both. I silently forgave him his denunciations referring to my skin color, heritage, and animal associations; he had lost a daughter, and I had gained the prize

I've told you of her father's dreams. He revealed that he had made inquiries about me via connections in London and through Portsmouth, London, Liverpool offices of a variety of merchant shipping companies. None responded that they knew me, to my good fortune. What's more, no word of my real occupation had surfaced. No letters sent to the Mifflins in Philadelphia had been answered. I did not sigh loudly enough when I heard this, but I sighed. Mister Allingame finally said, "You are a black mystery, dark, dark, dark, Joseph, but my daughter loves you, and I will accept that." He shook hands with me; the mother tearfully hugged and kissed me; that was that. Nancy and I talked of our plans with them, dined, and returned to the cottage and our wedding bed. Time was to pass quickly.

It became obvious—the subject had never been raised until we were wedded—that Nancy wanted a large family, many children, and as soon as she could, she wanted to get with child. This was the flint-strike to a smouldering fire that lasted the entire marriage. My case was that I needed to enlarge my business enough, so we would not be wanting or have needy children. Hers was for the progeny, memories, homespun family So, for the time we chanced it and were sexually active. I used sheepskins and bladders as a preventative. Nancy never complained. We were good lovers. She was like some thirsty Saharan at an oasis.

Our lives became filled with social events, concerts, dinners, evenings at home with me on the fiddle and Nancy playing her spinet, visits from Thomas Wilson home from his Royal Navy adventures, Francis over to play whist with Nancy's friends, Phoebe Marston or Mary Haverhart, with whom he flirted sinfully, and at least once a month, her mother and father, who had now treated me as family.

I had not received a letter from Mistress and Mister Mifflin in over a year. There had been a note that the British were occupying Philadelphia in the *Courant,* so I wrote the following at Nancy's urging:

✦ ✦ ✦

Dear Mistress Sarah and Mister Thomas (and Molly),

Forgive me for the tardiness of news. You might ween that I am dead by the long silence. I had thought it best, with the war in the colonies and my travels, to wait until I had sufficient news to relate. My business is growing, and I have added recovery to the import-export services I provide. I hope and pray the Creator has kept you safe and unhurt. I am. Know that when you receive this that I am happily married to Mistress Nancy Allingame of Islington, a small town just north of London. We might, when this war is over, visit since I miss the greene town and Nancy would love to meet you and see where I was raised. I hope you also do not suffer from the hardships I read about in the News we receive. I see that Gen. Washington and the colonial army have defeated the King's troops, and they have left New York and are occupying Philadelphia. Do they cause difficulty for you and Molly? Are Grandfather Samuel and my father Fling still alive? I am engaged in trade and have two partners; Messers Hyde and Wilson, and my recovery business and I are well. When you receive this please send my heartfelt salutations to Essie, Topher, and, Mister Mifflin, to Messers Franklin, Dickinson, and your other revolutionary (a blessed epithet) friends. I wholly support the 'cause'. I hope the war ends soon in your favour. Please forgive the long absence. I think of you every day, and still welcome the discoveries I make, with all gratitude for your generosity. Please write and tell me news of your lives.

Your most grateful, respectful, and loving adopted son,

Joseph

17 Canby, Islington, England <u>or</u> The Black Horse, care of Mr. William Humphreys, Charing Cross, London, England

PScrip: I have received no mail from you since I left. I hope that it is only the rigamarole of trying to send a letter so far and the arrant knaves we entrust our mail to. Perhaps if Mister Franklin visits, I can intercept him and receive and post news with him. If you see Essie, please give her my fondest regards.

🙦 🙦 🙦

I also needed to add a patina to my 'legend' for my wife. Frequent 'trips' with my business partners, my penchant for blood sports and late nights gambling, and a marriage bed that grew quickly cold wore on us. Early on we would go to the theater, concerts either in Chelsea or Vauxhall Pleasure Gardens, and, for a times, we were soothed of daily cares by innocent amusement. Nancy's parents seemed to warm to us, once they saw that we were 'settled' and would have us to their celebrations and Sunday dinners frequently. I did not hear from Philadelphia. I suspected the hardships of war, shipping restraints, and the vicissitudes of life to be the villains in this regard.

More and more, though, the Allingames and Nancy harped about children. I would merely change the discussion to business. I wanted none. The entire subject was a pall. For someone who loved ratting and bear baiting, nights out with my gents, I was a terrible husband. The comfort of home turned into a campaign of armies set to destroy each other, each laying siege t'other. I quickly exhausted all the property I gained in the union. I did besiege some £500 dowry. I spent none of mine. I missed the highway and its danger, and I missed the sea, both more than I enjoyed married life. In two years, the marriage dissolved. I had thought love would last, that I could change my life. Perhaps, again, I can blame my youth, or rather, my lack of worldliness and ability to desire a home and warm hearth. In the last few months, I lived again at *The Black Horse.* Nancy moved back to her embracing father, who now did not speak to me. I am certain Nancy received admonishments by the score. This is a practice, I do notice, persons use to feel superior rather than comforting. I moved out of Islington, anxious for new adventure.

There was no divorce, since it involved petitions to parliament and a great deal of money. Time we didn't feel we had. She was young. She had been hurt by me, and Nancy and I were satisfied that I would never marry again, and that neither of us would lay claim to each other. There was nothing wrong with our marriage save that we should never have married. We each were so different. She said she would seek an annulment and lie to the authorities that I had abandoned her. I did not quit the Meeting; I simply stopped going. So much for religion. So much for romance. Her father finally showed his real colors and said it was good riddance to a 'criminal nigger.' I have never again made the same mistake.

After my marriage to Nancy was over, I returned to Charing Cross. Bill Humphreys found me suitable and discreet quarters. It was with much joy, for I was well acquainted with folks I had abandoned when I went to Islington to live and was welcomed roundly wherever I went. But I was equally consumed by guilt over my profligacy, my abandonment of the Mifflins, Nancy, and any of my childhood values. It was if a cloud of insects followed me, stinging me painfully at times with a poison of guilt. I felt inured in my occupation, stopped my visits to Vauxhall and Islington, and in the sinks of London continued my fascination with gambling at blood sports, adding whoring to my needs—this because I had developed a lusty taste for women's bodies, having had a regular diet with Nancy for two years. I used a sleeve while I was married to avoid pregnancy then and was quite comfortable with it when I indulged. Then a bawd I met led me to one of her 'more expensive' pleasures.

One of my favorite haunts during marriage, and one at which I lost much of Nancy's dowry, was at St. Giles Rat Castle. It was the shabbiest and dirtiest of places, another basement, like so many others. Large, filthy, smelling of blood and animal and human sweat, dog feces, and stale beer. Odor leaking from the lights. The place one would think not entertaining. It was always full of a crowd, late at night and clamorous. Pulsing like one's heart. One could imagine the doors bellowing. The shouts of the bettors and oddsmen laying their wagers filled the room. When the rats were let out into the enclosure below the stands, there was a yell, and then low murmurs—a throbbing. A horde of rats swarmed together at one end, and the referee and a timer asked for silence.

The announcement might be: "Terrier Jessup will kill fourteen rats in one, I say, just one minute." The owner of Jessup readied the dog. Fourteen rats, some as large as a cat, were released into the enclosure. As soon as the dog was placed on the ground, the timer started. And with a bite, a shake and broken neck, and a drop, the terrier would go to work. Any half-dead rats were hit by the referee a few times, and if it roused and escaped, the rat was considered lively and had to be killed for certain. I usually was able to estimate the skill of the dogs, for I had studied the certain terriers which had been bred to be ratters in corn cribs on small Shropshire and Yorkshire crofts. Such fierce temperaments in such ladies' toy lap dogs, I suspect, were dangerous to any merkin that let it nest among its folds.

I made a lot of money that season without habit on the pike roads. And it fed my intelligence of the 'oh so noble' lords and ladies who frequented the rat castles. I spoke with many before we'd meet them on the highway. It was quite easy to determine a good touch at the bettor's stall, and to see what woman was attached to what man. Oh! The excitement. Such that I forgot my guilt o'er my too hasty marriage. Ratting was always popular while I lived in London. Some dogs as large as thirty pounds got the reputation of champions by killing hundreds a night for weeks on end. The blood literally pooled in the arena that evening when the record was set. Brat, a sable Beagle Rat Terrier of a muscular two stone weight, killed 120 rats in 6 minutes. I lost that bet, since several rats revived and were not dispatched. Unfortunately, I loved the sport so much, I wagered frequently and imprudently. Then, I got one of my small internal imp whispers, like fate guiding me. It was then I began to miss another of my loves—the sea.

Chapter 7

*In which Joseph meets a whore named Jenny,
sees a former associate in the gibbet,
recalls a Tyburn hanging,
and ruefully examines his life. He and Francis attend a dog
fight between Pearl and Negra, encounter some farm
toughs, and Joseph picks a winner.*

One night, before I sought out Francis Hyde, some months after my divorce, I planned to celebrate an evening's pleasure at a house known for a more reputable group of ladies of the night: a game or two of Ombre, some music, wine, and a fine dinner with one of them. It was my birthday on the weekend, so I named it a three-day sport. It would be a happy April day. No Arian demigod would enter with a sword to ruin it. The proprietress, Mme. Sylvia Duclassé, or so she called herself, had promised me a special birthday gift. To arm myself appropriately, I visited my brokers—both Nathan and Moses—and redeemed several watches and two of three rings I had harvested in the last week. One I would keep for a *petite pourboire* for my maid of the evening. Nathan told me to keep a gold ring I admired, with an emerald that was set stylishly between two classical nymphs who held the stone erect in their hands. I told him it was meant for a lady that evening, so he put it in a small box and wrapped it in a piece of bright green silk damask that had Egyptian figures on both sides.

I dressed as a gentleman and wore my hanger, and carried a small pistol made by one of the Charing Cross armorers to protect the £300 I had partially redeemed. This one, unlike the others I often carried, was primed and loaded with bird shot, for I did not want to mortally wound a thief, if there were one. That was unlikely, for transportation was being provided as part of a suite of entertainments Mme. Duclassé had promised.

Her price for such a service was £50 for the evening. She received her money the week before, so she could plan her theatrical plan of the various acts during the evening. I was only to provide something extra for my escort that night.

It was a clear evening, cool enough to wear my embroidered Turkish waistcoat and matching stockings—these purchased by Nancy last year for my birthday. Nostalgia always interferes with our memory. I also wore a short wig and the silver buckles I had gained from the Marine officer nearly two years before. Madame had me picked up at my lodgings in one of the new Stanhope Gigs. Unlike most I knew, this driver was well-mannered. When I entered the coach, I was greeted by a young beauty—my escort for the evening and companion for the night. Her name was Jenny. She was even fairer than Nancy, pale as a lily and blond, and of ample weight to be like a cushion as she snuggled against me, and she and I were quick to become acquainted in our conversation and otherwise. It made the ride luxurious, in the Roman sense.

Jenny wore a simple *chemise* of green silk. It was backless and in the fashion of the French, few undergarments, no bum-pads, no panniers, a scarf of lace and a small straw bonnet, embroidered rose sandals. She wore no wig and had luxurious, thick curly brown hair falling to her neck. I was aroused from the moment I saw her; my pego began jumping.

I still had rueful feelings by all that had happened in the last few years, but these clouds left quickly. I felt less man and more boy. Madame's residence was next to Covent Garden, and I heard from Madame later that Jenny had asked if she could be with the 'handsome blackie, Jo', for she heard much talk of me, and had spied on me while I played cards once with Francis. Her sister trollopes had told her stories, she said, of my race's prowess in love. I laughed, for I must say talk is usually false, as this was, when it is passed around like horses' oats. I was no different than most men.

When we arrived, we were welcomed by Madame and escorted to her dining parlour. By now Jenny and I had established an amiable harmony. I laughed at her mots, and she giggled at mine. We talked of London and our backgrounds. Hers was a common story. She had been raised on a sheep farm in Yorkshire and been home schooled. Her mother was a sweet woman, ill since Jenny's birth, and so after she was old enough to walk and carry, her father set her to tasks—the laundry, bringing firewood into the hearth, peeling potatoes. She had no dowry, no prospects, her mother had passed away two years before that day; her ague-plagued father was under the care of his brother, who had no room for her, so she packed a bag and took what little money she had and rode into London on a drizzly day and got work as a flower hawker near Covent Garden. Madame saw her at her stalls and offered her a place to stay, meals, and employment. "I have only been here two months and have yet to earn my keep." She blushed, and I put my arm around her, she clearly needing solace.

"I have a nice body and I am not plain. And I can learn what men want. Please don't choose another, Jo. I feel like it is fate that made you my first, and maybe you have a trick or two to teach me." Then she took my hand and smiled so sweetly, I could not deny her. I told her a little of my London history, but only incidents on the highway, and I talked about what I had experienced asea. We dined well on roast beef, Yorkshire pudding which Jenny said she could improve, vegetables baked with honey and onion, and a berry crumble. We both had wine, and Jenny had never had chocolate, so I ordered one for her while I sipped my Malmsey.

We then went to the card room, where she played as my partner at Ombre—still a fad for women—and then Whist. She helped me spend my money at dice, and sweetly accepted the winnings we had. We ended the night betting chances on Faro. Luck was with us both. I had won double the amount the night had cost. I gave her half and, after she asked, recommended several clothiers she might want to visit. We retired for the night to our room in Madame's house. When I was there, I gave her pourboire wrapped in green. She admired the cloth, carefully setting it aside and opened the box, discovering with much delight—and mine—the ring I had brought. "Jo, this is too much for such as me. I fear if I wear it here, it might be stolen." I told her I had spoken to Madame, fearing the same, but I wanted her to have it. Madame assured me that she would hold it for safe keeping if

Jenny asked her. Jenny thanked me several times that night in private ways I won't reveal.

Our love making was playful, for that was the manner she chose. She had said that since I was gentleman highwayman, I should be gentle when I stole her virtue. "But. Jo, you cannot steal my heart unless I choose to give it." She had embellished me with a sheep's sleeve bedecked with yellow ribbons to tie. As I lay abed, she removed her garments item by item, pausing between each to reveal some feature. Her nipples were pink and erect on her small breasts, her stomach soft and cushioning, her cheeks a pillowy melon from Spain, and her quim was soft, moist, and welcoming. I felt safe, since it was her first time. And I assured her I was free of any of Venus's curse or pox. At evening's end, I don't believe Jenny was sorrowful. For after exploring and embracing several times, I certainly was not.

That night she had sat with me at table. I had the winning cards, a good port, some moist beef, a playfully delightful companion for the night, and met some other important patrons. Of those who played at cards that night were one ship's owner, two colonists from Jamaica and Ste. Dominquè, and an army officer.

The colonists had talked at length, when they noticed my color, about slave unrest in the Caribbean Islands and compared it to the conflict on the mainland; the ship owner heard some of my interest and knowledge in sailing and presented his business card; and the army officer was obviously quite well-off, introducing himself as a Major Benedict Arnold, just returned from the colonies. He and the others were distracted by Jenny's beauty, to my advantage. Major Arnold lost quickly and a great deal. I remembered having met him that night when, during the riots some weeks later, I and some friends robbed his house. He was absent on that occasion, did not flirt as he had with Jenny, played no cards; he and his wife only accompanying our work with snores, one deep and rumbly and the other wheezing and melodious.

At Madame's he had regaled us with tales of spies in the colonies. Told us of some of the battles, of New York, of General Washington. He had known my grandfather, Samuel, who was Quartermaster for the Continentals, but not enough to tell me of him except that he was efficient in the way he handled provisions for the colonials. The Major was happy, he said, to be at home, since he knew one associate had been caught as a spy and executed. In all it was a memorable evening. When I had returned early the next morning, Francis had left a message that we should talk the next day. I was disappointed to hear from him; Jenny and I had had such a wonderful time that I was planning future visits and nothing on the highway.

In Dorking, the night after my amorous weekend, I had heard there was bear-baiting and thought it might be an entertainment more exciting than the other small animals I had watched. I rode out to an inn called the *Sable Cock and Hearts*, had dinner, and enquired of the proprietor, who I was told knew whereof the bear. He gave me directions. I found the place.

Much to my dismay, there was little contest, the bear being old and slow and the dogs vicious. I was both drawn to these struggles and had tired of them. When I saw the bear almost walking in his sleep, I thought of the cruelty of this 'sport'.

It was the same with badgers, and dogs, and bulls. Why was I interested in seeing clashes in which creatures were bloodied? Why were all these folk drawn to these exhibitions of blood? Even fist fighting was the same. It wasn't England solely; it was everywhere on earth. What was so ingrained in human beings to spawn such a fascination by war, strife, blood, hatred, death? It seems that there is some fluid humor in men especially that impels them toward violence. It is not the same in women who, lacking whatever this humor or substance, are nurturing and kind, comforting and tender, soft and welcoming. Why do we men do the one thing, and then seek out women who are the opposite? 'Tis a mysterious puzzle. It is as if the male action is a disease, and the woman's nature a cure.

I had watered Fern and, feeding her a carrot, was about to mount and leave when some local farmers shouted to me. The two thought it entertaining to people standing by to bait me by calling me 'Bear' and 'Black Bear', and the bear 'The Nigger'. My anger was strong enough that I almost made the mistake of confronting them. I was reaching for my pistol, but my father Mifflin's wisdom prevailed, and I left and galloped back to Westminster. I eventually cooled my fire, found Hyde, and we sought out a card game.

In our travels on Sunday, Francis and I passed an old associate, who weeks past had shot and killed a man for a mere 20 shillings. He had, unknown to us, been sentenced to the gibbet and was caged in it, hanging from its post. Now this was supposed to be no more than a shaming like the stocks, I understand, though they have used it on some hardened thieves or slaves, easily casting opprobrium on its occupant. I know some punishers have used the gibbet to display the corpse of a hanged man, to set an example to those who saw him. But others, like our friend, were in themselves set to punishment, slowly starving and thirsting a man who died for all to see. Ofttimes passers-by killed the prisoner out of mercy, moved by their cries for sustenance. It was chastening to see. I only saw—I remembered his name at that moment—Stiles Belshot in the gibbet for a moment. I could not help him, but it was enough to think hard on my profession. As we rode past, Francis asked if we should kill Stiles to ease his suffering. I thought of it for a moment, but cautioned him to sheath his pistol, saying 'the law has enough to seek us; it is a harsh judgment, but he is almost dead, and the same fate would shadow us if we did so.' So, we rode on, mute in our thoughts.

Strange also that I was in such a dark study, for I had had a wonderful weekend with Jenny, untouched by such solemnities. Nevertheless, my mood was pitch.

A gibbet was a curiously fashioned contrivance by a cruel smith, I think. Round the knees, hips and waist, under the arms and around the neck of the naked victim, iron hoops were riveted close about the different parts of the body. Iron braces crossed these again, from the hips right over the centre of the head. Iron plates and bars encircled and supported the legs, and at the lower extremities were fixed plates of iron like old-fashioned stirrups in which the feet might have found rest, were not the torture increased, compared to which crucifixion itself must have been mild, by the fixing of three sharp, pointed spikes in each stirrup, to pierce the soles of the victim's feet.

The only support the body could receive, while the victim endured, was given by a narrow hoop passing from one end of the waist bar in front, between the legs, then to the bar at the back. Attached to the circular bar under the arms stood out a pair of handcuffs, which prevented the slightest movement in the hands, and on the crossing of the hoops over the head was a strong hook, by which the whole fabric, with the sufferer enclosed, was suspended. And so, his hands secured, unable to rest his feet on the stirrups, his whole weight taken by the bar between his legs, deprived of food and water, exposed to sun, death came not violently by rope or gunshot, but slowly and agonizingly over many days. The specifications for the torturer illustrate the lesson for the offender.

I did not want this as a fate, or to be hanged at Tyburn where the punishment was a spectacle to entertain the crowd, which would gather far in advance of the 'lesson'. This reminded me of the torture slaves endured daily, some even more cruel. The thoughts chastened me in solitude every day now.

At Tyburn Tree, an oak where Wilson and Hyde took me once early in my association, wanting to frighten me should I be careless, we attended a 'hanging'. More like our evening's entertainment, they said, but it was not. Straw images of the accused and miniature gallows were sold to the children who came, and who showed an exceptional delight, like wicked imps, when the execution was performed. Oftentimes the mob pelted the executioner, as well as the accused, with offal and rotting food. It was a frolic, some thought, but not I; so, I thought more on how to find an exit from my trade.

Francis Hyde and I finished the day of my weekend celebration by riding to Middlesex, where we tarried two days making observations for evening adventures. We both were deep in thought and hatched a plan that when Thomas Wilson returned, we would travel to the continent, thereby mixing pleasure with our usual adventures. We could ply our trade with less fear and see some of France and Spain, to boot. Pleasure distracted our planning. We would talk to Thomas to get his wisdom. We also visited a bawdy house and went to watch two magnificent fighting dogs.

Now I have written about blood sports before, but this one, like my voyage to Jamaica, had a deep impression on my mind. I had received directions to the Warrington Pit from the bawd. When I and Francis arrived that evening and went to place our bets, three men remarked that "they like to see if the darky had as much grit as the Staffordshire 'Negra' who was going to fight that night against the champion White 'Pearl' Bull Terrier", and they said it loudly enough and observing me as I was about to wager, nodding at me and hoping the two of us might answer their taunts. They were rough country men, though, ignorant and unmannered, and I saw it would be perilous to rise to the bait, so I only nodded and bowed and smiled and looked subservient. I placed a £40 bet on the 'Negra', knowing that the size of the bet, as well as the object of my favor, would blanket their racist taunts. Francis Hyde's anger was greater, though. He started for them with pistol out. I had to calm him with words, reminding him of both Tyburn and the gibbet. The men took note and watched us as we left for the pit. I stopped to relieve myself, and likewise make certain my pistols were as ready as Francis's. Francis Hyde had always been very professional, of a steady temper such as I, cooling himself of any ire until lately. As with my humor, his had changed, and he showed less interest in continuing robbery as a profession. I resolved to stay close to him lest he act foolishly.

The pit was like a wasp's nest with the buzz of bettors. It was obvious this was to be a big night, since all the talk was about the final fight by the Negra and Pearl, the latter being much favored by the odds. Two preliminaries ended quickly. One dog would not scratch, and another would not fight. In both cases they were no contests, and both the owners and dogs left in shame, accompanied by hoots, whistles, and much rowdiness among the crowd. I must say that a scratch is a line in the sand that an attacking dog must cross before the opposing dog is loosed. In the first preliminary the dog did not cross the line and thus lost. In the second preliminary, the attacker crossed the line with a fury, but his opponent cowered and would not counter his attack. With those disappointing matches out of the way, the buzz grew until I saw the champion. Pearl was a beautiful specimen—and very strong.

Pearl was a tight-muscled Staffordshire Terrier, covered by healed scars that displayed the bull terrier's history of conquest. I felt some regret at my reaction to the taunts of the farmers. Until I saw the black Staffordshire proudly strut into the ring. Only then did I smile to myself at my pride in her color. Negra was a beautiful fighting animal, and animal she was, with rippling muscles, a short pant that showed her keen yearning for battle, and bright vigilant eyes. For the first round, Pearl would come to scratch first. Thereafter they would alternate. There was a rush to place even larger wagers. The setters held their dogs. They waited on Mister Killaney, the referee, who had weighed each. In that they were equal, no handicap was given. They readied. Pearl rushed the Negra before her setter had released her and nearly bit the Negra's setter. It was clear this was an experienced dog, but Negra fought and shook gamely and released when the setters grabbed their dogs after the round. Now it was Negra's turn to scratch.

Unlike Pearl, she crossed the scratch slowly, waiting for Pearl's setter to free him, feinted a cower, and a retreat, and at that moment grabbed Pearl by the neck and did not let go the entire round, holding vise-like with a bloody mouth as Pearl tried to shake her. I have to say I was proud of her. Though I knew neither dog nor setter, my fury was still up about my encounter with the country lads. One could easily mark the muscles in her strong shoulders as she held. Pearl tried to escape, but Negra hung on as if she had grown out of Pearl's neck. Pearl clearly was winded, having expended such energy trying to free herself. Both dogs were now lathered. One was bloody. Her setter sponged off Pearl more frequently than Negra, who was breathing normally but clearly excited. She was enjoying this battle. Her tail was wagging as she awaited the next set.

In the third round, Pearl scratched as quickly as she had before, but this time Negra ducked the attack and once more grabbed Pearl's now bloody throat. Again, Pearl tried to free herself without success, and just before the round was to end, fell exhausted. In a minute it was over. Negra was declared the new Lancastershire champion, and Pearl, still alive but badly wounded, was carried by her setter off to recover with more scars. I claimed my £800 in winnings and left. Shortly after we mounted our horses, one of the farmers who had taunted me nodded with some respect, as if to say, "Great fight, Blackie," then waved and rode off. We never saw the three of them again. And we had been saved from the gibbet, or worse.

Chapter 8

*Joseph, as a cook, goes to sea on several ships.
He visits the Caribbean, Italy,
and gets an education about real pirates;
he embarrasses himself saving a damsel in distress;
visits Philadelphia, finding only futility in reuniting with
his family; goes to Greenland,
and then joins George Gordon's anti-Catholic riots
on his return to London.
After a jaunt in the low countries,
he burgles the house of an infamous American traitor.*

Thomas Wilson had returned from being impressed by the admiralty to serve against the colonies and left his ship without liberty, on the run, in danger of being captured and returned for punishment. He was afflicted with sores from over much sunlight and almost unable to walk, steadying himself with a crutch. Thomas merely appeared at Humphrey's one day while Francis and I were bemoaning our own misfortunes. When we all met, I apologized for my icy behavior to him, and we all joined in the warmth of amity with a common purpose, viz, to avoid the law and leave London.

Instead of the continent, which Hyde and I had set our eyes on previously, we all decided to go back to sea on merchant ships. Francis and Wilson were good mechanics, and I, now a good cook, had Sails' crewman's tutelage to fall back on as well as two voyages for experience.

Thomas Wilson had found a tailor to make him long-sleeved outer wear which was light enough and ample to do a seaman's work. He wore a hat of sorts made like a farmer's titfer, or sometimes a turban like 'gyptians wear. He had a salve that smelled like turps and lamp oil that he put on his face. He was a mess. It was clear he would never return to the highway. He could work for merchantmen without fear of being reported, as they and his Majesty's Royal Navy shared no friendship at all.

Francis was anxious to go. He had served a short time as a sailor for his highness during the time I sailed to Lisbon and the West Indies, so he had decent skills as a gunner's mate and rigger. We three visited Nathan—who greeted us as sons, for we had not seen him in nearly eight months—and enquired about merchant ship positions. It fell to us that there were four, but none on ships we could crew in common. We opted for distant ports and made our contacts for schooners and brigantines whose routes were away from the Americas. As a compact, we agreed that we should meet again at Humphrey's in two years. By then we felt we could resume our work with less notice by the law, if we were at sea. To celebrate, we went to a ratting, feasted with Bill Humphreys, and then the three of us sought out a Covent Garden bawd who was delighted we had called.

The British had only just left Philadelphia, after nine months of occupation. News had it that the colonists had spent an appalling winter at Valley Forge. Since our weather seems to come from the sea, westerly, I suppose that is why we had so much snow. I took interest in that news, because I remember I had spent a day sledding with Mistress Sarah and Essie and Grandfather Samuel on the gentle hills around that blacksmith's valley forge west of the city. I remembered it, and the memory, now like a thorn of regret, hurt me. Though I wrote infrequently, I had never received word from the colonies. I suspect my letters to Philadelphia had been lost owing to the occupation and displacement of members of my family. Mister Thomas, and Mister Samuel, my grandfather, I know, were officers in General Washington's army. But I had no idea where Mistress Sarah, Essie, Molly, or for that matter, Fling Mountain or my birth mother, Belle, were. Most Philadelphians had relocated.

I was still intent on visiting my foster family and childhood friends at some point. I am certain that to them I was the prodigal child, but nevertheless... Back to my cohorts. We chose a bawd's house with clean women. This was important. We had all seen and heard of the Covent Garden ague or the Flap Dragon, the itch, being Frenchified, a dripper, or Venus's curse, and there were plenty of examples on the faces of men or whores one saw in the streets. So, we all took precautions. It would be hell at sea peppered off with pox. We sported for the night, returned late, and 'fore dawn the next morning we bid goodbye to Humphreys, who promised to board our horses and secure our goods. I took my fiddle and penny whistle and two changes of clothes, and enough money to suit. I boarded the ship Nathan had mentioned, reported to the Captain, a Frenchman named Pierre Latour, whose reputation for desiring good cuisine aboard credited me on a trip to Grenada. It was a three-masted schooner called the *White Demoiselle*. Prudently, I had quitted London, had signed on board a European vessel, and made a voyage to Grenada. From this period a' times till August 1780, I was employed as a sailor or cook on numerous vessels.

Captain Latour had heard of my reputation somewhere (I suppose the gossip network was among ships' captains rather than highwaymen), and Nathan had spoken well for me. So, on this first voyage, I was cook. The cargo was mostly trade goods: guns and ammunition, which I believed would ultimately make their way to the colonials via blockade runners. We also carried tradeable metal goods, and cloth, particularly woolens. Captain had sailed from Liverpool many times and fancied Lobscouse, so he gained, and I gained a good dish that I learned to make on that voyage. Liverpudlians that were on the ship were called scousers, because they also liked it. It is a stew made from a mixture of meats and vegetables, mixed as one chose to create uniquely. Mistress Mifflin and Molly both taught me that to succeed, one should be a skilled as one could be in any venture, and that preparing food gave one the pleasure of creation. I got the reputation—mostly from crew talk in port—as 'Black Puddin', for I also made both savory and sweet puddings, or 'African Duff', after the dough I used in them. I also used whatever fish we caught during our voyage in 'sea pie'.

When we left port in Grenada, we made one stop at Port-au-Prince in Ste. Dominquè. It was there where I heard my first about one Henri Christophe, a freed black who was—quietly, almost silently—planning a slave rebellion, and an associate of his named Dessalines. This is the first time I have aired that news—no one has yet read this journal. They would not like their names, little known except in gossip, what islanders call *suss,* bandied about. It was also there I saw that many blacks were *gens de coleurs*—men as wealthy as some of the white landowners, and many of whom held positions in councils and committees. I made a mental note to myself to return someday soon.

I decided to transfer to a British ship, which paid more since I would be both cook and mechanic. This ship was bound for the coast of Guinea, a southernmost reach of the Barbary pirates, the heroes of my childhood dreams. It was the *Darlene*, carrying molasses, sugar, rum, and coffee, teak wood (which is very dense), mahogany, and some copper, which I have said was popular for bangles, pendants, and rings among the native Africans. We returned to Jamaica twice, giving wide berth to American waters, for the war and shipping oft got entangled. We narrowly missed a ship of war and one privateer, but in all it was a pleasant five months' passage. The cargo was chestnut, walnut, and oak for furniture and fabrics. The only trouble we encountered was typhoons. In the few months I sailed those waters, there were six storms of such fury that we had to huddle like rabbits in whatever protected ports we could make before the storm's fury reached us.

Another thing to puzzle out. Nature seems to sleep so often, we do not notice it. I have heard from seamen of quaking earth that levels towns and flaming mountains that bury the earth in ash and liquid fire, and I have experienced windstorms that year that had blown almost everything to the points of the compass. Some say the Creator does this in anger, but I think this is a child's answer. Along with the slavery, hatred, wars, disease, sinfulness, and such, must we live a life with fire and ice and wind and quaking earth? Why are innocents belabored as the guilty, children and adults both?

Life is such a mystery; it will occupy my thoughts until I am no longer. When I see old men sitting in the parks and people laboring every day, I sometimes think that a man chooses his death day, from fatigue or frustration, after years of struggle. On that day, when he looks on the world and says he's finally had enough and releases his spirit to the ether; the Creator takes it for his uses. He says, "Shall I plant this in a new tree, in a grampus, a new child, or release it to wander where it chooses?" And then the man's spirit receives either a blessing or a curse. Yes, there are days like some I spent with Essie, Nancy, or Jenny, the men and women who raised me, my amiable friends, that are high pleasures. There is beauty in nature and art. But if I had to tally minuses or pluses on a broadside, as Mister Franklin had showed me once, I'm not certain the pluses would win. I'll think on't, as always. Though, as I age, I'm not certain my brain can solve it.

My last two voyages—Mister Thomas would be happy—were to Leghorn and Venice, and the experience opened my eyes even more to the world. There in the ports, I had enjoyable experiences. It was in both Livorno and Venice that I met persons who told me of 'pirates', and like many of my childhood dream, I learned the truth without the romantic patina.

Firstly, I must praise the red wines of Livorno and the food, for I had never experienced such variety in England. The plenty from humble gardens was astounding. I learned to like a variety of noodles they called pasta, with as many shapes and sizes as one could imagine, and always covered with sauces as numerous and various as the noodles. My favorite there was a green sauce I tasted in Genoa that had an exquisite aroma. It was made of garlick and various herbs, nuts and oil, and a salty cheese. It is unfortunate, I cannot fashion such dishes aboard ship, so limited are my foodstuffs... But I must return to my story. On the first night in port, I struck out to find a modest but popular inn where I could be entertained and sample the atmosphere of the area. At Taverna Tucino, I found just the place. After dinner I sat at a table overlooking the port, and in the cool of the evening watched the families and single Italians stroll by. This promenade was much like the habit of the British when it was hot and uncomfortable—a rarity in London. I idled and thought of things distant in time and far in space.

It was then a gentleman paused and asked if I was English. I had an empty table, so I invited him to join me. He was from a town to the east, spoke very good English, and we quickly acquainted ourselves as lone travelers and passed the time. I asked more questions than he at first. At the end, I must admit we were matched to each other like children in our curiosity. When I mentioned pirates, he stopped me, saying they were childish dreams. He knew firsthand of 'pirates', he sneered, and silently drank his wine until I urged him to tell me of't. He sighed and said he was sorry for speaking so coarsely, but he would tell me a story, so I should understand. He proceeded to talk slowly and quietly, a storytellers' talent:

※ ※ ※

I was born just down the coast in a small town called Cecina. It was a happy town in a Papal State and protected, we thought, from the outer world. When I was five, I would play near the port and watch the distant ships passing from Genoa in the North and this port, and see others that would be coming from Rome in the south, or rather Civitavecchia and Spain, or even England and the Americas. Then one morning as I began to dress, I heard shouts, clatter, gunfire, and the screams of women and men outside my window. Afraid, I called to my grandmother and mother, my father and older brother. There was no answer. I peered outside and saw men and women, both with ropes around the neck, being dragged, when they could not walk, through our street, and men with cutlasses killing men I knew, including my father, who I saw cut down as he fought hard to save my mother, who stood with ropes around her body naked and struggling to escape. My father was struck down. I could not control myself. I let out a cry.

Just then, the man who killed my father looked up into the house and saw me at the window. Leaving the bloody heap that was my father and the men who held my shackled brother and mother, an Arab with a cutlass started toward our house, making to pursue me. I, crying over the sight of my naked mother, her dress torn in pieces and tied like a goat, saw the bearded man enter our door. I ran to the roof and jumped from one ledge to a neighbor's, and another and another neighbor's, as fast as I could. The man cursed. I hid in my aunt's grape arbor, breathless and terrified. There, I waited until the sun went down and all was quiet in the streets once more.

As I crept out into the street, I saw the traces of the pirates' visit: It wasn't the happy little town where I had been born. Glass sparkled on the street, doors dangled unhinged, furniture lay broken. There was no house untouched by the raiders from the sea. As I made my way from my house, I saw my father's body beheaded. My mother and grandmother and brother were gone. There was torn fabric and blood everywhere. In my neighbor's courtyard, a boy's arm dangled from the portico, and I saw another dead man with his ears cut off. I was thirsty and hungry and desolate. I walked the short way to the sea as inconspicuously as I could be, but I found no one. Most of my village's boats were pierced or ruptured. The debris seaside was as great in the town. All the people were gone, save two.

As I entered the cuchina—the kitchen—of a restaurant near the piazza, I heard a dish break, and there at a table was old Georgio and Punta his dog, eating all that was there. He waved to me with a solemn look on his face. Punta jumped up to greet me. I wept uncontrollably. Once I stopped, Georgio gave me some water and bread with sauce on it.

He told me pirates from Algeria came into town and took everyone except him, who had hidden. I told him how I escaped, amid the curses and terror. When I said I would find my family, he told me not to bother, that my brother was already likely chained to oars in a galley, now and forever, eating a biscuit, oil, and vinegar once a day until he perished, and my mother was sent to a harem, now and forever, or auctioned to some slaver. He did not say what had happened to my grandmother, but I guessed at her fate. Their ships had come into port early in the morning disguised as merchants from Rome, flying the papal flag and speaking Italian. Once they all were threaded *throughout the village, with their numbers, they quickly subdued the town, ripping its fabric, and taking what they wanted.*

I cried and cried and cried. To this day—now some 30 years—I have not heard of my family's fate. I asked and looked everywhere—and I have travelled to many places they might be. Some captives were called yaleotti, set to work building cities or harbors when they were not needed to row galleys. Others worked as agents of their owners, selling water, harvesting crops. My brother might have been lucky enough. These putas made slaves of everyone they could capture: blacks, brown, whites, Christians, Jews, Muslims—yes, even their own. The razzia on my town was one of hundreds each year in coastal towns and villages, in France, Italy, Portugal, Spain, and as far as Iceland, I have heard. So now I hope you see how noble and estimable pirates are. I hope your childhood fantasies are dashed by this tale. It is true. I would not believe one of your kind nature would want to be corrupted for the lure of wealth. No, sir, you might think long and hard about the horror and sorrow you would cause by becoming one of your romantic pirates....

🍂 🍂 🍂

When he finished, we both sat quietly for some time, he lost in his memories, and I in serious thought. I had been chastened. He did not know that I had these past years done just that—albeit not as violently, but as despicably, for adventure and wealth, comradeship and excitement. I ordered another bottle of wine. Then we changed the topic to one we both enjoyed—women.

I left Leghorn the next day and sailed thence to Venice. This was even more exciting, finally seeing such a famous city with a fabled history. I found I loved to travel, and being a seaman, I had free passage. We were careful, as I noticed the Captain set extra watches while we were in Mediterranean waters, especially as we sailed 'round the boot'. Instead of four hours, the watches were every two to insure no one nodded off. Venice was a favorite target of the Barbarys. I thought on the Italian's tale of pirates. It now made me anxious, and the word 'pirate' no longer bred romantic notions in me.

In Venice, I had a true 'two days' parole from duties and made my way around the flooded city. During the time crossing canals and eating and taking note of entertainments, I decided on the second day to visit a pageant advertising a reenactment of Turkish and Algerian pirates. I dressed in land clothes and carried my small pistol for protection. I also wore a mask, for the Venetians have a love of masks and the ticket emphasized that masks were required. I found a shop that sold nothing but masks and costumery and spend almost an hour admiring the ways in which people can disguise themselves and betimes their real nature. I remember thinking then that it would have had a constant business with Hyde and Wilson and me, when were active on the by-ways. I picked one that matched my coat and was beaked, so I looked like a predatory bird. After dinner, I walked to the canal side theater. When I arrived, the entertainment was already underway and very realistic, with fireworks and explosions of a great variety—

much like ones Nancy and I had watched on the Thames and at Vauxhall—and a crowd whose women screamed and laughed in false fright and whose men grumbled. So real were the actors that one 'slaver' who was dragging a Venetian woman by the hair and swinging his cutlass, was surprised by me setting off my pistol—which I admit was a mistake and embarrassing and to no one's harm—and the entertainment stopped. All who were there turned and stared. I apologized to their sustained laughter. I felt the fool. They treated me as one of their own.

Later, I went to proffer my regrets to the actress and 'pirate' actor and was graciously received, for they noted that my *improvisare* was a compliment to their acting and the show. To boot, the actress told me she had really escaped the pirates when they raided her village some years before. She added, "Would that thee had been there with thy pistol," smiled, and kissed me. They invited me to dinner, which invitation I accepted. I resolved to put the *pirate* out of my mind and forget my dreams.

We left Italy and the Mediterranean after we stopped briefly at Gibraltar to offload munitions for the King's fleet, which was patrolling the waters before they sailed to the colonies. I briefly asked Navy crewmen if they had met Hyde or Wilson, but the responses were negative. I returned to the Downs and sought another ship.

After the British left Philadelphia, I made three visits, two only to secretly transport prisoners sentenced to the colonies for theft and other offenses. These, I understand, had either been indentured to colonists who were still faithful to the crown or pressed into army service for the British, who by then had lost many in the war. On the only visit I made that allowed me time ashore, I found my old home deserted, Fling missing, and Belle, my birth mother, moved. I was checked once by a Pennsylvania soldier and showed my manumission paper. The Mifflins had moved, their property co-opted by the army. Essie was nowhere that I knew, and my liberty was out, so I returned to my ship. It had been a disappointment. I was much saddened on the return to England. Before my time was up, the two years as Hyde, Wilson, and I agreed, I made one short trip on a small brigantine called the *Lady of Astolot*, under Captain Marris to Greenland carrying foodstuffs, steel sled runners, firearms, ammunition, kitchen pots, tea, rice, coffee, rope, English fruit preserves, and English woolens.

Greenland was the most interesting place that I had visited. Houses were painted in rainbow of colors—I was told—so that the fishermen returning home would be able to tell their houses from a greater distance. Their landscape had also been painted by the creator with a myriad of hues in gorse and mosses and lichens, so wherever one looked was beauty. The people were gay and friendly and fat. I was tempted to visit a trollope, because I fancy women with a little cushion, but the available doxies were so large I felt I might get lost in them. Almost everyone ate whale blubber in winter. I suppose it helped them endure the cold, which was even present at night there in the summer. I tried some, but could not tolerate it and spewed it out, to the laughter of those I was with. Cap'n said in winter the ice was too thick to come by ship, and dangerous as blades of Saracen steel. They welcomed the woolens we brought, for most only had animal skins and fur garments. I purchased a hat made from sealskin, which I wear on cold December nights. Weavers from the shires north of London made a variety of wool garments, also in bright colors, for these Greenland ships. The people there also had large packs of dogs, which were stout and muscular, like Staffordshires I'd seen in the pit but with very thick and long hair. An Inuit (that's the name for the Greenlanders) said they were the animals that pulled their sledges in the winter. It was not a green land so much as it was bright green, browns, and red and yellow mosses growing between rocks and snow.

Thence, I returned to London, and my old lodgings and in three weeks had been united with my comrades. We all had days of stories to tell. All of us had kept to our plan.

In August 1780, I, full of the fire of rebellion, joined the mob headed by Lord George Gordon outside the Houses of Parliament, although I cared not a whit for the issues of cause, being a Quaker, it was the growing rancor at the issue of slavery, long forbidden in England and her possessions, that raised my wrath which still quietly simmered--that and the opportunity to possibly gain some pelf during the riots or intelligence leading to later riches, which I found much to my advantage. This mob was the result of a dispute between the Papists and Protestants. It was a matter of the most sovereign indifference to me, whether the rebellion was just or unjust. The Papists had long been under the yoke of the crown, and now Lord Mansfield proposed to lessen some of the strictures: I and my associates eagerly joined the sport, rejoicing that an opportunity presented whereby I might obtain considerable plunder in the general confusion, or at least intelligence that would repay us later.

Lord Gordon, a zealot Protestant, represented to us in a speech of some length, an enumeration of the open attempts upon the Protestant religion, and the way the petitions of the injured had been treated by Parliament. He was flamboyant almost to moving me to mirth. Here was a white man excoriating other white men, none of whom was guiltless in sins against other men, and—in my growing hatred of them—moving them to mayhem.

He exhorted us all to follow him to the House of Commons. He said we should protect him while he should present, with his own hand, the parchment roll containing the names of those who had signed the petition, to the amount of about 120,000 protestants. The act itself, which he scurrilously derided, he shouted, "These acts would cancel the penalties to the Pope's army of devotees to march and allow them almost the same rights as Protestant sects and the Church of England followers". My mirth grew, as did the rush of my blood to move with the crowd. "The old strictures against popery should not be eased. Soon they will invade our properties and offices and usurp <u>our</u> rights and Protestants; nay even the crown will be endangered at the hands of the saint-driven pope empowered Catholics."

It was indeed a strong speech, and we could see members of the crowd throwing food stuffs and offal and stones at houses and passers-by. "Huzzah! Huzzah! Huzzah!" rang out. Most wore blue cockades on their hats.

His speech was answered with many more loud huzzahs. Repeated assurances of our zeal to support him and his cause came from throughout the crowd, and from those around me, I could hear slurs against the church and Mary the whore and the pope her servant. The mob growing by the minute, in number about 50,000; left St. George's Fields, and marched directly to Parliament. A most tremendous shout and more curses were heard from all quarters as we arrived before both houses. Lord Gordon moved that he might introduce the petition; but the house would not consent that it should be then taken up.

Once the mob heard that Gordon and his petition would be rejected and not heard, it became greatly inflamed. Several members of the House of Lords either standing before the crowd or arriving for the meeting were threatened and pelted with offal, and narrowly escaped with their lives. One was jostled from his waiting coach. Several gentlemen of parliament reprobated the conduct of Lord George in the severest terms; and Colonel Gordon, a relation of his Lordship, threatened him with instant death the moment any of the rioters should enter the house.

At length, when the question was put in the House of Commons, in defiance of the menaces of the mob, only six out of two hundred voted for the petition. The rioters moved into various parts of the city. I joined them on foot and watched as they destroyed and burned the chapels of Roman Catholics and their houses. We all raised hell on Catholics without regard to their religion. They were the enemy. I took especially note of houses in wealthier sections that might be later touched or burgled, though I avoided illegal arson and theft and mayhem. The five succeeding days were employed in demolishing some of the houses. It was the rule of the mob that moved, even though when I went with the crowd earlier, I was there to observe, perhaps filch, and gain targets for the future. I also understood this was merely another example of the bias men had of others unlike themselves. Quakers were targets too, but not this time.

Later in the rampage, the mob burned Newgate, leaving it open to the city and relieving about 300 persons confined in it, (some under sentence of death). An old associate of mine, a footpad much adept at relieving gentlemen of the watches and ladies of their handkerchiefs as well as their virginity, was among them, I was happy to see, 'though I did not greet him in the hubbub.'

The crowd, with which I had only marginal association after the first day, set fire to King's-bench and Fleet-prisons, and it committed innumerable other acts of violence and outrage towards those who opposed them—these mostly of the Papist complexion and constabulary. I noticed that officials of the more lawful bent were observing and taking names into books. I did not want to draw untoward attention to either me or my associates, so most of the time, I remained on the margin of the active mob, unchivvied by their fury.

I did save, all these years, an article from the *London Gazette* in which I was noted but unnamed. I will paste it into this chap book and line under the passage that refers to me.

※ ※ ※

......The Protestant divisions all joined at the Houses of Parliament and began to attack the Lords who were arriving for their session. They stopped the Archbishop of York, and grossly insulted him. They next seized on the Lord President of the Council, whom they pushed about in a rude manner, and kicked violently in the legs. Lord Mansfield was also daringly abused and traduced to his face. <u>They stopped Lord Stormont's carriage, and great numbers of them got upon the wheel, box, &c. making the most impudent liberties with his Lordship, who was as it were in their possession of near-half an hour, and would not have so soon got away had not a Negro Gentleman jumped into his Lordship's carriage, and by haranguing the mob persuaded them to desist. The Lord had been much ill-treated, and had his pocket picked of his watch and hanky. The Gentleman who saved his Lordship disappeared into the mob.</u> Several flags were carried in the different divisions, with the words "Protestant Association" "No Popery" "Support Gordon" &c., &c., &c. and the Scotch were attended by two excellent performers on the bagpipes. Lords were roughly handled, insulted, and personally ill-treated. We do not hear that any members of the House of

Commons received much insult, further than verbal abuse, excepting only Mr. Wellbore Ellis, esq., who the mob pursued to the Guildhall, Westminster, the windows of which building they broke all to pieces, and when they found Mr. Ellis, abused him and handled him very roughly. The avenues of the House of Commons were so filled with the mob from the outer door to every door of the House, the members of the House with difficulty tried to leave, but thanks to the good management of Sir Francis Molyneaux and the proper exertion of the door-keepers under his direction, all the passages from the street door, and round the House, were kept clear, and some of the mob fled. About ten o'clock the mob made a parade in different directions from the Palace-yard where they began to break-open the Roman Chapel in Lincoln's inn-fields, and pulled down the rails, seats pews, communion table, &c., then the mob brought them into the street, and set them on fire laid against the doors. About eleven o'clock the guards came and took several ring-leaders. The fire brigade contained the fire…

❦ ❦ ❦

Only Francis and Thomas know this. We three had enjoyed the pipers mentioned in this article. They were most excellently skilled. Many years have now passed since the riots, so it is of no concern. I gave the handkerchief to Jenny and the watch to Nathan, who assessed it at £30 5s. His Lordship had others; I am certain.

Alas, during this unrest, we could not rob the banks, which would have made our fortune once and for all. Some were too well guarded, and even though the rioters raised a huge hubbub, others had not enough of a distraction to give us the opportunity. One bank was twice assailed by others, too well guarded for our attempts.

On the seventh day our mob, which we had begun to call them, they being somewhat associates at this point, were over-powered by superior force and obliged to disperse. During this confusion and din, I provided for myself by plundering, at various times, about £500 sterling. A trifling of what could have been if luck had had it. Most of this was lifted from rioters too occupied to guard their purses. And some from observers too occupied with the ruckus to notice their pocketbooks taken. Other, more skillful footpads of our groups used their skill in taking some £2250 in total, so our inn keeper was pleased when we returned to Charing Cross. The landlord at the old place of resort received us very cordially.

The business of robbing again solicited my attention, and in the fall of the year, as I was walking in Wapping in quest of plunder, I accidentally fell in company with my old companions, Hyde and Wilson. They too had laid low, fearing growing interest in the removal of criminals from the city. Now that the riots occupied the law, we concluded it advisable to join ourselves to the gang at Harrison's, there to resume our occupations.

We heard much of the riches of the low countries. Holland now appeared an object worth attention. In November 1783, we went to Ostend, and thence to Amsterdam. On the road thro' Holland, we knocked an old Dutchman down and took from him 1100 guilders. I was angered by this violence and told Francis he knew better than to push an old man like some ten-year-old footpad. He agreed, apologizing to both of us. Thomas's skin sores had healed, and the weather in the low countries, being gray and damp, seemed to suit him. Until we reached Amsterdam, my race was of interest to people we met, but once there, owing to the great number of Lascars and East Indians there, no one took notice of me. The Dutch were a wary bunch who guarded their wealth carefully. And though famous as sea-goers, their merchants were sharp in business. We still did well.

The next day about 4 o'clock in the morning, Hyde attacked a merchant and obtained about 100 guilders; and the evening following, we robbed four gentlemen of about £150 sterling each, and three silver watches of small value. We continued living very freely at Amsterdam for a month, without effecting anything: during which period we were preparing to assail a bank. At length, by the help of various instruments, we entered it about 1 o'clock at night. We found an iron chest which we could not open. We brought away two bags of gold, containing about £1100 sterling. We buried them about two miles distant, suffering them to remain there two months. The noise relative to the robbery having by this time subsided, we took our money, entered on board a vessel bound for England, and were safely back in London.

It had been eight years since I had met Hyde and Wilson and set about my profession, and I, as well as they, were wearying of the highway in the spring of 1784. We had decided on the ship back to England to assess our cash, to convert our other assets, and to invest in real property, and quit this course of life we attended with so much fatigue and hazard. It was thought the most eligible plan. In pursuance of this idea, Francis Hyde bought a house and lot about 4 miles from London. I joined my share with Hyde's. Wilson purchased himself a situation at Cherry-Garden-Stairs. Each of us kept a house for the reception of gamblers, swindlers, and footpads as a separate enterprise.

The law having been harsh on the rioters, London now quieted from Lord Gordon's mob, and the rioters who were concerned in the rebellion were now daily arrested, tried, and executed. Since I had been deeply concerned in this mob, I supposed it probable that I might be uncovered next. I chastised myself at my behavior. Even if I had saved his Lordship, I lifted his watch, and though I had been raised a Quaker and taught tolerance, I joined the anti-Catholic mob like some scurrilous sort who might look down on a Negro and abase him. Old habits were hard to break, especially where gain was concerned. The heat of a mob can singe the most insulated skin.

In October 1786, we committed a burglary upon the house of General Arnold, who then resided in London. The colonists had raised Hell regarding this man. I remembered the man from the card game which Jenny and I had attended, when we heard his spy stories with some mistrust. It was a house I had scouted during the riots and notable by Thomas Wilson, who informed us that a rich military man and his wife lived there. A burglary was different for the three of us, but we applied ourselves, consulted with some experienced burglars, studied our plan, and then hired a small associate name Dubber, who by his thin and minor stature could enter and unlock the gate for us. Dubber squirted between the gate bars like an eel and unlocked it. We entered Arnold's house about 2 o'clock at night, with a dark lanthorn, and, from a bureau in the room where the General and lady were asleep, she more loudly snoring than he, we stole about £1500 sterling in cash, and a pair of emerald stone shoe buckles. I believe I mentioned that her snore was quite musical, entertaining us whilst we robbed.

I kept the buckles, and we split the cash, paying Dubber for his part. I celebrated with Frank and Thomas in high humor, for I learned later this General had narrowly escaped hanging for treason in the colonies. I tallied this trove as a contribution to my family's and friends' struggle there, though in s'truth I was the only one getting the true benefit o'it

Chapter 9

*In which Joseph and his friends travel
to France, Spain and Gibralter.
He meets with a genuine Barbary pirate who
offers him a position on his ship;
to his benefit, he uncovers treachery.
The three join his Majesty's navy and go to war.
Joseph takes one more voyage that changes his life.*

Late in the spring, Hyde, Wilson, and I met at the *Flounder*, a comfortable inn near Dover, to lay plans for the coming summer. Hyde was nervous since the riots, as was Wilson, and both importuned me of their fears of Newgate and the swift justice the magistrates had meted out to those who participated for Gordon and the lord's adherents. It was one of the reasons we had left London and met at the distant *Flounder*. Hyde reviewed how well we had done in our endeavors, emphasizing the burglary with a sly smile to me, and in short order we were all agreed to make our way to Dunkirk and south. Wilson sneered, saying the Frenchies were weak-livered, doted on women, had their humours, and certainly could bear touching. His behavior there was to bear out that he, too, doted on women. He showed his *billet-doux Français*—French letters—and both Francis and I groused at his embarrassing display of his sheeps' bladders—condoms on the table. "We are gentlemen, Tom, not ponces to noise about these privacies. Put them away. Save them for your doxies." We drank and talked preparations.

Francis went to hire a squint, and with a quiet sea, in three hours we were in Normandy. We disembarked near the outer quay, lighted our lanthorns, walked into town and fed the horses. It was still very early when we donned our road garments, bedecked as before to ply our trade.

Wilson and Hyde were in the lead as we rode out of the city, heading south to the town of St. Joan's execution. To some a holy city, but it reminded me of differences once again, intellectual ones. Our beliefs as well as our politicks set us upon one another. A day cannot pass without one saying that another is wrong about this or that. I meant to raise the subject for conversation as we rode, finding a way to pass the time, but we were interrupted as in life by opportunity. One is wise to snatch it when it comes.

It was 7 o'clock when we met a gentleman on the Rouen highway and robbed him without a cross word in English. "Arretez!" Hyde called out, and the man replied, "You are English, I can tell. Why are you here?" I was smiling under my mask as I replied, "To take your French money. If you have English money, that will also serve." Tom and Francis were merry at this, and oddly, the gaiety spread to our victim.

I jumped down and grabbed his reins, and we reaped about 200 French crowns merely as travelers to Paris. We heard the man swearing, "Merde! Merde! Les Anglais. Foutre sur eux!" as we left. Our merriment continued. Such hilarity supplants the fatigue of travel, of that we were certain.

Travelling by way of Brest, we found lodging early in the morning and rested most of the day. Although the channel crossing, touching, and ride were without incident, and the seaborne air fresh with the smell of lilacs and peonies, we were fatigued and wanted to be restored for this new adventure. I liked the countryside and the clean air, having been in sooty London too long. I was wearying of it. I needed new vistas, and perhaps new adventure. Wilson spent the evening with a doxy from the inn. Hyde and I slept in the loft we had rented.

At breakfast the next morning, Hyde, Wilson, and I came to agreement and made a pact that should either of them or I come to harm or danger, the others would do ought that might save the other, and we swore this on our faith and the names of our families. An oath, I finally accepted, for it was one assuring friends of my fidelity. I still felt some guilt rejecting my parents' faith by doing so. I remembered the day my father had joined the militia and how he must have felt when Mistress Sarah confronted him. Of my two associates after all these years, I clearly knew Hyde to be trustworthy and Wilson suspicious, not likely to be faithful, but tolerably square as long as one kept him under a cold eye. There was something in the manner of Wilson, though, e'er since we left the riots, that seemed to smell, and neither of Hyde nor I were certain we should continue to associate with him. But I had distrusted him before and found myself in error, so this time I continued to treat him as a friend—only with more scrutiny. During breakfast he amused us with his tales of sexual prowess, a habit that would gall us by the time we left France.

Nevertheless, when we met that afternoon, for Wilson had tarried with his whore all morning, we showed no difference to him in our behaviours. He was so lusty that when we arrived in Paris, he craved another trollope, said he would find some suitable muff to powder, and meet us for dinner at the *Coq d'or*. Hyde and I suspected he was poxed by now, since his favorite leisure was lying abed on the coney and breasts of some whore. I silently wished him well nevertheless, as he was an unattractive person, having fewer liaisons than others. Every being on earth are slaves to their basic desires. Once we settled at the *Le Coq* and refreshed ourselves and our horses, Hyde and I spent much of the morning looking at the magnificent sights that Paris afforded.

We started in the center near an impressive cathedral and walked near the university, thence to a hilly area with windmills and many small shops and businesses which were like London's. They did not have inns of the sort so frequent in England, but they had small restaurants with tables outside where we would stop when we were fatigued and have something to eat, and some of their excellent wine. All the while we were trying to assess locations and targets to ply our trade. Despite the architecture and novelty, it was a noisome city beside a stygian river, lined with quaint but putridly foul streets. It was as grubby as London, only with inhabitants who spoke a foreign language and cast hard eyes on strangers. Only the smiles of the women eased the grime.

We later met Thomas at our lodging, had a superb lamb and much wine, listened to an endless tale of the charms of his whore and his adventures with her and her French habits, some of which seemed quite impossible. At this Francis stood, bent and twisted into a contorted pose and asked me,

"Shall we do it this way, Jo?" and fluttered his lashes. E'en Wilson howled at that. It was a long story. Francis and I looked at each other, quietly deciding it was time to leave. We were on our way out of the city the next day.

That evening we went to the theater, for there was where we expected to gain some rewards for the culture we endured. We weren't disappointed. I encountered Count Dillon outside the theater while I smoked. He and I conversed about Mouliere and Racine, for a few moments—'Le Bourgeois Gentilhomme' was the play that night—I offered him a cigar, and in return relieved him of a gold watch and 12 French Guineas. I fled through two allées before he had even recovered by my touch.

The next morning was a bright one, wholesome again with smell of blossoms and bird music, as we rode at a canter on our way to visit Monsieur Le Governor Du Boyer at about 4 miles south of Paris centre, from where we had stayed.

Again, the country air made it a pleasure to be away from the smell of the city. I cannot say it enough: For all its beauty, there is no forgetting the cesspool of the river and the streets in Paris. One had to be in the country to appreciate the unsullied beauty of France, as well as England. People are the corrupters.

Our information on Du Boyer, which oddly enough was from Wilson via his whore, was that he, the governor of Paris, went to his papist mass via the southern Faubourg road every Sunday at 8 o'clock in the morning. So, it was there that both Hyde and Wilson chose to do the touch on Du Boyer while he rode to church that morning. I rested about

250 yards from the road, a safe distance, we had agreed, to which one could distract any interloper from stymieing our plans.

Hyde and Wilson, disguised only with face-scarves a'horse, stopped the governor, taking about £300 in bank bills from him. Once off, they signaled me, and I galloped to meet them. Having set our sights on Havre-de-Grace for our next visit, we rode with dispatch, since bold adventures such as these necessitated a clean escape. We arrived the evening of the next day, riding all night. Unfortunately, our plans changed.

The three of us had stopped to water and feed our mounts near Chemins-sur-seine, and in that village saw an advertisement posted outside the watering trough that noted the passing of counterfeit notes like those we had stolen from the governor. A coincidence, we thought, but not one to risk; so instead of changing them, we were induced to burn them.

Our experience with the French was unreliable, leading us to believe France may not be as fertile for our desires as England was, and we were not a gang like those associated with the famed Cartouche in the earlier part of the century who gained in esteem and fortune throughout the country. I also did not want to be apprehended, thrown in a French prison, and broken on the wheel for a few pounds. I persuaded Wilson and Hyde, one night when we were drinking, that it might be wiser to head across the Pyrenees to Spain. So it was that we next went to Bayonne.

We had to support ourselves. Thus, we did ply our trade as we travelled, but with care to disguise the horses and ourselves and perform separate robberies, each time posting lookouts from one or t'other. One night, Hyde robbed two gentlemen in a coach; Wilson, one lone rider; and I, a cabriole containing a couple. The total take was over £600 sterling. The hue and cry was so great, however, that we decided that France had surely become too dangerous. We therefore pushed southward over the Pyrenees with all speed for Spain, arriving in Madrid in four days.

With little knowledge of the city and much fatigued from our arduous trip, both Hyde and Wilson were irritable. I looked on't as another adventure, enthralled by the architecture and the large number of trees, many parks, and cooling green copses—so many that it reminded me of Philadelphia and that moved me into reverie. We found out that the layout of the city and various regulations would work against our plans. One regulation was the law against hats or any head covering that might conceal one's identity. There was little crime; penalties for petty thefts were severe. In addition, there was a curfew. We decided to leave, after some days playing with our riches, for Malaga, which was the nearest port; and thence, we would travel from there to San Roque and reach Gibraltar. Madrilenos were a stuffy sort and kept their wealth close and guarded, much like the Dutch.

The city, as I noted when we rode in, was walled too strongly. It had such few gates that a quick escape was nearly impossible. These too were shut every evening at 8 o'clock and carefully guarded. Every man was compelled to be in his habitation at curfew. Damned Spaniards. The next day was Sunday. I know little about what Tom Wilson did that day except pursue doxies, excited about passionate Spanish women, and Francis, still fatigued, slept.

I chose to go to a *corrida,* this being a common form of entertainment for Spaniards and different from the blood sports I had been errantly fond of in England. This was a competition between man and beast, something that attracted me on whim, but also as some deep urge in my spirit, something maybe from my history, like warriors fighting lions or other jungle animals. I was curious enough to take a chance that as a Negro I would stand out, and then I remembered that many of the populations' ancestors were Moors, darker that I.

I purchased a 'sombre' ticket and, the sun being very hot that day, a small flask of wine, and sat engulfed by the bright costumes, the antics of children, and the breezes that helped to cool the shady seats. It was a gaudy festival, with brassy music announcing various acts. The costumes on the men were ornate masterpieces that I would have worn once, embroidered with intricate designs, flowers and such. The men were very small in stature, like dancers I had seen in the theater, and compared to the bull, which was monstrously large and well-muscled, the man, the 'matador', was a penny to the bull's crown. The contest was not what I expected.

A first, men on horseback weakened the bull's shoulders and back with pikes. In Act II, men with short, ribbon-wrapped spears further bloodied and weakened the animal by running close to the beast and impaling with the darts as preparation for the man-against-bull conflict. By this time, I began to hope the bull was the victor; he was so weakened, so suffering—no wonder he was so angry. Blood and sweat ran over his eyes. One could easily see that this was a match that involved bravery only so much as was barely needed against a weakened opponent: a cat killing a three-legged mouse. In the end, the small man—the Torero—made several flourishes with a cape and received cheers from the throng, and then more flourishes to attract the creature. The bull charged several times, with the matador's bravery receiving many "Olés" At end, mercifully, the small man killed the exhausted and weakened bull with a sword. The creature's body was so abased that dragging it with horses from the arena only added to his undignified death. I left, disgusted; it was the last blood sport I would ever attend.

Disappointed in myself and in men who craved such things, I wandered the city until nightfall. I found a bistro where they served small foods. There, I chanced to meet the same Portuguese gentleman I had met in Lisbon when I had sailed there. Senor Rodrigo saw me at the long array, which the proprietor had set out, selecting a variety of the samples, for I always tried new food; it was late—despite the law—and he approached. I greeted him and found out more details of his travels, Lisbon, and, he remembered—the Barbary pirates. Rum, women, riches, the seas and excitement were what I had sought. We supped and drank, renewing our amity. Granted these years as a footpad and highwayman, I had accumulated much wealth, and my broker had it safely secured; yes, I had a wife once with Nancy Allingame; yes, I had ventured on the seas as a mechanic and cook; and I had much from life. I had also over-excitedly embarrassed myself saving a 'maiden' from such a horde, and I heard an Italian's tale of loss to the brigands. I was drunk and still interested. Rodrigo reminded me that I showed much interest in piracy when we had dined in Lisbon. We talked and ate and drank until very late. The proprietor had closed the back rooms to his restaurant, so we had no fear of the curfew law while we leisurely passed the evening.

I heard from Rodrigo words that it was certain if Francis, Thomas and I stayed in Madrid, we would be found out. For somehow there was word about, Rodrigo said he had heard, that some English criminals had arrived in the city. Knowing me only as a sailor, I did not betray that he was speaking of me and played the sailor still. I said I hoped because I was English, I would not be mistaken for some common thief. Then he brought up the subject of pirates.

It was widely known throughout Spain, especially along coastal communities, that the pirates I had so admired were not the privateers of old, but Arab princes who were primarily involved in the slave trade. They had been sailing corsairs for nearly 50 years up and down the weakly fortified coast around the Mediterranean, and for nearly 150 years—as I had heard in Leghorn—taking whole villages, often all the women who were there and the strongest men and boys—the former serving in harems. Mediterraneans as well as the Arabians seem to prefer the gentle flesh of the young and the hot-blooded Greek and Italian and French women who were favored by the Pashas. I could surmise that the sunlight has something to do with that, for in northern climes, less passionate preferences seem to prevail. I saw this in Greenland, though most of the women I met were large women, owing to a diet of so much blubber. Then, perhaps not.

It turned out that my inquiries in hopes of the Barbary pirates had put me in harm's way here in Spain, for my reputation had been noised about, and Rodrigo said it was me who might be in danger of being re-enslaved, a plight I had not known my entire life thanks to the intercession of the Mifflins when I was still a babe. These pirates had also sought out gunners, shipbuilders, seamen, and mechanics. Would I or my associates like work? the Portuguese inquired. If so, there was work a'plenty. I would ask. We parted and agreed to meet in Malaga in two days. As I told both Hyde and Wilson, when I rejoined them, they agreed and were as one with me to hear more of this, so we fled Madrid and made our way south to the seacoast, travelling the short way to Malaga to meet Rodrigo.

There, when the three of us met him, he said he would help. I was surprised that he was accompanied by a Pasha Al-Rasami, who was introduced as the owner of a fleet of small ships, xebecs, who needed crew and captains. There, that evening at the *Southern Cross* inn, the Pasha was unescorted and introduced himself. He ordered minted tea. After it was served, he took little time: "I understand from Senor Rodrigo that you would like to sail with us, this has been a boyhood dream. I also know from other sources—I have not told your Portuguese friend—that you have been a successful 'pirate' on the land, so to speak, and that among your attributes beside your healthy stature and your gentlemanly demeanor, you have been at sea long enough to have the skill to sail. You are an excellent musician and cook. And you are black, an advantage when dealing, as I do, with men of your race. I finally know that you ceased enquiries for fear that your state as a free man might be endangered by my habits of enslaving my captives for profit. What else should I need to know, except that you would be a more valuable man to have beside me on the deck than below the boards as chattel? With so much skill, do you still crave the pirate's life? It could make your fortune. This is an offer."

I was stunned by the breadth of his revelation. It made me fear the venture even more. Rasami told us he had other ships for my associates and assured us of our safety. I, in turn, said I would chew on it, got directions on how to contact him, and we parted cordially.

The next day I caught up with Francis Hyde, who had more intelligence about Rasami. He had met one Hassan, an Algerian who told him a story about the Pasha. It seems that he knew and had served under Rasami the previous year on a slaver out of Niger and had seen his cruelty, and that he was even more duplicitous than his words showed. I would have been enslaved shortly after I left port, Hassan told him—the Pasha had enslaved a black crewman from the Admiralty's fleet by a similar offer. Now the black captain builds palaces for the Pasha, as a working slave. He is nothing but danger. I thanked Francis for his warning. What was I to believe? I had heard Rasami's offer, and I knew the other tales. Yes, I could read and write—a wonderful asset among my peers—I was learned in the sciences and philosophy; I was strong and experienced; I could cook and sail, had few vices, and my hatred for the masters boiled. But. But I had too many gifts. Rasami could sell me for a very hefty price. I finally came to a decision. Soberly, I chose to give up the dream once and for all. To choose safety. Wilson and Hyde agreed that it was risky otherwise. Our decision, we thought, was prudent. We left our refusal by letter with thanks for his offer. Immediately that day, we three left for Gibraltar.

When we reached the rock, we knew from gossip that the guards were often fatigued there by the riotousness of their Saturday night leave and were often nearly witless from the pains of too much rum. We waited two days, and then we bribed the Spanish sentinel with a few pesos, entered British territory, and the next day sought an audience with the British Commander, one General Elliott.

He wondered what had brought us to Gibraltar. We told him we were British citizens, Englishmen, through and through, and had previously been mechanics at sea, had travelled to Spain for pleasure and partly for business, that we sought adventure and to serve his Majesty in these difficult times.

Our timing had been opportune, as Elliott informed us that in three nights, the fleet under Admiral Howe would be arriving, and that he could take us on as seamen. With that we idled locally for a day, then bade farewell as old friends, hoping to reunite when the war was over.

I joined the *Magnificent*, a ship of the line of 74 guns, commanded by Captain John Elverston. Hyde joined Lord Howe on the *Victory*. Wilson went on another 74-gun ship whose name I don't recall.

Duty was different than I had endured before. Military strictness was new for me, still young and feeling my freedom. I applied myself as a gunner, however. At sail I was assigned to one gun and learned to follow a gun captain name Portsmith. He enjoyed my humor: When I realized our duty was starboard, I joked his name should be Starsmith, and we all called him Starry after that. He seemed flattered. As other gun crewmen, we slept with our gun at the ready. During battle, we quickly unlashed our cannon, loaded, aimed, and Starry fired it. We sponged it. Then we did it again and again amid smoke and bombs and fire, the perdition of hell, like clockwork over and over, unleashing ball and shot in battle

When we weren't in battle, I mended lashings and fixed blocks and helped to haul. We were in six battles and successful in all. One was with a Barbary pirate sailing a xebec, who sought to make his escape when we sighted him, to his sorrow, for four of our starboard cannons destroyed his ship to the waterline with one barrage, quickly sinking him. Provisions were good, and food nearly as good as if I had been the cook. This was in the fall.

I tarried aboard the *Magnificent* about three or four months. During that time, we engaged with the French and Spanish fleets several times. We drove them out of the Straits, sunk their slower ships with hot shot, and captured the St. Michael, a Spanish ship of 74 guns. I saw neither Hyde nor Wilson again. In '83, the peace took place between England and the United States at Paris. The *Magnificent* sailed with the fleet for Spithead, where, directly after my arrival, I made my escape from her by bribing the guard with 5 guineas, and then swimming three quarters of a mile to the Isle of Wight. I knew I had illegally left and might be pursued, but I also was bent on changing my life, leaving England, and seeking a life more righteous. Let the damned pressers find me. Perhaps Philadelphia and my friends and family there would welcome me, and I could start anew.

From this place, I went back to London by the way of Plymouth. The landlord at the old place of resort received me very cordially. And I was home in Charing Cross. I still had heard nothing of Francis Hyde nor Thomas Wilson.

For months I made my plans. I rarely left the *Black Horse,* only reading in the garden or playing my music for pleasure. No rattings, dogfights, robberies, or doxies. I would settle the few accounts I had made, contact Nathan the Polack, consolidate my wealth, and seek a final passage west to my former home. I wearied of thoughts of adventure. I began to dream not of highwaymen and pirates, nor of wealth and the idleness of the rich, but of a simpler life. I also felt I might be like Equiano and set an example to free all my black and brown kinsmen and women. I would go to St. Dominiquè and Jamaica, and then to Philadelphia and perhaps, Boston. Those were my plans.

A month after I had finished arrangements, Bill Humphreys came to my room and left a letter from the Admiralty. It told me of the deaths of my two friends off Egypt in a skirmish with Algerian pirates—all men were lost, as well as the ships. Bill and I sat long into a dreary night toasting Francis Hyde and Thomas Wilson; we drank until we were totally besotted, trying to recall this touch or that on the highways, and when we entertained guests in the tavern. We spoke no ill of either of them. Thomas with the curse of being an albino— like some freakish circus performer. Francis, wise and adept, with his low laughter. The world was telling me it was indeed time to change.

After the war, I dared not sign aboard legitimate ships, fearing my past would creep up on me, so I returned to the south of Spain and sought passage to no avail. From there to Lisbon, where I regretfully signed on a ship called the *Lethe* with Captain Saõ Malno. He was bound to the west African coast and needed an experienced seaman. When I told him I had also served as a cook, he offered a bonus. I was being pursued by 'His Royal Navy', I had been told by the chandler when I was seeking a berth—thus the urgency to leave Portugal.

It was that ship I was aboard when I felt the urge to write this account. I am thankful now, even though I first rued my choice, for I saw first-hand what my ancestors have suffered these many years. 'Though I was lucky to have been raised as I had, my cultural soul had never grown. My life had been a confusion, a various mixture neither black nor white. Now that I have told part of this and made a full circle of it, I will continue my fresh birth. The next life is new. It was my actions that led me to this oddity: a Negro slaver of Negroes.

So, I am back where I began this tale. I am on the *Lethe*, captained by a Portuguese called Saõ Malno, who has nine years traveling to Cartegena, the Caribbean and Bahia, with a crew of eight. I am now a slaver. A black slaver? An anomaly. A sinner and a pilgrim seeking some answer that I can untie. Now, surely, my life has become a double fisherman's knot, tied so tightly as to need some sharp device to cut it.

Our "cargo" consists of 571 men, women, and children stored directly beneath me wherever there is space below the deck, in two compartments where they barely have room to move, like stuffed rags to fill the spaces. Those under the grates have some respite from the effluvium of odors. The smell is worse than any sty or London gutter I have ever known. On one side of the barricado on deck aft are some of the women; on the other, children and young men. These are shackled and watched closely for fear we will lose some to the sea, where many have been known to cast themselves. I sleep in a hammock at one end aft. I kept a cold eye on them at the beginning. Now my spirit has softened by their discomfort. They are always with me.

I have contracted with Captain that five of the young men—Olaudah and four others—are mine to 'own'. I intend to free them as soon as we make port. I have made a start on my penance by doing this, but I know I will have to do more. Nathan—my London broker—has instructions to send my small wealth to New Orleans; I have sufficient with me for the time. When we make port in Kingston, I intend to travel with them to St. Dominiquè, when they are fit, for there is a man there who is gathering freed men to liberate that island. I have also contacted former associates who are now in New Orleans to meet with them. After that, I intend to see the new country, the United States of America. I will find the Mifflins, who unfortunately have not heard from me in so long they must think me dead—that, or the worst reprobate. I intend to travel to Philadelphia to try to rebuild my prodigal life.

In the afternoons, we bring those below on deck and feed them all an afternoon meal of saltpork or fish and horsebeans. Any dead are thrown to the sharks. They also get their meal. Those who are very ill are sometimes treated, and then shackled and towed in a lifeboat. We must quarantine any who may have the pox or plague. The temperature below is hellish. Olaudah, a slave I have purchased, says that some believe their souls will return home if they perish this way, jumping into the shark-filled waters. Sharks follow us the way remoras follow them. It is not enough we provide barrels for their waste, but not every needy slave can reach them, so the deck below is soaked—not by the sea, but by vomit, blood, shit and urine, and every foul emanation of a human body one could imagine. A child fell into one of the slop barrels and died this day.

It was when this poor innocent, in fear the length of our travels, drowned in the worst possible way that I was touched to the bone. Why does the Creator allow this to happen, to starve children and inflate their bellies, to beset them with worms and flies, when all the poor creatures want is their mother's breast to suckle?

I continue to write all this down in my chap book. If you are here, you have heard my past. Be patient. I have much to do, and I will be as honest in my narration as before. I do it now because I bear such guilt and shame for what I do and have done, that I must confess before I return home. Yes, I am a black man. I was a child born of a slave, who was freed and had an advantage of the riches whites have, and which I squandered in my youthful freedom. I now am a mate aboard a notorious slave ship and see the horrors of my heritage

This voyage is nearly over. At twilight, a ship begins to come alive: Every sound is magnified and distorted by the wind and sea. Shadows creep out on deck from the thwarts and stays; sheets, and halyards hum with the wind, howling in storms. Every flap of the jib, every creak of a shroud adds to the macabre aura of this ship. On the *Lethe,* one must add the clink of chains, the wails and moans of the women and men and the mewling of the children. My heart is nearly numb, lying still with suffering. I feel enrobed by the humid darkness of this starless and moonless night, and by the black of Africa which I carry with me below decks, and the black and empty universe above and behind me.

Chapter 10

Joseph leaves the Lethe,
accompanied by five slaves he has freed,
And travels from Kingston westward to Trelawney
and cock-pit country to meet the Maroons.
He stays in a village learning about them,
has a disappointment,
gets his fortune told and suffers nightmares.

It was that five weeks on the *Lethe* that sealed my feelings about the trade of human beings. But feelings are not reason, which philosophers of our age mark as paramount in unlocking the mysteries of our lives. When we made port in Kingston, I felt a confusion of anger, sorrow, and disgust. Beyond that, I teetered between loving the Mifflins for saving me, tutoring me, comforting me, and giving me an engendered Quaker serenity; and an enmity for being black and raised white, and then my continued robberies, with only a few worldly possessions to gain, which I allowed to corrupt me. Would that I had had more maturity when I met Hyde and Wilson. I might have toured Europe as Mister Thomas had hoped and returned to Philadelphia a finished citizen of the new country—not a martyr like Crispus Attucks, but a black hero from Philadelphia. I might have had my adventure during the colonial war; I might have shown my wit there and been decorated, or I might have died a noble death, an example for the poor black slaves hoping for a future with dreams of a better life. Had I survived, I could have written about it to inspire them, like Ignatius Sancho and Olaudah Equiano. Making my mother and father and Mister and Mistress Mifflin proud. Mister Franklin would have printed it. Mayhaps I could have been read like Mister Paine and Mister Jefferson. I had learned the one thing that is ofttimes bandied about: Youth is wasted on the young. Moreso, when you're young, you only believe your own verities. Older truths from the aged mean nothing in your salad days. There is much to do now to make amends. I have a heavy penance to serve in Philadelphia. That will be later. I have written some of my account and I have purchased freedom for Olaudah and four others. Now, there is still more to do to finish this purgatory of a trip before I can get freedom for more of my race. Maybe freedom is not enough for a human being; maybe we must all learn to become a different animal than we were created. Maybe once we learn that, then we have earned the right to pass onward.

On the ship, we had much of the work that goes with such a cargo we had carried. I first paid Captain Saõ Malno for Olaudah and the four others I had purchased. Olaudah had some English, Bantu, Hausa, and some creole, so he translated for me with the other four. Captain then made him a trustee; thus, I learned much of him and the trade in odd-time conversations.

Before I could free them, I felt I should name them. A name makes you proud when you bring it honor. I pondered this and began. The smallest, I named Giant for fun; the tallest was Olaudah, so I named the one closest to him in stature,

Two; one of them was always surly, so he was Rogue. And I named Ban thus because he spoke Bantu. Olaudah drilled them with their new names for a short time so they would remember their free identities. They stayed on board to be cleaned while I went ashore to get suitable clothes for them.

It took me some time, but in a port such as Kingston, almost anything could be had if you had money. I showed some silver to a merchant, and he led me quickly to a clothier for sailors, which I was fortunate had the shirts, britches, shoes, and hats my group would need. Others such we could buy elsewhere. When I returned to the ship, my new associates smelled less like the humans I had been used to on the voyage. They were scrubbed and clean, exuding lye soap. I distributed the clothes and indicated where they should help with the duties on the *Lethe*. Afterward, we would go ashore and eat. I set about writing manumission papers for each of them, having Cap'n witness the documents, and indited copies.

Even though I was to free them, they set to work like the slaves; they were cleaning the ship, disposing of the dead— only 16 in all the whole trip, our business losses. Most had been thrown to the sharks as they were discovered, There were only three bodies left. Three women, one who on the last day who had been sickly the entire trip, and two who had been raped by their community slaves below. Only one child perished, falling in a slops basket.

The rest of the cargo, the other slaves, were lined up on deck and cleaned, de-loused, examined, dressed, fed, and the men, well-oiled and left shirtless for market. Those who had been ordered before the trip were then transferred, after payment to Captain, to their new mistresses and masters and left the ship. Some of these, per instructions by their owners, had been branded—not by me—before the voyage. Cap'n had been kinder than most I had seen, for they were not disfigured by the mark, he having it placed high on the leg instead of on the face.

We shackled those remaining and delivered them to the holding pens at the 'market' near the harbor, in single lines of misery. Later that day, Saõ Malno would have them auctioned and collect the proceeds. We finished by off-loading firearms and ammunition, metal ware, woolen cloth, and furniture and home goods for the colonists.

Captain said he was never going to carry such a cargo again, so we then had to thoroughly clean the ship, disinfect it with tobacco smoke and fragrant herbs, fresh water and soap, soap-stoning the deck and as much of the hold as we could clean, and then rinsing with turpentine. We had purchased that and other ships' stores that had come from North Carolina colony. The *Lethe* had to be clean enough to haul rice, molasses, rum, sugar, coffee, and tropical woods, teak, bamboo, mahogany. We opened all hatches, cleared all the scuppers, set men ready to pump on the bilge pumps, emptied all slops, and with buckets and mops doused the entire ship below the gunwales—this after we moved beyond the main harbor.

One would not have known the ship as we returned, for it smelled newly made from the pine naval stores. I and my five men prepared to leave. The rest of the crew still set about finishing the cleaning. I received my pay and wrote out the papers for the five slaves I had purchased for £165; for each,

Cap'n only charged me £33 rather than £35. I gathered my belongings, fiddle, and my money. Captain Saō Malno kindly wished me well and helped me arrange for horses, gave me directions and a map—writ clearly—for the western-part of the island. He also gave me a letter of introduction for a gentleman, Charles Darney, who lived at Black River near Whitehouse. About this gentleman he said naught, save that he had heard he had a plantation that gave work to free slaves. We parted ways. I thanked him, wished him Godspeed, as he for me.

I immediately joined my five young lads to walk into town to plan our journey. I found a restaurant that catered to the blacks at market. When we arrived at the *Blue Peak* to order, the proprietor, a freed Jamaican, seeing my color and retinue, said he knew just what we needed and proceeded to bring us Ackee, potatoes, three roasted chickens, and fried plantains, with several pitchers of beer, and fruit to refresh us—good victuals for hungry men. The seasonings, I had never tasted. Nutmeg, allspice, cloves from India, very hot orange peppers that made one's eyes water and reach for more beer. I and the freemen ate with gusto. Their eyes grew big. They remonstrated in Ibo and Bantu, so Olaudah explained that we would be travelling, and that I desired they should be well-fed.

Afterwards we sought merchants who could supply our adventure. We purchased blankets, good victuals for travel, and six rifles and ammunition, flints, and cloths for shelter, large blades one needed to cut brush, and various sundries needful personally. At the store where we bought the blades, *machetes,* the Spanish called them, the storekeeper sharpened them like swords. I am certain they are common in this clime, for I have never seen them in Europe. They were used for cutting cane, by the slaves harvesting sugar cane, the proprietor said, and if we were going to Trelawney, we would need them, for Jamaica was densely forested once one left the coast. They also would serve as protection.

After I inquired about the country, the proprietor suggested two mules and a compound he said would protect us from the insects. He knew the parish around Trelawney, where I had said we were headed, and remarked that that was Maroon country. I told him I had heard they were free slaves, and that was why I was headed there. He poured us some beer while the men loaded the goods, took pause, and talked to me quietly about the Maroons.

In brief, he told me they were their own men, free for many years—tall, strong, and very dark. With that, he pointed at "Two"; like him, he noted. "Dey raise food and trade freely at markets and plantations. Slaves here, dey on marronage—dey go 'way two days from de work, and then cum back. Trelawney one of der main villages; English cede to dem after last war. It is not de comfortable peace, dis one. Trelawney is de jungle and 'cockpit' country; the pits be deep cones in de earth where one can fall in or easy hide in him, if one need be. And dey are well used. A Maroon can hide a foot fron' of you, and you don't know it. He so, so dark and de jungle so, so thick, he invisible. Imagine stalkin' a man who disappears," he laughed. "Dey Maroon drive dese soldier crazy. Dey will be cautionary wit' you until dey can trust you. Be careful' dese men. You have 'white' manners and a 'white' habit.' Maroon may not trust you. Dey easy trust dose mans wit' you. Dey slaves. Dey—Maroon mans—also hab' de habit of returning 'scaped slaves to plantations.

Tell your men to have cawtion, cawtion when der." With this, he nodded at the other men.

I thanked him for the warning and took my leave. We had only a few hours of daylight left, so we travelled just out of Kingston, found an isolated grove of trees, and made camp for the night. Before I slept, I had Olaudah tell the four others to stay close, for we were in dangerous country. The next day, we travelled via Spanish Town and turned south to follow a path along the sea.

The path was rough. The road, one could not call it that—uneven path—was often overgrown. Gnarled roots tripped us and slowed the mules. Olaudah would dismount with Giant and Two and hack at the brush for an hour to get us and the animals through, and then, suddenly, there would be a meadow, miraculously clear for several miles, the sea leeward and lush, green darkness north of us. If a painter limned the landscape away from the sea, his rendering would have to allow for countless greens, brightening and then shading almost to black.

When we approached a settlement, we were cautious, as the merchant had warned us. There was no reason six strange black Africans, some speaking no English, could expect to be welcomed in this the epitome of slave islands. We passed quickly through several villages. There were always stares and curious inquiries when people saw us, for although I was not dressed in city wear, I and the men looked different than the Jamaican folk. It is curious how humans can always tell when one is not of their own.

Two days' travel, and the next day we passed Black River. I did not use the letter introducing me to Mister Darney. In asking for directions of a woman carrying an impossibly large bunch of fruit on her head, I got an interesting response. "Yo wan' go dis man house? You sure? Massa Darney has 'nother name sometime. Dis name 'Da sting of da whip'. Maybe you and dese boys keep going. Not go dere." With that, she crossed her arms and looked me up and down, as if to dare us. I understood completely. I thanked her and told Olaudah and the others to stop; it boded ill luck. We travelled farther on most of the day, until we found the trail end on a long, wide, nearly white beach near Negril. We had reached the western end of Jamaica. Here, we decided to rest the animals and ourselves there for the night. After we fed and watered them and made a lean-to shelter, Olaudah and Two cornered and grabbed me and, with Ban, Giant, and Rogue looking on and laughing, threw me into the waves. After I walked out, I laughed too, and stripped as they had, to enjoy the coolness of a swim—six free men delighting in the luminous, cooling water. It had been a taxing few days.

Next dawn, after a cold and damp rest at Negril, we turned east again to make for Falmouth. From there, southeast would be Trelawney, cockpits, and the Maroons. It was easier going on some more established roads, and we were able to canter and occasionally gallop for part of the time, the mules alone slowing us. By midday we came upon a small village and a market and rested, answering questions about the journey from Kingston, news of the world outside—what little we knew—and ourselves. Ban and Two, being as dark as night, vigorous, young, and bold, attracted many of the young women, who in their bright scarves and loose frocks were unashamedly flirting. Only the language difference hindered them. We ate some tropical fruit, watered the animals, rinsed ourselves, cooled, and left. Where we had spent time was Falmouth, it turns out.

With Falmouth behind us, we entered the interior. Our adventure began. The heat bore on us like an oppressor. Gone were the cool breezes from the sea. One blessing, at midday, there were no insects. Later, though, as we made our way deeper, there were times they clouded us like an impish army set to driving us nearly mad. We fortunately had the compound our Kingston merchant had given us, and once we had moistened our skin with it, the bugs retreated, and we had relief.

The country was jungle growing out of limestone which had formed huge 'cockpits'—deep, overgrown craters and hollows. The going was slow. We walked our mules for fear we would fall into these depressions everywhere along the way. The further we moved into the interior, the more numerous the perils. Our animals especially found it difficult when we erred on the path that would lead us to Scotts Hill or Crawford Town or Nanny Town, where I hoped to meet with some leader who would join an alliance, I hoped to form anti-slavery forces.

Cockpits were poetical names. They reminded me of the sites of the great gatherings in London where I wagered to watch fighting cocks kill each other, or ratting arenas. Conical theaters where blood struggles could be held. These here were places of death also, when uprising Maroons had slaughtered ambushed soldiers years before, a time when I was still just a babe in Mistress Sarah's arms. These Maroons I was going to meet had set their ambuscades, trapped and fought the

British until they sought an understanding. I can't say there was peace, because some Maroons to the south, I'd heard, still raided plantations, poached on acreage that was supposed to be off limits, and did this when the British paid them to be 'peaceful'. I ask you, when a man treats a dog by beating him instead of respecting him, will the creature be obedient—or resentful and unlawful, steal and kill chickens and take shoes and hats for things to chew?

Since we were dusty from our ride and the animals were hot, we sought some fresh water. Giant, cutting brush with a fury and scouting ahead of us, found a pool with a spring in a small clearing, perfect for refreshing us and our animals. We could rest. I rose to drink near the small falls that fed our oasis. As I drank, the bushes in front of me suddenly seemed to unclothe from green foliage into a tall black man, whose skin showed hundreds of scars. I had never known he was there in front of me. He looked at us all, and in English asked us who we were. We were so stunned by his appearance that I think we looked like children at the circus, gaping at a strange animal. I stood there as speechless as one in a dream where one can't scream.

When I recovered, I spoke to and told him we were here to meet a leader of the Maroons. I wished to speak to one who led them. After minutes of consideration and a long examination of every one of us and our animals, he smiled and shook his head. "No man. Leader, she Obeah woman. Aboso', him also." But he motioned to us to follow him, revealed a well-worn path we had entirely missed, and started to walk along it into the jungle.

It was my supposition from that response that I would be meeting the Obeah woman, a group leader who I had been told was like the local witch, healer, and second-in-charge in these communities. It was so. When we entered the clearing that formed a meeting of three paths, there were small wooden houses, a few daub and wattle huts, and a large hall, which the man pointed to and said, 'dance hall', where there were several tables on which artisan ware, fruit, some fabric, and copper that had been fashioned into bracelets and pins lay. Beyond that, standing on steps at the hall, was a very black, very large, turbaned woman. She was fashioning something out of copper wire, and as she bent to pick up a feather, I could tell from her massive thighs she was even larger than she looked. She had a dignity about her. The man pointed. "Obeah."

Rogue quailed and backed away, explaining to Olaudah and me that she was magic, that she had power, but I thought only that, like an aura around her, was her authority. She noted our arrival and started to walk toward us, while the man we met tied our animals. She wove her way around all of us—slaves first, and then me, her clothing moving like water and her eyes marking all the details. She handled my britches and jacket, the while also measuring my body and whatever she could sense. She smelled us all, and then in a spout of words started talking in creole with the man, so fast and so long that I began to think this adventure was more dangerous than before. It wasn't. But Rogue, and now Ban, shrunk to quivering boys. Two cradled their shoulders to show them they needn't be afraid.

The man whose name was Mose' said that the five slaves were newly free—she smelled it—and that I was very much a confusion of *bakra*, white men, and slaves. She would talk to me at dinner, to which we were all invited. I was certain she was the person to speak to, knowing for certain that after this brief meeting, she had learned much in her assessment of us. Olaudah and the others stayed close for safety at first, then slowly began to roam about the area, while I unpacked a variety of things I had brought which I knew Maroons needed. I then rested. Mose' brought me some water and a pipe filled with what he explained was tobacco, but better. "Ease tire' body, ease pain, make things happy." So, I, to my delight, smoked some of their 'tobacco'. It surely relaxed and enlivened me and my thoughts. And its effects reminded me a little of the opium I had tried in a London Jelly house. We rested all afternoon.

At time to sup, once assembled, about 25 or so men and women and a few children came to the dinner, which they all brought variously. They also had some very good beer. Everyone had their ease, at once making me feel that I was among friends, like Francis Hyde had so many years before. It was sumptuous: chickens and pork, rice, beans, ackee, a food they called 'bread fruit', hot peppers, and something they named 'jerk goat.' After dinner, we told stories about our lives. They were extremely curious about us all.

Of the boys, they asked of their homes in Burkina Faso, Ghana, Niger and Congo, their tribes and family and the ocean voyage. When Olaudah translated, the smallest Maroon children would sometimes hide their faces, or they would be rapt, eyes large and holding their breath. I noticed Obeah watching it all intently.

Of me, they asked mostly of the country that had been at war to the north, and of London, France, and Spain. Those subjects ran thin; it was then, addressing this to the Obeah woman, I explained that I had brought gifts: pots, pistols, flints, and fabrics for them, since they needed such. They learned of my time in Philadelphia and London, of my education in the slave trade and my hatred for it, my history of robberies, sailing, and of what I knew of the five men who accompanied me. As a bonus, I learned more about them: that Nanny's-niece, the Obeah woman, was from a long line of rebel Maroons, and that because she spoke some Ibo could converse with Rogue and Giant, the latter reminding her of a great Maroon warrior of the past: Cudjoe, a short, broad, and strong Maroon leader.

She explained that many slaves here were free to take a day or two away from some plantations, calling this *petit marronage;* at other times, their masters might let them have a week; she called this *grand marronage,* in the French manner. From others I heard of the farming and fishing, of the towns Accompong and Crawford, of leeward raids, hiding stores, stealing from plantations, boiling water for salt, or using wood ash instead, and the Dancing Palace we were using for dinner. It was then a man taller than I and Two entered the hall, and the group grew quiet. I introduced my group, and he nodded and said, "I be head, name be Aboso'." After a few minutes, he had heard some about us from Nanny's and Mose', and sat down, picking at the food.

He invited us to live for a time in the village, but he made it clear that we must stay separate. We agreed; I would keep my thoughts private for a few days. I wanted to see how they lived and what the situation with the neighboring British plantations was.

After dinner they played on drums and shells and, with that as encouragement, I unpacked the fiddle and joined them. We drank beer and smoked our pipes, laughed and joked and danced. It was merry. I was beginning to feel a kinship that reminded me of my days in Philadelphia—yet somehow different.

We stayed there several weeks in all. When I had written the manumission papers for each of the slaves and named them, I made certain they could clearly speak these words:

" *My name is. . . and I am a free man. I was recently purchased by Joseph Mountain of Philadelphia, who freed me as a citizen of Pennsylvania. Here is my paper."*

And I made certain each could say his name. Only Rogue had difficulty; I think he is slow. They read thusly,

> This is to attest that I, Joseph Mountain, a citizen of London and Philadelphia, swear that
>
> this man, named. . . .
>
> was purchased by me on the ship, Lethe, in Kingston, Jamaica harbor, this day the thirteenth of July in the year of our Lord 1788, and immediately made to be a free man with no encumbrances.
>
> <u>Signed JO Mountain Capn</u>
> <u>Loduvico São Malno. witness.</u>

I admit that as a Quaker I am not to take an oath, but no one knows my beliefs. With a witness, it was a legal document. I cautioned them all that they must keep this safe and only show it to lawful men, and I gave a fair copy of each for them. During that time several of the slaves, particularly Giant, Ban, and Rogue, forgot their fear for romance and made friends with some of the girls. One very pretty young woman had a glad eye for Giant from the first evening. Now they were seen frequently holding hands.

I learned much and freely shared my London experiences with Mose', Nanny's-niece, and Aboso'. It was a time when, despite overtures for peace and smiles from the British, there were still raids on the Maroons, but this group lived peaceably. We counted six days as a free time without any threat.

But fields of crops were burned, and villages vandalized. The Maroons had a rigid class system. Once, under treaty terms, they were meted out responsibilities: Accompong, for example, grew coffee and pimento; Trelawney Town, tobacco; —not the plant we had smoked—and Crawford Town could raise cattle. There was a tax also. This arrangement, Mose' told me, had fallen apart. Now, more and more frequently, Maroon men in various parts leeward and windward on the western end of the island had returned to the old ways. They raided plantations, stole goods, firearms, cutlasses, and one man had even used a machete to hack a soldier's arm off.

I chose the moment, when I was being told things like these by Aboso', to tell him my plan to unite all slaves in a federation. That I intended to travel to Ste. Dominiquè and seek out slave leaders to do the same. And New Orleans, and Philadelphia, and Boston—all places where there were large groups of free slaves. I told him I had changed my mind about the whites. There were reasonable men among them, but I hated slavery and those who supported it. As did some of them. Only an alliance had the strength to prevail with blacks and whites at peace. I thought it would be easy to create some land in the north where we could live as peacefully as the Maroons did. Aboso' spend some minutes thinking. Then he told me he would tell other important men from other villages and see what might—*might*—be decided.

Evenings continued the same way as the first night. I grew fond of this tobacco they smoked and liked the vigor and creative thought it gave me to plan the mission. I laughed frequently with the Obeah and played my fiddle every night; Olaudah and Two tended to stay close to me, almost as if they feared I might come to harm. None came.

So, after a week when Aboso' was gone with Mose', I spoke with the men about leaving for Ste. Dominiquè and thence to the newly free colonies in the north. More and more frequently, I heard the abeng horn the Maroons used for communication. It meant that Aboso' and Mose' were meeting and talking with others. I was heartened. That evening, after smoking and drinking much beer, Nanny's-niece showed herself to be a great storyteller.

She talked of Cudjoe, pointing to Giant, saying he could be his son—he looks so much like him. She talked about the war they had and how they thought they were free, given a treaty and land—even she received £200 to be the Obeah—but then the disappointment came when the British lied and showed their treachery, how they could no longer be believed. She talked proudly of her aunt Nanny, who was so fierce she wore a belt with 12 knives and had made bracelets, which she wore around her ankles and wrists, of the teeth of the British becarra (whites). "Dis one soldier, she cut him head off in one figh'." How she had been named for her because she made true predictions, even as a child, and had a strong spirit. And she could chase away *duppies*, ghosts.

I told her we had to leave to go to Ste. Dominiquè, as soon as Mose' and Aboso' returned. She replied that we could leave the next day. He would be home that night. She also said she liked my plan. She had arranged for Piggin to take us on a boat, and said we were all welcome to stay.

The next morning, as Nanny's-niece predicted, the men had returned. We arranged to talk that night. Three of my men—men who now had romance, not fear, leading them in life—asked to stay. I tried to persuade them with travel and adventure, but nothing came of that. "Are we free?" they asked. I told them they were; that I was only concerned that they would be happy.

Thus instructed, Olaudah and I divided our goods, leaving much for the lovers, and then the two of us packed. He looked at me, curious that I helped. To allay his doubts, I explained that we were equal and did equal work. There was a red sky that night—a good omen—so we would sail in the morning. Obeah told me she would be happy to read my fortune. "After the talk tonight, yes, I am curious about the future."

That night was a mixture of disappointment and amity. As before, there was a plentiful setting of roast pork, chicken, rice, fish, plantain, pease, and ackee, mango, and guava. Beer and what I called their tobacco: 'Happy.' We talked and joked, and Ban, Rogue, and Giant, who were going to join the group, were closely kept occupied with their new women, I must say, very discretely occupying themselves with touchings, squeezings, and one can only imagine what other things there were when we first are in love. Obeah watched them with joy, as did Mose' and Aboso'. She assured me they would be happy. We played music for a time afterward, and the small children ran off to play 'Hide and Find'.

When the group finally dwindled, Olaudah, Two, and I sat quietly with the head man and Mose' and Nanny's-niece. We talked about the cruelty we all had seen and experienced, I less than the others, for my life had been one with the oppressors. Both Mose' and Aboso' said that others in Trelawney Town, Crawford Town, and even among plantation slaves had almost been one in the judgment of my plan for a federation. "No," they had said. They had their own federation. Men would fight hard for their own land, but less so for another's. Jamaica was carried in their blood and hearts. Aboso' spoke, heaving a sigh and looking at me with a familial understanding, "We got dis islan'. You got your country. It free, now. We got dis' town. You got your Philay town. We wish you all happy time. You will do good. Be well." I knew enough that his words were final. I thanked him and told him I understood. I would try again when I reached Ste. Dominiquè on the morrow.

I sat for a time, and then turned to Nanny's. She took my hands, let me get settled, and stared at me intently. She lit some herbs so they smoked, and wafted the bundle over me while she spoke in a tongue I did not recognize, then in English she told me with close scrutiny: "Yo will travel home, not home, see a white man, feel the lash many times, one time, try go home, meet a woman. Yo find love. Yo fin' mother one. No mother two, father two. Yo plan grow without you. Young girl point long finger at you. Sun sets on a road like a long rope." Then she shivered and grasped my hand with such strength, I thought it would break. I sat for a moment, as did she. She drank some beer and laughed and shivered, "Oh, my. I am too ol' for trance. Him tire me." We laughed. She in her reverie, I in a puzzlement.

We parted, and I slept. I thought what I heard from her many times before I drifted, worrying about some of it, but I didn't sleep. I don't think I slept, for I *felt I was awake, playing my fiddle at the Black Horse, badly. I would play a C and it would be an F, then on the whistle but the same, an A was a G, the whole song dissonant, and then a constable had me in chains standing beside Fern. He laughed when I tried to speak but could not, and clasped me in a gibbet where people gathered to pelt me with slops. I saw two in the crowd who looked like Mistress and Mister Mifflin without faces, and Fling Mountain holding his cup up as in a toast, and Essie who was fondling herself like some whore in Wapping. Then I was free on a long ship rigged like those of the 'gyptians, where the captain had hanged a crewman. He motioned to me to cut him down. "Aye, aye," I answered and climbed high in the forestays to get him. As he hung there, he was whiter than Wilson but clearly a native American, and his face was cinnamon and had my features. I tried to escape, waken,* and I did, panting. I was soaked with sweat. After that, I fell back asleep once more and *found myself along a stream, robbing a Quaker pastor who had my mother's face, Belle, my birth mother, she pointed at me and as she did became a young woman—I know not who—and started screaming. She pointed to a place behind me. I turned to see whereof she pointed and saw a Tarot card as large as a broadside, warning of crimes. Its design had a young man hanging by one leg—a card I had seen when Sybil had told me my fortune. I, struggling in the preacher's hands,* awoke. I calmed myself by breathing deeply (as I had learned to when I was excited) and mopped the sweat off my face. It had been a *cauchemar*—a nyght-mare—I had never had one before. The first light was showing through the window. It was time to go. I had much to ponder.

Chapter 11

Joseph sails to Ste. Dominiquè with Olaudah and Two and
discovers a colony in which blacks
are free and have wealth and sway.
Meeting one of the gens de coleurs, he and his associates
learn much of the island's history.
Ogé, a priest of the local Voodou religion,
listens to his plan
but disappoints him once more.
A loa named Grace befriends him.

A weary ghost was what I was that morning. All night, Nanny-niece's words stayed with me, made large by the Jamaican tobacco and my disappointment. Yet, the nyghtmare was a puzzle, like a monkey-fist knot Sails would tie at his leisure. Were the predictions true? Like all these soothsayers, she was probably guessing at some things, using what little she knew of me, read my reactions and inflated their meaning, and jumbled them up so it would sound mystical. But some things rang true. How would her prediction affect my plans? And then there was Sibyl's reading of her Tarot—but that was playful, lusty, and she said it meant nothing. I had enigmas after puzzles after posers after questions. They could wait, or perhaps they would reveal themselves when the time was ripe.

And dreams such as the one I had? That was another puzzle. What was a dream? Was it a spirit that visited when a sleeping person was totally disarmed and unaware? I know there is some history that ancients like Caesar and Trajan and Alexander believed their dreams, but could I trust a dream to guide my life? I didn't even know what its meaning was. I left it. Back to my story. I was leaving Jamaica for Ste. Dominiquè.

Now was now, though, and Two, Olaudah, and I had to leave these good folks, much as I had left the Mifflins long ago. We said our goodbyes, and I received thanks over and again from the three boys I had freed. Now, they were starting their new lives in a new land on this new day. I gave each their rifles and ammunition and horses and livery and 20 crowns, so they would have a start in their lives. They thanked me through Olaudah's translation. And Rogue moved me to tears when he knelt and bowed to me.

I hugged Nanny's-niece long and hard. It was then I remembered doing so with Molly and Mistress Sarah before I left home and wished I had held them longer. Mose' said 'Peace' and then 'Suerte', a word from Spain for *luck*. Aboso' quietly nodded. He then pulled me aside. "Dem in Ste. Dominiquè angry. You see dis' man at Por' Prince, him Hougan, Voudou pries', name Ogé. He go France once; him ha' much power. You talk dis talk w' Ogé. Maybe it yo' plan good for dese peoples. God go wit' you." He nodded; with that, we were off with Piggin and one other man toward Falmouth.

In two hours we had arrived at the shore to locate our boat, a shallop painted green. It rested among four others, outfitted for fishing. Twee, Piggin's aide, said that they used them for smuggling goods, so the British could not tax them. On seeing the age and condition of ours, I paused, for I knew it might be unstable in heavy seas. I said this to Piggin, the boy Obeah had sent with us. He replied, "Dis boat, she go Dominiquè many time, she strong, she fas'. We safe." I accepted his word, but I would be certain Two, Olaudah, and I were ready for worse.

We could only load one mule, leaving the other and the horses with Piggin. He, in turn, passed their reins to another young boy, who smiled like the sun that day. I felt blessed. I told him they were a gift to the village. The boat had been beached by the night tide, so we used the mules to float it as the varnished dawn showed itself above Jamaica. Only one other boat was on the water, being rowed by a fisherman while another younger man payed out the nets. With a breeze rising, once we were loaded, Piggin set off with a brisk wind to the east, running with it.

The little boat was faster than I thought. It was a perfect day to sail, blowing a clear breeze from the southwest and a swift current, not a cloud on the horizon. Piggin and Two and Olaudah sang at times, and my two freed slaves talked at length, passing the time. I set my self as watch, but gave it over, for I started to nod. I was almost completely occupied with my dream and my thoughts about the future, to no answers. During the voyage, Two and Olaudah had bailed the entire night near Cuba, since the boat's draught and sideboard were shallow. I suspect Piggin or others used it to enter shallow waters to smuggle and raid. The ocean remained still, even through *"home, see a white man, feel the lash many times, one time, try go home, meet a woman. Yo find love. Yo fin' mother one. No mother two, father two. Yo plan grow without you. Young girl point long finger at you. Sun sets on a road like a long rope."* When I woke to relieve Piggin at the tiller, I felt rested and thought no more on't, though we had a constant breeze and ran before it the entire trip. I could remember Nanny's-niece's words, but still had no meaning: "Yo will travel home, not home."

The sail still took all night, quiet and smooth, 'til around 5 of the next morning, we landed in Doussous, Ste. Dominiquè. Doussous was a tiny, squalid farm town—hardly four huts, all wattle, some very lank pariah dogs, a naked child playing in drainage offal near one of the huts, and a man whose left eye was milky white, who was moving a stick around on the ground afore his hut. Two told me and Olaudah that it scared him. I had to agree. On a map, Doussous was on the tip of the gator's lower jaw. The 'jaw' is what the western end of the island looks like. We would travel by land to Port-au-Prince in the throat. I would seek this Hougan named Ogé near the upper jaw. This all did not seem a good omen to me, and Olaudah was also muttering.

At Doussous, after we unloaded and packed the one mule, I gave Piggin and his helper, Twee, ten gold crowns to help the village and told him two were for himself and Twee. They thanked me with such humility and dignity, they could have magically been gentlemen at Vauxhall before royalty. Two, Olaudah and I left after Piggin and Twee had set sail and, with children and chickens and hungry dogs, we formed an odd parade. The man with the milky eye spat, and then spat at us, muttering. Olaudah matched his curse with his own charm; he spat.

We ignored him. Half an hour later, after the dog and chickens left us, we set out at a good pace, following the road north on the trail to Port-au-Prince. It was shortly after that we were stopped. 'Arretez!' echoed against the hills from a French soldier who stood on the road. In creole, he asked for our papers, but as in Paris, when Hyde and Wilson were there, I spoke to him in French. He asked our business: "De quelles affaire vous occupez-vous ici?" I responded, "On va parler en Englais, pas le Francais ou Creole." I told him I had just come from Jamaica, that I had been robbed and was lucky to find help, that I shipped indigo and sugar from Port-au-Prince for a French company, that I had to meet my contacts there—he had no way of unfolding my lie. He looked at the men with me and very, very carefully read their papers. After some minutes, he let us move on, cautioning me that there were riots because of the drought, and the *gens de couleurs* were upset over the assembly's ruling. He bowed and offered apologies, drew a map with a shortcut to the port, and saluted us on our way. We stood there until he disappeared once more and remarked to no one that we had been welcomed

In a short time, we were on the hill overlooking Port-au-Prince and the clear water beyond. The port was much more sophisticated than Kingston. And I could see it was busy. There were several ships there whose flags were flying from the top masts: the French tricolor, two American flags with their blazoned stripes and circle of stars, one British, and one Spanish merchant flag, yellow and two red stripes. We rested for a few minutes, enjoying the vista, and then proceeded into the city.

After we found lodging in a luxury hotel and arranged for rental horses, Olaudah, Two, and I went out to shop for suitable clothes. At my direction, they were outfitted as the local *gens*. I unpacked my modest London ensemble to make a good impression once we found our Voudou priest. I spent some small time instructing my two associates in good manners, which all men politely used to avoid untoward attention.

It was late in the day before I was lucky enough to find someone who knew of and could direct us to Ogé, to a village to the north called Gonaïves. With that, the three of us dined, fatigued with our sea travel and the newness of Ste. Dominiquè, and had classes. Two and Olaudah required tutelage in eating, drink, dressing, Creole, basic manners, civilization, and behavior. I felt like the owner of two puppies. Questions about everything; translations to boot. They were quick to learn, however, only needing my direction after a few hours. I sensed that there was always a weight on them— it seemed—when they quieted and would gaze off as if in a smoke trance, perhaps taking some African flight to a missed land or child or loved one. Their musings spurred me into my own reveries. We three had lived through a journey to the lower world, and had met with devils and devilish acts that could never pass into forgetfulness. That night we were cossetted by a deep sleep.

The next day we spent partly in leisure, partly in more classes for my two associates, and sitting in a café. It was there I met Laurent Moreau. He was a true *gen de coleur,* as tall as

I and as dark as coal, so dark the shadows on his skin were deep violet. He had seen me take a table at the café with Olaudah and Two in their new clothes and, before we could order, introduced himself. He had a walking cane and tricorn, a hanger embellished with a tricolor, and a blue velvet coat and britches—I could have worn the same. He spoke excellent French but shifted to fluent English when I greeted him. I invited him to have coffee with us. He agreed.

Monsieur Moreau was a planter of indigo who, having been once a slave, was freed by his master when his master died. He was also bequeathed 100 hectares of good lowland with his new freedom, only east of the city. As a member of the local council, he had some say in local politics, was married and had a son and daughter, who were 7 and 10. I told him part of my story, how we had just arrived, and said we had an appointment to see the Voodou priest Ogé, who I understood held considerable sway among the locals.

Laurent agreed that it would be a wise meeting after I told him I hoped to form a federation in the Caribbean and America of anti-slave members to fight bigotry and slavery. Jamaicans seemed to have their own path to freedom planned and would not join. I asked him if he thought the people of Ste. Dominiquè would. He didn't know. But he thought I ought to know some history of the island. It was then he told me this:

"I believe this island is poised for a revolution, as our brothers in France and the colonies to the north have had. We were built on slavery, and now there are many more slaves than masters. Even now, there are rumblings in the north, near where you intend to meet this priest. There are two important groups here: the *gens de couleur*, of which I am one, and slave owners. The former is mixed African and white heritage with diminished rights. The slave owners, some of whom are black *gens*, have formed a Club Massaic and refuse to grant rights to anyone with your (pointing to we three) and my African heritage, even though we may have more wealth or influence in the community. There are some here who want to rise, lop the arms and legs and heads off every 'master' with cutlasses and machetes, fill the streets with their blood, clog the gutters with their entrails; there are others who peaceably seek your path and mine in council. This is the foremost slave nation now, with all of us divided. More slaves were brought here than anywhere. Some of us married whites, and some were born to whites, and now some of us want the rights of whites. Even now there are people who argue against extending the same rights the French engraved in the *Declaration of the Rights of Man and Citizen* to people of African descent, because we are foreign and not French. Be careful. Your plan for a peaceful alliance is noble, but perhaps naïve in this world. There is a boil forming on the body of this country, filling with anger and violence every day. Eventually, it must be lanced."

I was stunned. Monsieur Laurent Moreau was as serious as a lord from parliament, and as eloquent. I had no argument. I examined my own motives. Perhaps I was doing this as penance for my crimes. By chance, could I not really understand why I felt as I did on the *Lethe?* Should I merely return to those I abandoned and build my own life with someone I loved? I will follow through until I finish in New Orleans. May haps the answer will come, as I thought it did on that deck at night, from the cries of slaves.

I said I would see, after I visited the priest. I told Monsieur Laurent that he also should be careful in the months to come. War is terrible. If he is right, war will come with all its savagery. He gave us directions.

I checked at an office which Nathan had said might have my money. Andre' Tresser told me he had not receive anything from Nathan, though he had been in touch via ship twice in the last month, and that it was likely in New Orleans at Nathan's banker. This annoyed me, not so much by the money's absence—I had plenty for the three of us and our plans—but more that the arrangements had changed. I had never had reason to distrust Nathan.

Next day, we followed the directions to Gonaïves, travelling with our mule, on three docile horses along the coast road to Cap-Haitien, avoiding people as much as we could. So unspirited were the horses that Two joked that the mule or we walking could outpace them. There were still small follies and disturbances by people in one or two crossroads. Some folk were beating drums or blowing horns, but no one was hostile, and the three hours we rode were uneventful, but much slower than I had hoped. As Jamaica was, the island showed lush tropical greens to our right as we rode north, and aquamarine to the sea breaking white over the tops of reefs to our left. At Gonaïves, we stopped to water our horses and let them graze near a well. The horses were lathering in the heat, so each of us were careful to gently cool them with the buckets there. All around us, we could see signs that the area was populated. The land was pitifully tilled and planted with calabash, which spread like an ugly invader. This was not the carefully tended and weeded gardens that we had our food from in Jamaica. There was evidence of drought and less jungle, since all the tilled land had been cut and burnt, leaving wide swaths of ash and charcoal with only a few plantings between. Much of the tilled land was eroded by the afternoon downpours. The well-spring where the horses and we drank was popular, attracting villagers—both brightly attired women, and dusty and sweaty working men. I asked directions to the house of Ogé, in French. I saw only addled faces. Speaking more slowly elicited a response from two men. My slower French was the reason. Their patois was mixed with creole; I should have known. They people at the spring merely looked and nodded to a lane by the horses, pointing and in their happy voices, saying in a lilt "La! la! la! la!." I took this as good fortune.

Refreshed, we walked down the brambled lane, overgrown with weeds and tree roots in places. Ogé's house had been painted red and blue and yellow and orange, had a variety of crosses, stars, obscure symbols and signs randomly painted in black and green on it. It had bundles of herbs hanging from the eaves. The doorway was dark. There were geese and chickens and several goats in a fence on the side. A numinous aura seemed to shimmer about this house. It exhaled incense and unusual and exotic odors. Yet Ogé's thatched shelter was inviting, for there were tropical flowers around it, and it had been painted in swatches of bright colors that drew one to them. The watch geese had set up their usual disturbed honking. Visitors! Honk! Strangers! Honk! Someone! They stopped us with their alarm. We only had a moment to look at his house before Ogé appeared in the doorway. It was as magical as the instant in Jamaica when the Maroon Mose' had appeared out the greenery. (I think now that men of color in Jamaica and Ste. Dominiquè learn a trick that allows them to fade out of sight and memory when they are stared at.) We were all momentarily unsettled.

Ogé was a medium-sized man, of Negro blood but so light as to have been almost a brother to my old associate, Thomas Wilson. His hair hung in small twisted and plaited ropes, light tan, and in some places braided with ribbons and glass. He smiled, "Je vous ai attendu." When I spoke English, he changed to that.

"How did you know we were coming?"

"The Abacou horn from Jamaica."

In my puzzlement, he only smiled and said that he was a priest, and that a priest's Loas tell him many things. At this I asked, "What is your religion?" A brown and black dog appeared and looked at us, flashing a tooth. She had strange hair, like two separate dogs joined together. The brown hair was straight, and the black curly, like mine—a Negro dog. Her name was Grace. Ogé said 'La bas" to her, and she laid at his side.

I told him I was a Quaker. He nodded.

"Je suis Voudou. Qui cherchez-vous?"

I told him, "Vous, Ogé." He motioned us to the side of the house, where there was shade. We followed him, leaving the horses in the pen with his geese and chickens. We both laughed at their squabbling; when I did that, the animals all quieted. We joined him and had the water he offered as he started to tell us about his position as a Hougan. I learned some Voudou very quickly, as we were told Loa are spirits that are models for living. There is a Loa for peacefulness and one for bravery. They are as many as human yearnings, and they represent the perfection of that characteristic, like Catholic saints. That was enough. He was sincere. I believed him when he told me a Loa had told him we were coming.

We talked of the trip and Port-au-Prince and London, of Olaudah's and Two's and my history, of the slave ship. Of me being raised as white, which he said was not so rare, especially among quadroons who here in Ste. Dominiquè own much land and wield some power. But these *gens* are still looked on with fear, not amity. As the subject was warm, I mentioned my plan of forming an alliance of all *gens de coleur*—free or enslaved—to find a way to remove the bigotry, slavery, and bias from men, that the Jamaicans were not interested, but that Ste. Dominiquè had started on that road, as had the colonies to the north, that France had a passion for freedom and human rights, and that Ogé could lead it here whilst I made my way to the newly governed American colonies. He grasped our hands, wisely saying nothing. A few minutes of thought made him rise and enter his house. I knew nothing of any response; there had been none. Olaudah and I stared down the lane, while Two listened to the rest of the translation and sat in the shade at the side of his house.

Grace ambled over, tail wagging, sniffed first at Olaudah and Two, then me. She spent some time savoring our scents, certainly knowing our muskiness after a time. She turned a few times to settle at my feet and stared expectantly, anxiously awaiting. I have an affection for dogs and always had, though I have never been in one place long enough to own one. They, just as Grace was at that moment, are always expectant—waiting for some morsel from someone's hand or a pat to show them affection, or even a command: fetch, come, stay, that would give them some play. I think they are like Milton's angels 'sent disguised in forms so various' to tend to us lesser creatures of God's creations, comforting us when we are frightened or succumbing to some plague, loving us e'er. I am certain there are times like this when they are telling us something—like 'keep patient'—but we are too ignorant of their spirit language to comprehend their message. I had no morsel for her, but I did scratch her coat while we waited. She sighed and slept.

Ogé reached into the fenced yard, shooed a goat and Two's nearly sleeping horse, and grabbed a fat red chicken, which he held for several minutes to calm it. He entered the house and returned several minutes later, inviting us to eat with him in two hours. "Monsieurs, reviens en deux heures et nous allons parler." With that, he told us where in town we might pass the time, and drew a small map to show us the way.

He returned to the house as we rode back down the brambled path. When we reached the road, we followed it on for a mile or two to a small, sturdy building which was painted as gaudily as Ogé's house. This one did not have the mystical signs, however. The garden was shady, faced a light breeze from the sea, and invited us with its music and aromas, so we drank local beer, and washed and attended our toilettes so we would be presentable for dinner. We passed an hour or so. I did not want to be late for Ogé's dinner.

When we returned to Ogé's house, Grace barked her greetings and settled in the shade, again studying me for some response. I looked in at the door and saw that our host had an elaborate altar on one wall, and a few chairs before it. On the altar was blood and feathers. Ogé saw me and explained, "Dese people hab a ceremony here some days. I sacrifice chicken to read signs what you tell me. I am cooking same chicken for dinner. Get signs and get dinner—no waste." He smiled, as did I. We all went out to sit in the shade, in the less unbearable heat. I wondered how Grace, with her ample coat, bore it, but she endured the heat and flies and fleas and humans. She had two fur coats like those I'd seen on Greenland dogs.

Ogé asked when we would leave for the colonies to the north when I inquired whether Câp Haitian had boats that went to New Orleans. Yes, "One time dis week in three days. Not worry my answer, wait. Tomorrow, I will know, and you will know." We arranged to meet the next day. Our business was over, I knew, by his manner. We socialized and told stories, ate the chicken and herbs and garlick and potatoes for dinner, which was very good. I was told its sacrifice fed the Loa to get an answer. We learned that Grace was Ogé's 'angel'—a loa—as all dogs are for the people who own them, and that free blacks and mulattoes, *gens de couleur*, and petit whites all were seeking an explanation of their rights, now that France had embarked on a revolution to match the Americans. He had been to France and had attended their Assembly and received assurances they would have 'equal rights' with all men, but when he returned to Ste. Dominiquè and addressed its Colonial Assembly, its hypocritical whites and others sought to deny them these rights. The rights were these (and I set them to memory) as he recited them:

Men are born and remain free and equal in rights. Social distinctions are made for the general good. These rights are liberty, property, security, and resistance to oppression.

Political associations should preserve them, not hinder them. Every citizen may accordingly speak, write, and print with freedom, but shall be responsible for such abuses of this freedom as shall be defined by law.

And, since property is an inviolable and sacred right, no one shall be deprived thereof except where it is a public necessity, legally then only on condition that the owner shall have been previously and equitably indemnified.

Olaudah translated with my prompting, and Two applauded. Grace moaned. I suppose she, in her animal brain, recalled the Bard with 'what fools these mortals be'. Ogé went on to tell us the provincial assembly was afraid that some free blacks may be richer, more militant, and more numerous. Ogé told us that fear breeds fear, and some planters were now abusing and executing mulattoes. Marronage had increased. Ogé would think on my plan, he said. After dinner we told stories. Then, it being late for travel and us having no lanthorns, he offered us beds for the night—we could rest there on pallets he had in a room in back.

He made a tea with a large bean he called gogo. He said we would sleep well and dream big. We talked some more and then, to my surprise, Two started to talk to him, partly in Creole and Dahoumey. I could only parse part of it, but Ogé spoke as if he were fluent. For some minutes Two chattered on with excitement, making gestures to the man and the surroundings. We drank some tea. He continued and finished. Then Ogé spoke to Olaudah and me to translate.

Two, he said, misses his home and is thankful he met you, Jo, or he feels he would be dead. He has a very strong feeling Ste. Dominiquè is where he should live, the jungle, the people, the air, so he wants to stay. He is afraid, however, that you will be insulted, feel betrayed, and insist on him going with you. He wants to be here, but his love for you pulls like a pet 'sur la ped et sur le coeur.'

I am not one to be moved, nor to weep, but I had begun to look at Two and Olaudah as sons. Perhaps this was what Mister Thomas felt when he hugged me and waved to me on the deck of the Chalkley. I hugged Two and squeezed him so tightly he groaned, and releasing him, nodded my assent, and asked Ogé to translate. "My friend, I bought your freedom, and you have it. Neither I nor any man can take it from you. If you want this island, I wish you the best fortune. I will miss you and think well of you. One thing you should do is to make someone free; make this world better." Two showed a happy relief when he heard my thoughts, just as I had been as a boy when I left home. Ogé then told me he needed someone to teach and an assistant. With a smile, he nodded at Two.

We drank his medicinal tea and fell to sleep with large and colorful and pleasant dreams, awaking refreshed. These people in Jamaica and Ste. Dominiquè have teas and tobaccos that I should import. I am certain they have medicinal as well as amusement value, and probably started as nostrums and tended toward pleasure.

Two would stay the next day, so Olaudah and I decided to explore a little until our host had a decision. There was little to see, save for tillage, jungle, and ocean shore. By mid-day we were at odds for something to do, so we sat in a restaurant drinking beer and lazing. When we returned to Ogé, we were greeted by Grace, Two, and him, and sat in the shade anxious for good news. There was none.

Ogé wore a gown with threads of many colors and embroidered bird designs. Two wore a plain one, obviously from the Voudou priest; he wore it proudly, though it was the symbol of diffidence. It looked as though it were made for him. The emmisarie and priest, Two's new mentor, had decided to be formal and spoke in French, "Mes assoçies et moi dissent **non**. Nous avons cette île. Quand vous arriverez á la Nouvelle-Orleans, vous aurez la vôtre." I translated for my fellows that he'd said almost the same words as we had been told in Jamaica.

Ogé then expressed his regrets. Then he told me that there were very big plans, other plans that his fellow gens would hear of some short time in the new year. He said, 'Bonne chance,' and left us to finish our goodbyes to Two, who had a smile on his face and tears in his eyes.

When we rode away, Two waving in the distance, we saw that we had an escort. Grace followed for a mile or so. Now she was a very close friend, for I had given her some chicken skin under the table at dinner—which gesture will make you a friend of a dog forever—and she sensed my disappointment and sorrow in leaving Two. As our horse started to trot free of brambles, she barked once, sitting in the dust and staring at us as we rode out of sight to Câp Haitian. I supposed we had a loa with us for our travels.

In Câp Haitian we booked passage on the Prophet, a fleet brigantine bound for New Orleans. The captain had heard of my skill in the galley—in fact, he asked if I was Black Puddin'—so we arranged that I would cook him four dinners for Olaudah's passage. His name was Scott Barnhouse.

For two days we enjoyed the town. I taught Olaudah Whist and Faro and how to lay a wager, for I knew from sailor's words—tar signals—that New Orleans had gambling, and women, and wine, something he and I would soon enjoy. There were average restaurants, but we had good French cuisine at one, which we returned to for two nights. I must say the French make good wines, many of which we sampled during the day. We went to a Quaker meeting. Olaudah was puzzled that we sat in silence, with only one gens speaking out in favor of freedom for all citizens of Haiti, a name he called Ste. Dominiquè, as the French had given it there. He asked me about the silent congregation. I told him what I had learned long ago: "In the quiet, we look for connections between those around us, or inwardly to our own self, or to the Creator. Once we do that, the feeling becomes stronger, and then we may begin to examine the world and our own relationships in a new way. Our worship then may take us beyond our own thoughts, our own selves and insular ideas, to help us examine and respond to the world around us in new ways. The man who spoke was moved by his feeling and thus, stood and spoke them."

Olaudah said he liked the feeling he had, especially the way everyone around him wished him well and shook hands with him when the service was over. We quietly walked down along the jetty and remained silent with our own thoughts while we looked out to the ocean and the ships at anchor. I do not know who or what Olaudah was thinking of, but I truly missed Philadelphia and the life and people I left there. We returned to pack our few possessions, went down to the tavern to have one last drink, and then retired. We set out on the Prophet on a Friday after dreamless sleep.

Chapter 12

*In which Joseph and Olaudah arrive
and thrive in New Orleans.
They learn a new dance, Olaudah is stung by Amor's arrow,
they attend a festival and meet two gens de couleur libre,
Pierre Castigny and Javier Rosinant.
Jo says goodbye to a young friend of his blood.*

Nouvelle Orleans, such a surprise! Olaudah and I both gaped as we walked and sweated in the febrile heat. It was French without a doubt. The gardens, ironwork, and colors alone were enough to persuade us. I expected a colonial town like Philadelphia, here in North America. It was so different. France and not France. And I alone noticed one more sign there for what I wanted society to be.

There were *gens de coleur libres*—free people of color—everywhere, in every neighborhood, shop, street, and business. As Olaudah and I sought a place to eat the first morning, I mentioned this to him, and he said, "P'raps your dream is real here when the war end." I corrected him that not everyone seemed free, and that this was now a Spanish colony. We found a small place with tables outside and had some porridge, fruit, bread, and beer, while we passed a time watching nursemaids, cooks, liverymen, messenger boys, and housemaids going to work.

Speaking of meals: Remember I wrote that I traded my galley skill for Olaudah's passage with Captain Barnhouse on the *Prophet*? It was a week's passage. In that short week, we ate well because of the barter. I cooked three meals for Captain, and he liked the last so well, he ate the rest of what had been left. There were fresh foodstuffs and viands as well as ample pork, ham, lamb, and island fruits. Compared to other ships, in the *Prophet's* galley, storage and space was more than a passenger cabin, this owing to Barnhouse's habit of travel only among the islands, Mexico, and the southern part of the American colonies. We would stay here for a time, but I made certain to attain his schedule from New Orleans to other ports.

I will write about the third meal, a *barbecoa*, as the Spanish islanders call it. We had a shoat that was well fattened and meat-heavy. So, on the iron, we laid out a slow fire down to glowing coals, which tended let the pork cook slowly. Over this at a little height I spitted the shoat, and for several hours—nearly four watches—roasted it, adding a green herb like pine that they call *romero* to make a fragrant smoke from time to time. This was not all my invention. I had seen it done by Nanny's-niece over a pit of coals and banana leaves in Jamaica. After all those hours, the meat was so succulent and tender it began to fall off the hog. I placed in a pan roasted roots and drippings mixed with salt, island peppers, allspice, and molasses, until the aroma was heavenly. I served this with a plentiful rice. The captain praised it highly and shared it with the guests and crew. There was enough left that we had it a second night. I was happy to see all the folk—white, blacks, Chinese, quadroons, South Americans, and central Americans, rich and poor—enjoy such a feast together in harmony. Olaudah especially liked it. He and I favored the skin of the pig, which had cooked like hard biscuits and had a wonderful flavor. He cracked it with a belaying pin, going back for a second and a third time for more.

I am writing this at night. We found an inn, the *Toulouse*, near Rampart and St. Louis street, beside a large cemetery 'the direction of the bayou', and opposite a square where there is supposed to be an African festival on Sunday, two days hence. Olaudah and I were dressed appropriately—imitating London and Port-au-Prince fashion—so few if any took note of us as we walked the streets. We slept long and deeply that first night.

Our Saturday was spent visiting restaurants, taverns, shops, and a large market where local folks sold various foods and wares. Especially cloth and trinkets, and sundries that women love. They were the object of our attention. We also noted a dancehall called Tr'maries where they gambled. I was tempted to use some of my skill as a footpad and highwayman to lift a purse or two, touch some *gens,* or rob some churchman, but I kept my own resolve and did not. I had kept my purpose thus far and allowed no lapses.

Reform, as I must, can harbor no excuse or backsliding on my resolution. One venial sin—as the papists call minor indiscretions—can lead to another, and another, and so on till one's map changes, one loses direction, taking a lower and lower road 'til one is mired, like I was when I first started this adventure. I must remind myself at every opportunity whereof I'm bound.

The city seemed to be half burned. There was much rebuilding. Brickmakers appeared to be filling their molds at every corner. When I tipped my hat to a young man and asked about this, he told me that last year on Good Friday, the city had burned, destroying almost a thousand buildings. 'Now they will use brick instead of wood.' It was odd to see an empty house space with an intricate iron fence around it and weedy garden, but no building. So many. That day, we also went to the port to arrange passage north. The 'Americans' were not allowed to sail to or use the port, so we made arrangements with a Spanish chandler, who did business with the other captains who traded there. Olaudah and I were to sail for Bilbao in six days on a merchant frigate, *Melissa*, with a Captain Sabatini. We were making the trip to Europe partly to show Olaudah London, and partly to retrieve what Nathan and Moses had banked for me. My plan was to sail thence to Philadelphia. I arranged that day to see what the problem was with Nathan's pledge to me. There was no notice in Ste. Dominiquè, and the agents here in New Orleans said they had not heard, nor could they contact Mister Nathan. A puzzle, but not one unsolvable.

The New Orleans populous was rowdy. People shot off flintlocks just to make noise and, in their parlance, 'raise hell'. Save for the *gens* and the white ladies and gentler men about their business, most of the town had fur-traders, ne'er-do-wells, gold-hunters, gamblers, smugglers, soldiers (now without a cause), drunkards, opium sots, whores, and the worst—slavers. I heard New Orleans was the largest slave market in the new country; later, I found that honor went to Charleston. That puzzled me when I saw that many of the more genteel folk were ex-slaves from Ste. Dominiquè or the southern colonies, or second-generation quadroons or octaroons from the French city's past or other Caribbean islands. These were free people of color minding businesses, tending their own plantations, and having cotillions. They were not the shackled, tortured and lashed men and women I had seen. I and Olaudah chose not to visit the slave auctions—something that would only thicken our anger. Yet this "malarious wet thicket of willows and dwarf palmettos, infested with serpents and alligators," beset by floods and hurricane storms and nearly insufferable heat, teeming with myriads of colonies of mosquitoes and no-see'ums, is growing and has a surface of fine fabrics and baroque metals, polite manners, and old European culture to be cosseted like a delicate flower for a blushing young girl. For dinner I took Olaudah to a restaurant known for fine Savarin cooking, using it as another of his 'lessons'. We were questioned in a social way, but both us chose to leave some past blank. No one need know that he was a recently freed slave, or I a past highwayman. The company we were in treated us as gentlemen travelers, as they should have. Good evenings end, and we retired.

The next day was a Sunday. Though a Quaker, I did not attend meeting. Olaudah did not treat it as a special day. We dressed less formally, wearing only breeches, stockings and shirts, loose at the collar, the air being torrid and thick. I had our innkeeper pack some bottles of wine, fruit, cheese, and bread in a basket made of sea-grass, and a corked jug of fresh water. I had waited to read Two's letter and put it in my pocket for later. It would be a good thing to read it to Olaudah under blue skies. I didn't need directions, because we were headed to Congo Square just down the street, barely three hundred yards.

This was a surprise for Olaudah. He hadn't known of slaves given a day's freedom from the surrounding plantations on Sundays and allowed to gather in this park with freed men and others of color—differently from Vauxhall—to play and dance to African music from the tribes. I had rightly guessed my transported companion would like it. He did, beyond description. At one point he had danced and celebrated so joyously, there were tears in his eyes. It was here he tried to teach me a new dance, although I don't expect I shall see it in Philadelphia or London in their civilized ballrooms.

It was called the *calinda;* a young woman had shown him. This dance is so, so very sensuous and suggestive, especially with a woman moving her hips and the man thrusting his. One could have no imagination and easily know what was happening. Normally, I think it should not be done by two men, so after one or two steps, I sent Olaudah on his way to dance with the new woman he had met. For myself, I was happy just listening to the music and watching all those enjoy their day of freedom.

I read Two's letter. Whereof he found a scrivener, I know not, but it was well written, and I am pasting it in my book:

By your leave, Sir Joseph,

I must speak this speech to you in this letter, of which it is written by Timothy, a young man who is known by Mister Ogé, Sir Joseph I must leave you to live

in Ste Dominiquè for I feel after the deathly voyage that the people here are most kind and loving and free and understand where my life has been, you saved me,

me and Ban, Giant and Rogue who have left in Jamayca and Sir Olaudah who is a very good person. You are going to the Pensilvania colony to you home.

I wish you God's blessing and fortune! And also to Olaudah ~~whether who~~ a teacher and friend.

If our Creator allows I will see you again some~~time~~day And I thank you Mister Joseph for my freedom most of all. I will make a good life. I am at Ogé's when you write.

Grace keeps looking for you. She a good ~~lea~~ dog.

Your mos' obedient and humble free man,

Two

Two's word touched me to tears. Olaudah, returning from his dancing, asked whereof and I read him the letter, which in turn did the same to him. We sat there quietly for a short time, but the drumming raised our spirits again and we stood, rocking to the thrum. It was then I was tapped on the shoulder and turned to meet two of the city's *gens de coleur*: one named Pierre Castigny and the other, Javier Rosinante—both landowners with small plantations, one near Bayou St. John, north of the city, and the other south toward the ocean. While Olaudah spent time celebrating and dancing to exhaustion, making eyes at young women and joking with men from West Africa, I spent time letting Pierre and Javier tell me about the war, the colonies, and their lives in this Spanish province. I returned the favor with stories of my life during the last fourteen years. They especially wanted to hear about exotic cities I might have visited, and of course, Paris and London. I shared our victuals; they, their brandy.

By the late afternoon, when many lazed in that meadow and some dozed, talk had turned to my plans and the mistreatment of men and slaves. They said that Ste. Dominiquè was a hot island ready to spring into flames, as was Jamaica, that many islands—in one way or another—were seeking a solution, and that the American colonies were still in a quiet war over slavery. They invited me and Olaudah to visit their farms on the morrow. I decided to do so. They would send us a carriage to meet us at Rampart and St. Louis. The heat and wine and brandy finally did their work. Fatigued, we parted like European gentlemen; Mister Thomas would have been proud of me and Olaudah then. After we were back at our inn, we were refreshed by a short rest.

That evening we visited Tr'maries dancehall to dine and gamble. I spent time after we dressed to teach some simple games like Poker, Roulette, and Faro to Olaudah, counselled him about cheaters, and to bet wisely, for Faro was made for a cheat. Ingenious ways had been developed. I showed him how at Faro a man might attach a fine horsehair to a chip, and once a bet is made could remove it with a flick of his hand, or how he could do the same with a copper when he places it to change his bet. In a twitch, the bet can be changed twice. We played several games. Olaudah was a natural. He showed a talent beyond mine, so I was happy to spend the evening at cards without concern.

I told him, "I'll watch the game before you play to make certain the bank isn't using a short or double shoe to deal cards. This is probably a fair game. You can watch me bet and decide." I told him to have fun. He learned well. I returned with 300 Francs; he, with 230—all to our profit. That night, we slept like happy and peaceful dead in the inn we'd rented near St. Louis Cemetery.

We were received to our carriage in the morning by a thin, sienna colored boy named Homer. He was only a few years younger than I when I had left Philadelphia. He had been taught his manners (and I pointed this out to Olaudah, saying that manners—not color—were what mattered in men). Homer pointed out a variety of sites on the way to "Merry Oaks", the plantation where were to be guests for the day. Merry Oaks was Pierre Castigny's plantation north and east of the city. He grew a small plant with terribly pungent red fruit—a pepper called capsicum, which he said was excellent with fish and beans. He was experimenting with a pickling process to preserve its zest. Ten families worked his land and lived in houses he provided. Each family had a three percent share in the profits. They are free *gens* who work 150 hectares.

His house was modest compared to those we had seen on the way. It was comfortable sitting on his gallery, where we ate some beans, rich and spicy shrimp midday, and drank cider, which he proudly said was from his apples. We rode horses for most of the afternoon, exploring his property. I saw his orchard. I had to steady a restive mare that nearly bolted when she saw (and for the first time, I saw) a large alligator that had lunged near the bayou, and which Pierre quickly shot. Pierre muttered to himself while he walked over, prodded the creature, and then spread his jaws so I and Olaudah could see the teeth. Pierre asked several workers to drag it with a wagon back to the house, giving instructions to clean it. Olaudah and I tasted some of our first gator tail that night—strong fish.

At dinner, Javier Rosinante asked if we should like to see his plantation the next day, and we—not having any engagements—agreed. Homer drove our carriage home and draped a gauzy fabric over the surrey's canopy top to keep the mosquitoes out. Smart boy.

Paulito, an equally smart and well-mannered boy, met us in the morning in a surrey, a carriage whose style was more in keeping with the owner's heritage. It was much more ornate than Pierre's—shall I say more Spanish? Olaudah said he felt like a king. The greying sky showed clouds that reminded me of squall days a'sea. It smelled like rain, wet nature, and rot while we rode, but the storm held off, lingering like a wet ambush.

The plantation was near a very large lake—an inland sea, almost—that the boy call "chatrain." (In truth, it was Lake Pontchartrain.) Then we saw cane fields running for several miles. Paulito said they were not all Senor Javier's, only some, and he turned into a lane. There we saw Javier and Pierre waiting for us in front of the house.

After we settled, the rain had started heavily. Even the gallery was drenched, so we stood in the entry which glittered of gold-leaf everywhere like the baroque churches of France and Italy. Paulito helped another man take our wet coats, and Javier escorted us into a small room with large windows. These were open to give us the benefit of the cool breeze attending the weather. As we sat and talked, we were served brandy and watched the storm cross the lake toward New Orleans. Javier told us about the hurricanes that beset them and said—from reports he had heard—that this storm would pass quickly, that it was not one. Ships' masters mooring in port were the source of such news; otherwise, people were at the Creator's whims.

Javier had 125 hectares for sugar and another 50 he planted with vegetables like okra and tomatoes, beans and maize. Except for swine, fowl, and kine, he and Pierre traded foodstuffs and workers as needed.

While we spoke, Javier launched into a small harangue about Janine Lachat, a Voudou priestess who had emigrated from Ste. Dominiquè, who was frightening the whites with curses and fictions, that she was upsetting the *gens de coleurs* so that they were beginning to see moments of race hatred by frightened whites again. We were quiet, silently hiding our embarrassment during this rant, until Pierre guided him into another subject. He asked Olaudah if he liked New Orleans. It appears there is a knack for diplomacy of conversation that is characteristic of American women like Mistress Sarah, and French emigrés.

Olaudah was pleased in these circumstances, he said, especially the plantations and the lakes. He said he liked to grow things when he was young, and he thanked both Javier and Pierre for their *gentilesse* (his using the word surprised me).

Javier brought in a bottle of a clear whisky which was very strong and thinned it with juice, or, by Heavens, we would have been deaf and dumb besotted. He returned to the subject of Janine Lachat. It was then I mentioned my thoughts about an alliance to fight this hatred of whites by blacks and blacks by whites, and the experience I had on the *Lethe*. We discussed these matters like members of parliament, with Javier pretending to be a white planter and Olaudah playing a slave to entertain us. It was a cruel masque at times—especially, I think, when the cruelty of slavery came up and Olaudah's brow knitted in anguish. But then the conversation moved to my immediate distrust of Thomas Wilson, my deceased associate of the highway. I now know his pallor and color in its whiteness seemed wrong, and I did not realize that to whites, our color seems wrong. I was as guilty as they in distrusting him. Yet I worked with him all those years, biased by his appearance. Had I not been so biased to white, he and I could have been closer.

Then we agreed it is the same with women. They are considered less trustworthy and less intelligent and less vigorous than men, Javier said. Yet I have oft seen them do twice the work, calculate faster, and keep their faith better than men. Certainly, my erstwhile wife was such a woman, and I albeit a man, weaker. I was full in my tale: they heard about the young female slave child who I entertained with a sailor's whirligig in the morning and had died unspeakably, drowning in the slop's cask. The women were the source of comfort and nurturing in the world. And they would always be the source for peace.

From that we moved to religion. Didn't America start because one man thought another wrong in the way he worshipped? Did we not as Christians lead crusades against the Muslims, killing on both sides, over the years? And do we not distrust the East Indians who have monkey and elephant gods?

Then the topic shifted to war, and to the character of man. Javier asked a maid for another flask of spirits. It was the same with nations and immigrants, religions, and sport.

Even some animals express bias. Was it something the Creator stained us with? Maybe, as Scripture tells, it is what man added after his loss in Eden. When we rule, we cannot abide a difference in government. When we are in school, there must be a rivalry. The food you eat and the soap you use is better than mine, so I must give mine up. It spreads to things like clothes and animals and colors. The list that man makes to find differences is endless, because man was planted with the seed by his Creator to prefer a rose to a tulip. This was an ageless topic, perhaps inexplicable, baffling. My cause might be hopeless beyond my quarter. Javier rose unsteadily. It was time for dinner, with some foods some of us would prefer not to eat. It was time to sup, or we would surely be besotted with these thoughts and the whiskey.

Olaudah seemed bored, so Pierre began talking about his favorite philosophers and writers. He mentioned Rousseau and Locke. He asked me what religion I clung to. I told him I had been a Quaker in Philadelphia, but nothing since. He said he was a Deist—an enlightened man like so many in those years—a near cousin to me, a Friend. As soon as he mentioned *enlightenment,* we both started talking and Javier, like a referee at a blood sport, intervened and cooled us. The conversation moved on to freedom and the neighbors to the north. "The Americans think they are free now that they have won a war for liberty," Javier started, and Pierre said that most men there still say about black Africans what Voltaire said of our race: "*Leurs yeux ronds, leurs nez épaté, leurs lèvres toujours grosses, leurs oreilles différemment figurées, la laine de leur tête, la mesure même de leur intelligence, mettent entre eux et les autres espèces d'hommes des différences prodigieuses.*" I translated for Olaudah, pointing to each feature like a teacher (Their round eyes, their flattened nose, their lips which are always large, their differently shaped ears, the wool of their head, that very measure of their intelligence, place prodigious differences between them and the other species of men.) "But they are wrong in this thought, Olaudah, as you can see. Here we are sharing our thoughts and speaking thus because someone shared their gifts with us," raising his finger heavenward.

"If you get hungry, thirsty, are deaf or blind or insensate, in need you will be enslaved, for those who satisfy your urges and desires then become your masters. Everyone is a slave at some time. Only when you add profit, and transact that relationship of the needy and provider, do you find a greater evil, as we have had throughout the world." And then our conversation left slavery and changed to whether money corrupts (I had much to say from experience). Even Olaudah raised an eyebrow. Olaudah added, "De Somalis, dey say 'Poverty is slavery.' Is truth."

We sat at dinner, where the conversation continued. Again, Pierre, who had studied in Paris, quoted and looking at Olaudah, saying, "'It is slavery, not to speak one's thoughts', a Greek dramatist once said, and now you realize your freedom, Mr. Olaudah." I asked where he had studied. Pierre was brief: "Le Sorbonne, Joseph, before the revolution. When blood and mayhem were clotting thick in the streets."

We had Vichyssoise, only pausing to eat our cold soup, a vin blanco from Spain. A salad of leaves, tomatoes, cucumber and cooked shrimp that Javier said were from the ocean nearby, fried chicken with the piquant peppers Pierre had brought, and fried okra, which Olaudah praised as good as what he grew in Africa, and the conversation came in fragments until we finished. I had purchased a bottle of fine French cognac as a gift, Olaudah presented his house gift (a book I suggested when he asked what he should get, Locke's *An Essay Concerning Humane Understanding*), and we retired to the dry gallery to finish the night.

Javier spoke of America, which he said had gotten rid of a king with his needs for power and self-aggrandizement, but then pessimistically predicted that since she cast her fate with the goddess of fortune, she would someday endure a period of a leader like a king who had fewer scruples and more greed. Perhaps many. This would be the fault of the variety of people who won't vote for honesty and right, but selfish desires and bias. What are kingdoms but great bands of robbers?

We all were sated and, with all our discussion and thought, it seemed, pensive, sipping brandy while we watched will-o-wisps. Javier was the first to yawn; then, of course, we others followed. It was getting late; we began to say our good nights. Javier gave a book to Olaudah, thanking him for the Locke, and told him he must learn to read and then he'd never be enslaved. It was Aphra Behn's *Oroonoko*. After I read from the title page, Pierre, who was the more didactic, looked at Javier and said it was not by Behn, but by Pierre Antoine de La Place and should be called *Oronoko, ou Le Prince Négre*. "Twas not English, but French," he disputed. The two *gens* quibbled and sparred over the book for a moment and, realizing we were smiling at the silliness, stopped. "Socrates said 'Tout ce que je sais, c'est que je ne sais rien'." Pierre laughed, as did we all, and we parted.

As we rode away from such a fine day, Olaudah asked what Pierre had said. I told him: "All that I know is that I know nothing," and he slapped his knees and laughed.

Olaudah had liked the day with Javier and Pierre, and his lessons were learned quickly, so in the next two days before we were to leave, we talked often about what he hoped to do in his life. He was welcome to travel with me as I went north. I assured him he would be greeted and loved as family. His thoughts differed. Now that he had seen how the *gens de coleurs* had a society here in New Orleans, and that Two lived in Ste. Dominiquè, he felt he could find a path to follow in both places. He feared the white, obstinate southern Americans and sensed there was something brewing in Two's island. He liked Javier and Pierre and Roselle, the girl he had danced with at Congo Park on Sunday. As I, he liked cooking. Perhaps I could share some of that with him.

Our lessons consequently grew more intense. I added cooking, more English, manners, how to choose clothes, avoiding cheats, some pickpocket routines, no gambling (for that had nearly ruined me), and we talked about nature, identified flowers and animals, recipes (which he had written in a leather chapbook, as I do my life) and had him read to me. My passage had been delayed by mechanical problems on the boat we were to take. I took this as a gift from the Creator to allow me more time with Olaudah, who I began to feel a paternal and a fraternal care for.

We read the news of the new nation and talked about people I had met as a youth—Mister Franklin, Mister Thomas, and others I had seen around Philadelphia during the year I left. I guided him to buy books and to remember what Javier had said when he learnt the book. He had finished it and wanted to return it.

I contacted Janine Lechat on a lazy afternoon when Olaudah slept. She lived north of St. Louis Graveyard by about a mile, in a ramshackle wood house that showed some burn from the previous year and, like Ogé's, was a rainbow of colors and an array of runes and signs. She was there and answered, "Qui est la?" when I knocked. "Joseph Mountain," I responded, and she stepped out. This was the woman Javier had cursed so long? Frail, so bony one could snap her with a squeeze, she had long hair tinted purple and arrayed with some sparkles. Her white gown draped her like a wire mannequin. 'Do you read fortunes, Madame Lechat?"

"Oui," she said and stepped aside so I could enter.

Once we sat, in my nervous state, I told her I had met Ogé in Ste. Dominiquè and that I was here only a few days. She said nothing while she lighted scented candles around the room. She nearly glided when she sat opposite me. "S'il vous plait, en Anglais?" "Of course, Joseph," but first we had to settle on price. Once that was over, she asked me of Ogé and I told her, and of Two staying with him. She then got up and fanned smoke over me, being certain to touch all of me with its fragrance, then she sat and took both my hands and looked in my eyes.

"Yo spirit is better than ship and your heart heals. You have painful loss across the great waters yet return to love. Yo see the mother of you and are struck, then a long road, dreams, time, theft, moon, the lash, lies, and the rope." She shivered, and when I paid her, she gave me a candle to burn once every day to protect me. I left with worry about the lash, rope, and disappointment. What could it mean? I troubled myself with these thoughts as I walked to my inn.

I met with Javier and Pierre separately at a creole restaurant that evening, while Olaudah spent the time with Roselle. If he agreed, Olaudah could stay with one of them and continue his studies with a local teacher. If he chose Ste. Dominiquè, Pierre would provide introductory letters to a man named T'oussaint in Câp Haitien, who would give him a hand. Elsewhere, they had no contacts, save for one island off the coast of South Carolina and Georgia. After a year of studies, they both agreed that he could work in a warehouse, or shipping, or as a caretaker for their farms. He would choose his own path. I gave them £300 to provide for his expenses, books, clothing, and sundries. Javier and Pierre spoke to each other again very rapidly in Creole, Spanish, French, and English for about a half hour while I enjoyed the food and wine. Exhausted, they finally stopped. I smiled, knowing this was their manner.

They agreed, but also said they would supplement what we could not foresee. All agreed, we talked about entertainment in town and where we might walk to other than Tr'marie's after our meal. We walked for an hour around the quarter and near the port, returning to the restaurant to meet Homer with the carriage. I thanked them and walked to my bed, thinking that hatred and pain, almost all negatives, were diminished by love.

Olaudah told me quietly that he and Roselle had a wonderful visit, and that she had kissed him. At that moment, I knew then he was staying. On the morning, we ate on the inn's gallery and remained there for several hours. Olaudah had much to decide. I was leaving the morning after tomorrow on the tide.

By noon he had decided to stay in New Orleans with Pierre, "To learn to speak French like all dese peoples." I told him about the expenses, warned, as Mister Thomas had me, about lending and spending and gambling, women, men, and sin—a true Polonius, I was. Mister Franklin would approve. And asked him if there was anything he wanted. There was not. We planned to visit Pierre the next day. He packed and wrote a special note to thank Pierre for the loan of the book. I sat on the gallery, leaving him to his writings, thinking of when, like him, I too was about to embark on life, though differently.

After he was finished with his letters, I suggested he should have a full name; he would choose. After some thought, he said he would make two new ones. His new name for his new life would be Paul-Joseph Rousseau, because people spoke well of "Deh Saint, and for your name, and for Pierre's philosopher." I bowed to him, placed my hand on his head, and said, "From this moment this man will be called Paul-Joseph Rousseau." I then took pen and paper and rewrote the manumission papers I had written for him on the *Lethe*, returned them to him showing him his new name clearly writ, and took him out to shop. Since Paul-Joseph was a large man for that time, we went to a tailor named Jason Nimes, who Pierre had mentioned, and had Paul-Joseph measured. Monsieur Nimes was accommodating. With Paul-Joseph's direction, we picked out four pairs of britches, four waist coats, two coats, stockings, belts, three pairs of shoes, one banyan, one negligée hat, two cocked hats, one cape, five shirts (one fine), four underdrawers, three handkerchiefs, three cravats, one pair of spatterdashes, one stock, one ruffled shirt, one suit, one plain kerchief, three rough trousers, and two muslin shirts—the latter two items for every day wear—and because the occasion may arise, one periwig. I purchased a new pair of breeches, two shirts, a Monmouth cap, and a woolen coat for the voyage. Monsieur Nimes nearly swooned. But he recovered very quickly when I paid him in British silver. He agreed to deliver our purchases and those clothes he would make to Merry Oaks and Monsieur Castigny. We then went to a bookseller near St. Louis Square.

At the store unnamed, but owned by a Mister Wolfe, we spent some time: Paul-Joseph like a meadow bee moving from flower to flower, and I, selecting some few books I remembered from my days studying at the Mifflins' that I would leave with Pierre to educate a lad I loved like a son. I chose a translation of Rosseau's *Social Contract*, a copy of Thomas Paine's *Common Sense*, Gibbon's *Decline and Fall of the Roman Empire*, Johnson's *Dictionary*, Olaudah Equiano's *Travels: The Interesting Narrative Of The Life Of Olaudah Equiano*, Bartram's *Travels*, Gay's *The Beggar's Opera*, Pope's *Poetry*, Fenning's *Speller*, an English grammar, a guide to handwriting, Hodder's *Arithmetick*, and *The New England Primer*. I told him that when he was ready, he should choose a book of prayer. I emphasized this and told him it would be most valuable in difficult times, beyond all others, as it focused on something greater than earthly woes. I also gave him a copy of Laurence Sterne's *The Life and Opinions of Tristram Shandy, Gentleman*, to entertain him. These, as well as some classics and books on science, would be carried out to Castigny's. I had no fear about leaving Paul-Joseph. Pierre had taken to him as well and would give him a good education, teach him French and sundry things. When I returned next spring, I knew he would be an enlightened young man.

It was late, so we retired after a small supper. The day had taken all of Paul-Joseph's energy. I was emptying of feelings once again. I mused on what my visit north would be. And I slept.

Homer stood by the coach, waiting for us. We stowed Paul-Joseph's belongings, checked that he had his papers, and rode out to Merry Oaks on a day softly sunlit and breezy. The air was fragrant like many before in England and France. I took it as an auspicious omen.

Pierre bounded down the steps from the gallery like a puppy welcoming new friends. He shook hands with both of us, saying 'Bienvenue, bienvenue.' When he finished, I introduced Paul-Joseph Rousseau, and he grasped him in a warm embrace. We went to the shade on the gallery and had some tea, pastries, and fruit. Pierre had already received the books, saying he would teach Paul-Joseph French every day, thanked him for the note he had written, and took us to a small building behind his home that had a small stove, and two rooms for him to live in. There were shelves that held Paul-Joseph's new books, a table by a window looking out at the bayou and trees hung with moss, three comfortable chairs, an armoire, a bed, washstand, cupboard, and oil-lamps. His eyes grew wide and then teared. He turned to me and held me close for some time.

I did not want to prolong this farewell. I took my leave and said I would write. I told them both I would return in the spring, only months away. The last thing Paul-Joseph said to me was 'My new father, my new life,' and handed me a letter. Homer took me back to the inn. I was empty.

Chapter 13

*Detoured, Joseph sails to England on the L'Printemps,
revisits Charing Cross and the Black Horse,
which he finds under new management,
seeks out Moses and Nathan to his great distress,
but saves a homeless child, then finally sails to Philadelphia
and falls back in love with Essie.*

Life now whispered that I should return home. I left the *Toulouse* and walked through the Quarter to the chandlery and waited to meet the captain, whose merchant frigate would speed me to the continent. Alas, when I arrived, I found the boat had left without a word to me, and I castigated the Spanish chandler with curses. I believe, except for a Gad's tooth or Bloody!, I had not been angry enough to take the Lord's name in vain before that moment, so angry was I. But I got face to face with the chandler and said "You gob-spitting, tarnal rigger, bastard! Trying to cheat me. God's death on you, you weasel!'

He rejoined, "Nigger, I should never have treated you like a true *gens de couleur.* Get out of here!" I pursued it with, "Tu est un con. Call me Nigger? I should shoot you." I felt sweat break out on my face and angrily turned to see who had tapped my shoulder. Another gentleman, standing back as I turned in fury, said, "Whoa, there. I can fix this." Then he told me he was leaving on the tide for London with a cargo of molasses, cotton, rum, and rice, made a hilariously vulgar joke about Spaniards, offered me passage, and thus partly defused my ire. He made me laugh. I said I would go. I paid him for the fare, which the chandler had by now quickly returned to me. I introduced myself, and he told me he was Captain Letours. After he finished his business, he escorted me to large frigate named *L'Printemps*, which was still being laded, and once aboard, showed me to my cabin. He also was a conversation diplomat, like so many women I had known. I apologized to him for the cursing and my anger. "Je connais. C'est rien," he replied with a smile. Then, for us both, "Bon voyage!"

"Bon voyage, Monsieur Captain Letours et Monsieur Mountain!" I replied. He beckoned to a crewman who retrieved my bags, and we walked to his ship. He had his duties; as he left, I followed him on deck to watch the crew work and the French-American city fade, to stir my memories of the smell of the sea and the cries of the gulls, to bless those I left and others in their freedom.

The words I wished to Captain Letours came true. *L'Printemps* was a fine ship, fleet and yare, and the crew able under fine command. One storm badgered us off the Canaries for two days as we turned toward London, and one other passenger, a Mister Hobbes, was seasick most of the time, but the three weeks sped by. I did no mechanical work or cooking. This was a holiday for me. Except for Sail's tutoring on my first voyage, this was much the same. Idling, I fished as we crossed the green river flowing northward with its sargassum and flying fish. I landed one large Dorado and two sharks, which fed all of us aboard. There was naught but one

Negro aboard, and as the cook, he served some good and some better victuals than I could. It was common during the days I served a'ship to see many African crewmen—all free. This thought, as well as what I saw in the islands, New Orleans, and in the larger cities of Europe I had visited, rested my unease about the prospect of ever ridding bias from men. I have returned to some of my Quaker thinking, enough to help me put the reins to my anger, careless living, robbery, and uncivil habits. I read my prayer book, following my advice to Paul-Joseph, missing him, limning pictures in my mind of him studying or working at Javier's and Pierre's. I should cast off my foppery and return to the plain dress, I was taught by the Mifflins; I should try to attend meeting and read and study the Bible; I should avoid strong drink; I should investigate myself to find the light of God; do I believe enough to do this? I oppose violence, oaths, war, slavery, now, but there must be more. I may not be a saint when I return to Philadelphia, but I will a better man than I have been all these years. I do not excuse it as youth. Paul-Joseph is someone I can point to as one example I have helped and set on a path to a better life.

Besides fishing, I occupied my time as usual watching the activity topside and reading. I walked the deck for exercise and did my best to stay fit, for I wanted to be "tip-top," as the gentlemen in England put it, when I arrived.

When we landed in Dover, I did not disembark. I wanted to reach London without the clatter of a coach and the discomfort of the roads. Captain Letours said he was going on to Gravesend, so I would continue. There, I hired a surrey to Charing Cross. The *Black Horse* was still convenient, but under new ownership—a Mister Goodkey. Humphreys had retired and was said to have settled in Nova Scotia. Damon Goodkey and his wife Anne welcomed me and provided for my comfort. He also lent a mare, named Nancy, to me for the day. I was twitted a bit by her name and unsettling memories of another by her name, but she responded well on the ride. I didn't use her name. I told her it was not her fault. I rode out after I was settled to Rag Fair to see Moses and Nathan. It was time to use some of my wealth to do good.

I stopped first at Moses's—my, Hyde's and Wilson's broker. There, to my vexation, I found he had returned to Warsaw, with no associate left in London nor any of my wealth. There was naught but timbers and ash where he lived before. No one neighborly had any response of value when I question's Moses's flight. I held my temper, joked to Nancy that I was mounting her, and rode on to Rag Fair and Nathan's. London was quickly changing. Streets disappeared that I had known before. Twice I met cul-de-sacs, and once found a street I entered that led me to a maze of lanes and courts, so I spent nearly an hour returning to Moses's. Still frustrated at my loss, I rode to Vauxhall first, believing I'd find some solace among the tree-lined arcades and copses. Not to be.

Vauxhall was tawdrier than ever—or perhaps I had outgrown its charms. Doxies and their pimps, lusty young couples lying half-naked in the copses, footpads by the dozen populated my park. Most were children. Young lads and lasses in rags, hardly 5 or 6, homeless and begging crowded visitors. There were few clockwork animals that worked. Some remained, but were broken and would never perform. I doubt anyone as genteel as Nancy rode there, so I returned to my errand. I only briefly let my past with my wife linger in my thoughts and took a different route to Rag Fair, and pulled the bell-cord at Nathan's business. I was being sorely tested in all my resolves.

At first, there seemed to be only his shop in disrepair. I could observe dusty counters and few goods through the dirty window. When the door opened, I was stunned. His youngest son, Isaac, skin and bones and slovenly, asked me my business—he did not remember me—and when I mentioned my name and explained my business, with a shrug of his shoulders he showed me in. It was obvious there was no business there, and none for months and months. I asked where his father was. The poor boy started to cry and told me his father had gone one day, a year ago, and never returned. He had packed things from his shop, told his wife that he was going on a trip, kissed him, saying, "Be a mensch. Keep your faith; care for your mummy. He never came back. Mother died in Newgate last month. I don't know what to do." Then the lad leaned against me and cried so hard that as much as I was silently cursing Nathan as a Polack, an Israelite and Jew and swindler Jew Christ-killer; I could not be hard on him. It was clear now. I had lost everything between Nathan and Moses. Ah, but so had Isaac. I comforted him and doing so eased my anger.

When the boy quieted, we closed the place. I had him sit afore me in the saddle and returned to Charing Cross. Anne Goodkey took the boy in immediately when I explained his circumstances. Was this what happened to me with the Mifflins? Damon was equally kind and showed him to a small room behind the kitchen where he could rest.

It was then Anne explained that they could not have children, and Isaac was a found treasure. It was a fortune like that which made me the adopted son of the Mifflins. I still boiled with such anger at Nathan and the other Jew that it took several hours of occupying myself with Anne and Damon before I could think about a way out of my pickle. They had solved one problem with Isaac; but I had a greater one. In our silences, our eyes communicated what to do.

I had only about £50 sterling and some loose francs and pesetas, my clothes, my pistols, my fiddle, and some sundries; a watch, a cane, and little else. But . . . I had my skill and wits. Fuck the missing brokers. I had a tankard and some ham and biscuits, then saddled Nancy and rode to my old associates' haunts. There, from a footpad I had known, I found out that Nathan had been killed shortly after he left London. A footpad in France had bludgeoned the old Semite and taken all his goods, and mine. I enquired about blood sports and card games in the offing and found two games set to be played in Gravesend that night.

I would increase my silver and sell my pistols, hangers, cane, and books, for a goodly price, owing to their current value. That would leave me enough to support the Goodkeys' kindness to me and Issac. That night, after I supped, I repaired to a brothel in Gravesend and entered the games. It was a long night full of reneges—not of cards, but of my resolves.

This was a time to use what I knew to gain back the wherewithal to carry them out. Would the Apostles have followed Jesus if he had not saved them in a storm and filled the nets with fish? I felt a clarity in my resolutions. I would not cheat at cards; nor use my pistols in a robbery. Given that Nathan and Moses left my situation a mare's-nest, I had to find a way back to Philadelphia, and some money to do it. I won that night. I used only my reason and no tricks to win. Fortune blessed me with luck in the cards. I won £213 sterling. And then I got an unexpected gift. I found a purse. A gentleman next to me at the gaming forgot his purse when, besotted by brandy and haste, he left the brothel. It made me raise my eyes when I found it. In bank notes and guineas, his loss was an addition of £160, enough to get me home. Against temptation, I inquired about the gentleman with the bawd. She told me he was drunk and left most quickly for one of the ships at Gravesend harbor, saying "'e was late for his boat to Spain, 'e was. Nearly diddled me out of his supper bill; paid it on the run, 'e did."

Hearing that, I knew I had no way of returning it to him. I kept the purse with no guilt. After I left the bawd's at Gravesend, I rode to Islington and passed Nancy's house. There was candlelight shining through the sitting room windows. For a moment I was tempted to knock at the door to say goodbye, but the weight of the guilt I had made me the coward. What happens to two lovers in a marriage that make their love fail? Is it immaturity, penury, faithlessness? Or, I think, as was partly our case, that one of us had dreams the other did not share—children, family, adventure. Another question to ponder. Why does life raise so many of them?

I left and went to the fair to visit a ratting. Here also, I had second thoughts. I decided instead to return to the *Black Horse* where I could do some good. With Damon and Anne, I set aside £100 for Isaac and his care, giving an extra 20 guineas to the Goodkeys. I packed my goods. Next day, I crossed the square and, seeing my old armorer's shop closed, rode to Whitechapel in Castle Alley and sold my pistols to Henry Nock, the gunsmith. Like parting with an old friend, I sold my fiddle; rode to some of the crossroads and fords where once Hyde, Wilson, and I would await and touch our prey; stopped for refreshment for Nancy, my good mare, and me at inns I knew; and finally rode Nancy back to Charing Cross. I said goodbye to the mare, joking she had been ridden hard without complaint. When I arrived at the inn, Isaac had had a bath, fresh clothes, his hair trimmed; he had been fed and rested. His simple manner made him quiet, but it was clear Anne had taken over a mother's duties. I told them all I was leaving early the next day. We all sat down to dinner together. Anne, in the Friend's way Mistress Sarah had done at supper time in Philadelphia, asked us to hold hands and silently thank God for our plenty. During our supper, I found out they were Quakers, 'Friends' as they said. I too, I told them, and we blessed providence and our Creator for bringing us together, even for so short a time. I explained to Isaac that these people would protect him if he chose, that I was going across the ocean, and that he should be the best man possible in his life. I said goodbye, thanked them, and left before dawn.

My ship lay low in the water full of cargo. The tide was on the rise. Captain Ephraim Hutter welcomed me aboard the *Virtue.* As was my habit, I stowed my effects in my cabin and returned to the foredeck to watch the sunrise, city, and crew sail us out of Gravesend. Captain Hutter and I learned much about each other in the three weeks sail to Boston. Dutch by birth, he lived in Delft, where his wife Clare and he had raised two boys and a girl. The girl, Isabel, was the youngest, and still at home waiting on him faithfully during every voyage, which he made twice a year now that age had slowed him. He had Dutch friends in New York. One of his boys was an artist working in Delft and the other, who lived there also, made porcelain pottery. Both were happy craftsmen. This and the return from Philadelphia would be his last voyage. He said, "T'was time to stop wandering, sleep late, and love mein wife."

I shared some of my life—but not my sins or recklessness—told him of my early life in Philadelphia, my life as a cook and mechanic at sea, and something of my experience in the Indies. He had been once to Aruba, asked me what I felt about slavery and sugar, and listened when I told him my thoughts. He suggested that perhaps I'd like to cook. I said I might. I also told of my hopes to be a good son returned from my profligacy, and perhaps live out my days as a good Quaker, son, citizen, and, perhaps now, father to someone. I wanted to be active in the Abolition Society, which had a large membership in that city. I wanted to leave something good in the world before I left it. Captain praised these thoughts but warned that the 'new country' was sometimes euphoric in its new freedom. "There is a type of lawlessness among the spirit of the people, an attitude that 'we have won our freedom and now are free to do anything we desire.' Many feel they have free speech and say the wrong thing, and by turns, trample on other's rights. It is the same as lords and ragamuffins, masters and slaves, those who have and those wanting; they are like horses let free. Some are trampled when the gate opens." I took his words to heart.

When we stopped in Boston, I told him to buy two ducks for the voyage south to Philadelphia, and I would cook him a meal as payment for his amity.

I arrived in Boston the 2nd of May last. The *Virtue* in one day was lighter by half and loaded only one tonne of goods, mostly fabrics, some flint-lock rifles and pistols, and casks of black powder. There was nothing left for me in the islands or in New Orleans, except for the few friends I had there. In the United States of America in the south, where a black man was still treated less than a dog, there was ingrained slavery, certainly nothing for me except demeaning laughter. I was headed to my birthplace. For two very cool days, I walked around the city to learn what had happened there during the war and to taste its flavor. My first stop was to Bunker Hill in Charlestown, to see where this glorious battle for freedom had started. I passed some quiet time there thinking, knowing that an alliance was impossible, but wondering how I could make a difference for men—not just my African brothers, but men as a homo-geneous whole. People still avoided or suspected me from my skin, even with my fine manners and speech and embroidered coat and silver buckles. After some time, I wandered toward the harbor. I wanted to see where Crispus Attucks had died, the first casualty of this mighty cause, because he was a black man, a sailor, as I, and was willing to fight for rights. I had seen impressment and how it was no less than legalized enslavement by the British Admiralty to fill their ships with crews, willing or not. This was unjust—just like the tarnishing of Attucks' name afterward when John Adams raised his image as one of the rioters to help defend the crown's soldiers who fired the fatal shots. Others had said he was only observing his fellows taunting the redcoats. At end, the injustice—over race and history—still hangs. Attucks died on the street near the State House, and his body was carried to Faneuil Hall. I stopped by both, hoping to raise some spectre of the past, and perhaps converse with it, but there was nothing but the hustle and bustle of daily life around me.

As I walked to the harbor with its land-cradled ships at anchor, I stopped for my evening supper. Two tankards of good stout, a pigeon pie, and a bowl of wonderful quahog chowder full of fatback, potatoes, and greens made me ready for a restful night aboard the *Virtue.* When I boarded, Captain and crew had finished the lading, cleaned the ship, and he was reading his charts. He introduced me to two new passengers, two fat Muscovy ducks, who he said I must name for the week.

I thanked him for the courtesy and said, "Supper and Dinner," dubbing them with their names. He smiled, and I retired.

Next turn of the tide, we were off, and I followed my routine of rising at dawn, watching the crew, and ordering my hopes, which were nearly like brief prayers now. I hope the Mifflins gracefully receive me; I hope all is well for the city and my mother and father and Essie, and my friends; I wish well for Paul-Joseph and Javier and Pierre, and Nanny's-niece, Two, and the world. The ducks sat watching me as I saw the city drift into mistiness. And I watched them with some misgivings. They were happy creatures, unknowing, and soon to meet their fate.

The cook, a Chinese, had no qualms about expediting it. When I was asleep the second day, he sent Supper and Dinner to their maker, cleaned them, and hung them to age in the galley. I spent the day after defatting them with slow heat and glazing them with some molasses and oranges, and serving them to the Captain, two other passengers, and the cook. We had five bottles of wine. All of us told stories from life. We toasted the departed birds. Sated, we retired early.

It was a warm midday when we reached the Delaware and turned for the port. The picture from my last visit had only changed a mite. Ships were being loaded and unloaded, but there were no transported prisoners being introduced to their new homes, no slavers, no royal navy. Philadelphia seemed a bustling, buzzing hive. It was indeed a green city, as Penn had desired.

My monies were growing short, but I had enough to buy an old roan mare. She reminded me of Janine Lachat, who had told me a fortune which I was still puzzling out, so she became Janine. After a good scrub and brushing and a portion of oats, she also looked better. To improve her life, I wove some ribbon in her mane and fed her two apples. Gone was the day on a swift horse to ride when I could count on some unfortunate traveler crossing my path to be robbed by Mountain, and I could bid him adieu with some grace. I had a humble horse; I was humbler.

Then I set out through town, I had to keep my manumission papers at hand, for I was often stopped and questioned, especially by my manners, my speech and my clothes, which seemed better than most whites. At last, I had finally made my way from the port to Philadelphia proper, which now was almost double the size it had been when I left some thirteen years before.

Now I saw it on horse; the clatter and hoo-hah reminded me of Liverpool and Madrid and smaller cities in Europe. The people seemed happier, however, and it was clear that freedom suited the state as much as it suited me, and would suit my race if it ever came to be. Maybe it was, as Penn had wished and named it, the city of "brotherly love." I carefully rode past places I had known in my youth and frequented, stopping by those I had remembered—Society Hill, John Bartram's garden beside his house, Carpenter's Hall, the City Tavern, Franklin's Hospital. And I rode passed the Mifflins, taking care to wear a hat down on my face and gloves and a scarf to somewhat disguise myself. I did not want to be recognized, for I know how ungrateful my silence o'er all these years had been. Timing was important. There was some other family living where I had been raised. I asked of the maid, whereof the Mifflins? She said they had moved out to Fairmount up along the Schuylkill. I understood this to be Samuel's, my foster grandfather's, where I had seen the badger. I tarried at the port and spend a short time exchanging some tales with one of the seamen. From there I rode past the Dickinsons' and was there surprised to see a somewhat familiar face. A tall, green-eyed woman, nearly as tall as I, slim and attractive, but slightly graying in her hair, was throwing water on the pavement outside the house and started sweeping, cleaning the walkway as I trotted up on Janine. Looking up at me, she spoke, "You took long enough coming back, Joseph, much as we all thought you dead all these years."

"Hello, Essie," I said as I dismounted. She stopped sweeping and walked up and kissed me. "Come in and rest awhile, and tell me what you can." We went in, and she opened a jug of porter and then led me to the back garden. "I won't tease you anymore. Lord, listen to me, the way I'm talking. And you jes' like a regular Philadelphia gentleman." She fidgeted with her hair and then excused herself. While I waited, I mused that she still attracted me with her wit, rough beauty, and gentleness.

When she returned, it was obvious she had changed to a clean apron, washed, and combed her hair. We sat in silence for a while. The first sound was both of us speaking in unison: "I did miss you." Then I told her she should tell me first her stories, which revealed a tolerance for what had happened during the war. "Molly is married to a lieutenant in the Pennsylvania Guard. She has two twin boys, one tall and artistic and t'other, a red-headed scrapper. Sarah and Thomas moved away and never returned after the British took your old house. I think they may be living in Fairmount—though I have never seen them in town—Samuel, Thomas's father died jes' 'bout 'most eight months past. You might try there if you want to see them. Blessed Sarah was sorely saddened by you. They got no letters. She would be standin' there talkin' to a body, and then break down weepin' for no reason. She did this until the British left that June, then never again. I suspect she thought you and they was all allied, p'raps a Yankee hater. Mister Thomas was occupied with General Washington, so we rarely saw him, and when we did, he never mentioned you or showed a care. I looked for letters, too. Then, with the occupation, I gave up hoping."

"I can imagine. I have wronged many."

"I've heard no word of your real mother, Belle, or Fling Mountain, 'cept he was put in the gaol by the soldiers when they were here, for drunkenness. He may still live in the Northern Liberties, there by the river." I told her that I sent several letters and a note to her and the Mifflins, but when I received no news, thought only that the war had disrupted everything.

"When you didn't return, I married. You know, Joseph, I was always sweet on you, teasing you and tempting you with things. Still am, a bit. My husband, John Wheaten, died only a year after our wedding at the Battle of Brandywine. Didn't have the time to make babies. The Brits did not take this house, so I stayed on after they left in the spring. I would be much pleased if you could stay for dinner, and maybe a night or two before you travel."

Again, there was silence.

"I'll stay; but I must find out if Mother Belle and Fling are still alive, and if Sarah and Thomas will welcome me back. I couldn't live here without their forgiveness. I have a little silver. Let's go down to the tavern to sup, and then walk the city?" And we did.

That night Essie made a bed for me on a divan; we drank tea and talked for hours. Her tales of the war made me realize I might have been sent to London by the Mifflins to get me away from harm. I talked most about my sea experiences. Some about Jamaica and Ste. Dominiquè, and New Orleans. Essie had thoughts of all the cities she'd like to visit; Paris and Madrid and Rome. I painted a pretty picture of those places to feed her thoughts and be kind. I had not the heart to talk about the fetor in those cities, as well as London stink. It was well after midnight when she retired, and I slept.

The next day she woke me with the aroma of chocolate steaming hot and the smell of bread from her oven. She also had fresh apples from her neighbor's tree. We sat in the garden behind her house in our bed clothes and continued our histories, I omitting the robberies and the slave ship. Essie had business that day at the Athenaeum, and then the printer. She said the latter was Mister Franklin, who I had met long ago, who was gaining in fame and who flirted with her. 'Old Ben likes the girls. If you were one, you'd be sure to be pinched. He will try for your breast, but the fanny is his favorite target.' And then she laughed with me until tears came. She said his devil would advertise the goods she wanted to sell and could no longer use. She said money was scarce, 'cept when she could bake goods or sew and darn. I told her that I understood, now that I no longer went to sea, that I, too, would have to seek some employment in the colonies. After I dressed, I saddled the mare to go to Reading and seek my mother Belle, and said I would return early enough to see Fling, if he was not in gaol for drinking. I would meet Essie at her house for supper.

Several hours of riding to Reading reminded me of Hyde and me on the way to Yorkshire. What profit we had those days! I went to my mother's house, but it had been fired and destroyed during a British march; neighbors told me she had moved to New York, and one had her address. She said I could find her there. I thanked her and took the paper she wrote. Reading was a town that had no charm and had nothing for me, so I returned by way of the Germantown highway, a fine road with little traffic. Janine did not look it, but she could gallop. It took little time returning. When I arrived in the Northern Liberties at Fling's old house, I was sorely disappointed. He had passed. He was my real father and had passed to what glory there may be after the grave. I spoke no prayer. Sat in saddle for 'a time, thinking how hard life could be, silently sent prayers forth for him, and rode away. He had always been a stranger.

Thence on to Essie's. She was smiling to greet me and kissed me on the lips, long and softly. "It's so good to see you and wait for you on a day," she said. I told her of Fling's passing. He had been buried in a Potter's field. They found him dead on Front and Brown, just below Germantown Road, at the roadside, a flask by his side. She asked of my mother, and I showed her the address in New York. "I have to try to see the Mifflins tomorrow. Would it be proper for me to stay another night? . . . neighbors talk, Essie."

"You may stay as long as you wish, Jo. I like us together. I shouldn't have been such a tease." "Tease as much as you want," I told her. "I'll stay the night." We supped and talked. And just as casually found the bed, where we loved each other tenderly. As I lay there with her, this time I spoke of my errant boyhood and Hyde and Wilson, playing the fiddle, some little about robbing the rich, life under the Admiralty, my foolish attempts to join the pirates, and finally, the *Lethe* and the changes it wrought in me. How like a flash of light on a dark sea; truth, freedom, and virtue were revealed, and I promised the Creator I would alter my life to improve man's life. For some of it, we laughed at the recklessness of youth. At the end of my story on the slaver, I found myself clutching Essie and weeping for the first time since I had left. Together, we drifted; then slept deeply.

On the morning, I kissed Essie and told her I was going to Fairmount. I would be back by afternoon. I was steeling myself for a righteous response. Yet I knew, like some popish sinner going to confession, I should face my penance and be shriven.

It was so pleasant, I stopped for some time as I crossed the Schuylkill at the bridge, and then at the road along the stream the local folk call the Wissahickon. This was the forest I remembered walking with Grandfather Samuel when he taught me to name so many trees. I still could call out their names. This was where we young boys swam and had our hideaway. When I did this, muttering to myself, Janine would turn her head and look at me—thinking, I imagine: what is this lunacy? I let her travel at her own pace that lazy day.

At the by-way to Samuel's home, I turned her. When I dismounted, she grazed as I asked the woman cutting flowers whether this was where the Mifflins lived. She stood erect, eyeing me suspiciously.

"It is, sir."

"Are they at home?"

"No sir."

"When will they return?"

"Don' know for sure."

"When would you guess?"

"Free, maybe four week, I es'pect"

"Where have they gone?"

"Whereever, maybe Nort' if that's where Boston be."

"Is there someone else here I may speak to?"

"No, sir, jes' po' me. That enuf?"

"I don't know."

"Yo don' know a lot, do yo?"

"Young lady, do you know anything that can help me, or do you know nothing?"

"Well I know that yo don't know nofing enuff to acks me what yo wan' to know."

I was tired of this terse conversation, so I told her that I would return in a month, and that she should let Mistress Sarah know that her son, Joseph, has come home and wishes to beg her forgiveness.

The woman stopped her gathering and said "You Josip?" I nodded.

"Den you come back. Fo' sure, Missus be very delightful to see you."

She went back to her flowers, and I rode home by way of the Pennsylvania College, down new streets and lanes. I turned to the harbor. There I reserved passage for New York on a ship thence. When I returned, Essie had a cool, wet rag to wipe my brow and a tankard of cool ale. We were lovers now. That evening after stories had been told, we lay between cool sheets, and I looked at her two pink nipples she had teased me with, kissed them and her, and loved her.

The next day, Essie and I visited the docks. Watching the crews unloading and loading, she asked if I missed it. I told her that everyone most certainly misses pleasant memories, that when I returned from New York, we would fashion our own. We passed the day in one of the squares near our old neighborhood, the one between Fifth and Seventh streets near Walnut. When we were younger, it had been a midden where local merchants and families dumped their refuse, but it appeared the war changed their attitude about the city. Now neatly raked and planted with beds of flowers, shrubbery and some trees, it gave us an arbor to enjoy our day. Essie had filled a basket with cold meat, fruit, bread, and porter. She was lovely and loving. I rested on the grass with her.

I was chary but asked her, nevertheless, if I could leave some of my silver with her. "For safe-keeping." She took no meaning otherwise. When I packed that evening, I left her with everything except what I needed to live modestly for a week, and my passage back. That evening was like the last. I felt in love for the first time and was happy. When I left for my ship the next day, I was hopeful for a good life, forgiveness, and amity before me.

It was August 1789. I left Philadelphia in the *Briton* with a cargo of bread, molasses, rice, and flour, owned by Mister John Murray, jun., and travelled to New York to find my mother, Belle Lee.

Chapter 14

The Briton, a fleet packet delivers our hero to New York, where he acquaints himself with the denizens, eats Chinese food, and searches for his mother. He experiences an opium dream that bewilders him even more about life and his destiny. He is stopped in time.

The *Briton* was a mid-sized packet and very fast. Her Captain, a Mister Sloan Skitter, was very able in the rough waters along the New Jersey coast. He made his business from passengers like me who traveled the short trip between Philadelphia and New York. We left from the foot of South Street, a place that had fond memories, for it was there I learned the yarns of sailors, stories of pirates, exotic ports like Analanjirofo in Madagascar, where many pirates are buried on Ile Sainte-Marie, Mombasa in Africa, and Chanderonagore in India, and other tales that fed my imagination. After a reach down Delaware Bay, we were once again on the ocean I knew. I remember Sails, my first sailing teacher, saying that sailors appreciated Madagascar's vast numbers of good fat beef, chickens, eggs, and fresh fruit. He said pirates would say, "Gone to Madagascar for lymes," and leave that message at places they hid, because they loved to attack ships from India and Africa there. I got lost in reverie for a moment and realized we were nearly to New York. I spoke to Cap'n Skitter after asking his mate permission, and he was happy to spend some time at the helm learning where I had sailed.

I did not get to know him, but I did learn of his schedule, and told him I would return with him in a week or two. In two nights, I was in New York, the *Briton* anchored in the East River. Along the way, there was much to see that had been damaged by bombardment during the war. As we came near the port, especially, skeletons of boats burnt and warehouses demolished lined the harbor. We anchored, I was told, at the tip of Manhattan Island. When I left the ship, I was within walking distance of Pell Street, the address I had for my mother—I was told by Cap'n Skitter's son, a lad named Robby, who helped his father on these short trips, that there were many Chinese there.

I set out enjoying the new town at a goodly pace, for it was late in the afternoon. I sought the address: 13 Pell Street (steps from Division and East Broadway). 'Holt on to yer money. Chinamens don't like Yankees or blacks or anyones 'cept themselves,' Robby had said. It was a longer walk than I expected. When I kept the *"northerly"* course, as the boy put it, I encountered some of those who had not only the misfortunes of war, but of an enemy occupation. My spirits dropped. There were many homeless in tatters that hung like shrouds, and children so filthy one could easily think them piglets, loosed from the stye to scramble for food or any man's leavings.

To raise my mood, I entered a tavern and ordered a brandy. The greeting I received was less than cordial, with patrons whispering loud enough so I might hear words like "slave" and "blackie", "criminal", and I expect because I wore my city clothes, "British bastard." And none of the patrons was Chinese. I finished quickly and took off my coat to carry, not wanting to attract attention, even though the breeze from the water was cool.

I tarried as I walked further on, looked in at a ruined church whose only resemblance was the remaining stained glass on one wall. It was much like the skeletal remains of some glass whale. It was there I began noticing many Asians in the area, and discovered from a hawker outside a restaurant that this was where indeed many Chinese lived. Many of African blood, free of fetters like me, but at a glance less fortunate also.

It being mid-day, I ate at a place they called Phoo Suk. The food was exotic, and I tried duck with lychee, rice, and apples mixed with sweet meats. It was delicious. They offered warm rice wine, which did not suit my taste. Beer was less dear. And cooler. It was a pleasant place, where many who waited on me bowed and smiled and bowed and smiled, so I passed the time there to rest and smiled and was smiled at.

I spent time safeguarding my purse as much as a warden, for there were Asian footpads, I was certain, on the lookout for a visitor to touch. I thought over what I would say to Mistress Belle when I finally saw her. I asked the proprietor where 13 Pell was. He took me to the door, and pointing and nodding many times, smiling and bowing, said, "Go one street, right, go two streets, go left, then go right, right, and left," and bowed and smiled when I left. I followed the path and had to double back, ask a passerby who smiled and bowed, and finally found 13 Pell. Not what I expected.

Next to the door, a small brass plate had the address and the words *Hua-yan jian* with Chinese characters. The door was framed with the bodies of naked women and mythical animals and flowers carved into some wood which I had never seen. When I entered, I was greeted by a small Chinese man who bowed and smiled and, seeing my clothes and complexion, spoke politely to me in English, "How may I help you, sir?" "What is this place?" "Ah, this place flower-smoke room. We have naked women do what you ask, and we have opium to smoke. You may have one or both. Separate or together, no matter. What do you prefer?"

'I am looking for a woman named Belle Lee. She is from Reading, Pennsylvania, and she is older, no longer a flower. I have your address for where she lives." I showed him the paper. My host's smile had disappeared, but he was still polite. "Why you want her? You police?" I stood up as tall as I could and told him proudly, "No. She is my mother. I have been gone many years. I wish to see her."

"Oh, you finally come to see her. At last. Now? She not here now."

I was struck by these words. Will everyone be absent from my life, now that I am trying to return? I asked Chuan, for that was his name, whence she had gone, and he told me she left this morning on business. That she was expected to return this evening. He crossed the room to me when he saw the desolate countenance I wore and said come enjoy some tea to wait, maybe have a pipe or two to clear my thoughts. I ordered tea.

While I waited, I read the *New York Gazette* and the *New-York Daily News.* While I read, there were a few customers who were escorted to the back of the building by wonderfully delicate and powered women with pink cheeks and long-lashed dark eyes—in kimonos that were shimmering pieces of artistically worked cloth—who in mincing steps seemed to enfold their clients in their silk robes. They kept whispering the words *ya-p'iàn,* which Chuan explained was the word for opium.

I read an interesting story in the *Daily News* that told of three condemned men which were executed near Brooklyn Heights in the same place where there had been a fierce battle during the war. Their friends were begg'd to be anatomized. It raised my curiosity about doctors and medicks to use dead bodies to study, and I thought for a while that it might be a possible occupation for me if I went to Pennsylvania College on the Schuylkill. Dr. Mountain, imagine that!

My thoughts wandered. I did not want to leave; it might be hours; I wasn't hungry; I had counted the pictures on the wall; I had examined them. I counted the tiles and re-counted, lest I was wrong. There were 46 or 47, I don't remember. I decided that while I waited, I would smoke a pipe or two. I called Chuan. I paid for three pipes and privacy, no flowers. Nevertheless, a beautiful girl named Lotus, no more than sixteen, with skin so white, my own looked ebony next to her, escorted me to a small chamber near the back of a long room with many tiers of smoky occupied pallets disappearing into the mirk. When I had been a sailor, I frequently was told of places like these. At the fancy Jelly Houses in London, there were often fops who, having smoked opium or the Jamaican tobacco that the Maroons used, would dreamily wander into the card rooms while Francis Hyde and I were gaming. They were as silent as somnambulists; when they spoke, it was incoherent dream-like nonsense, then. Now there was an enfolding silence, marked from time to time by slow exhalations.

The room Lotus brought me to was lavish in its décor, and clean. She made green tea for me and placed cushions so I could sit comfortably. She sat with her paraphernalia at the small table, unwrapped the opium. Lotus then smiled at me while she kneaded the paste, trimmed the wick on the lamp, and placed a third of the smoke on a wire that she turned into the flame of the lamp until it nearly bubbled. As the first wisp of vapor began to lift, Lotus gently handed the pipe to me and helped me hold it. She instructed me to suck in the luscious perfume while the vapor rose, and I began to see clearly what paradise must have been.

As I watched her scrape the pipe and prepare another, time vanished. I finished my third and lay seeing Essie. Lotus had poured my tea and had gone. I thought about my plans, and of Two, Ogé, Nanny's-niece, Pierre, Javier, Mistress Sarah, Paul-Joseph, Fling, Belle—what will I say to her? —Francis Hyde, Humphreys, Tom Wilson, Paris, Fern and our rides, the many ships and places I had been; I thought of them with such clarity that I reached for Essie, only to find her missing. The stink of the streets was not there. The air seemed perfumed like the lilac-scented air of the French countryside. I thought of my absence and my thefts, my selfish days and nights, of the blood sports and their cruelty, and of the *Lethe*—that nightmare of suffering that was for me the paradigm of man's cruelty. I saw this all through the smoke dream, dozed and awoke to revelations of my sins and wept. I drank some more tea which Lotus had made, and then idled and continued my thoughts. It was then that my fortunes wove themselves into my dream and I experienced the truth of knowing, for I saw a courtroom with me in it and no return. It frightened me. Lotus sat beside me and calmed me and made one more pipe. The last removed my fears. I once more was in an Eden. Calm, dreamy, misty, lavender and perfumed haze.

Chuan came to get me after a time and led me through a massive room like those I'd seen in storage houses on the docks in France and Italy, with nearly all the space holding pallets stacked three-high, each holding a man sleeping or dreaming or smoking, and so hazy that I believed I was myself succumbing to the tantalus perfume of opium smoke. Then the old Chinese led me through a door with its smoking men seeking paradise to the front of the house, where a woman stood in a moire silk gown waiting for me. She smiled. "I see you've become a man, Joseph, so handsome." She crossed the carpet, hugged me and kissed me on both cheeks. "I thought you were in Heaven or gone to me." She paused to look at me. "Now that you are here, let's sit; let us try to erase all the blank years." So, we sat and erased them for an hour, and erased some more.

I learned her story. How Fling, always drunk, beat her and then left her alone when I was born. How Samuel Mifflin let her stay until I was walking, and then dismissed her. She had no way of caring for me, so she agreed to have Mistress and Mister Mifflin adopt me. She had moved to Reading to avoid Fling, worked as a mid-wife, then in the war as a nurse. She once rode to Philadelphia to visit me, but the Mifflins and I were all gone to unknown parts. After the war, there was nothing for her there, so she came to New York. She could get no work. When hunger and homelessness taxed her beyond relief, she joined with four other women and sold herself. Once she became addicted to the smoke dreams, it was easy. "Forgive me. I did not know you, Joseph. I tried to survive."

It was four years before Fortune smiled on her. The owner needed a manager. Her body was too old to please the men who came there. "I persuaded him I would be someone he could trust, and he put me in this position. I balance accounts, train the young women who seek us out, oversee their health (which means some men have to go elsewhere), and have some comfort from the pipe." I didn't press her. In turn, she let me glide over the robberies and transgressions, as Essie had. *Forgiveness* is a woman with a wide apron between her knees. She holds the small fruits of her virtue there, to generously bestow on men such as I.

I wanted to get her outside, to do something. "No, Joseph," she said, "I feel safer here." She ordered tea and we talked all night, while Chuan saw to his business—a generous man, and kindly for his occupation. I had seen some like him in London who lived only for the money they could suck like insects, like blood, out of women's bodies. It appeared he was different. I told Belle I was returning to Philadelphia and Essie, that I meant to stay there, and that when I did, in a few weeks, I would send her money to return to live with us. She could live with us, or not. She had a room, she said, next door at No. 15, and that she could safely get the money there. At dawn, I quitted the den and kissed her goodbye. I said I would see her after noon. We would walk about and see the

New York I had heard so much of. I needed sleep, and not the kind I would have there. I left and walked uptown through a warren of small shadowed and threatening streets, aware of all around me like a hunted bird, until I reached a green bright park and found a small hotel, where I slept for the morning.

When I woke, a soft light had seemed to fall on me, for I had met my mother. I was certain I could help her reclaim her life. It is odd that I had been fated to live without the dire needs so many people have. But poverty, ignorance, distress, and thirst afflict so many that one wonders how a being has the strength to persist in living. Then if one is lucky, he reasons out where he has reached in life and why, and understands why it was not what he thought it would be years before. Maybe one day at an age, one says to blazes with it. "I've had enough ignorance and cruelty, stories of the treatment of one man to another or some dumb animal or child, gives up, and then dies, choosing to die instead of trying to bear more of it." I felt that my mother and Essie had many years of a good life ahead. I dressed, had some bread and meat—I know aught—and ate an apple as I walked toward Pell Street and mother's home.

I noted the wealth of some of these New Yorkers and the absolute rag-tag poverty of others—especially the children, who wore little but rags, had no shoes—known from their smell, not their demeanor, had they washed. They begged, but I resisted giving away my scarce money, though I sorely wanted to take each little one for a meal and some clothes, each Paul-Joseph in another's lives. I remembered the day before I left New Orleans when we went shopping, and he stood stupefied as I helped him pick out his new clothes. My memories buoyed me as I made my way.

Mother was ready as soon as I knocked. She too seemed afloat on the breezes that came from the harbor. She suggested the walk, and I followed. We avoided the mud and horse dung and wandered along a causeway past some shops and restaurants for a while. We purchased some bread and cold meats and a bottle of wine, and ate, as the Italians would say, *ala fresco*, looking over the sights on the East River. There were many fine ships there. I told her some of my sailor's history.

Mother tired easily, so we returned soon after. She would not have me in her quarters, saying it had to be cleaned. I believed she was embarrassed. Outside her door, we embraced and kissed and took our leave, knowing in a few weeks, life would change for her. I walked up Thompson Street to a large park which was full of life with a bounce in my step. For a while I watched the mothers pushing prams, a juggler who kept dropping his balls, and some small group of street Arabs and guttersnipes. After I read the *Gazette*, I sunk into a reverie about Mother's fortune and those who told me mine: Janine, Sybil, Nanny. All women who had a gift. Like their nature, they were sensitive to life and thus could look into a man's heart, if he was open to it. I had been on a long road; I felt no lashes save for my guilt and had seen no long rope. I nodded, then dozed, awoke, and nodded again.

I dozed on a bench. When I awoke, the sun had almost set. The square was nearly empty, the shadows getting long, and the light vibrating. I roused and got my bearings and started for my lodgings. Just then a young lad, no more than seven or eight, his hair a bramble and his clothes mere shreds, stopped in front of me and asked:

"Sir, if you please, do you have the time?"

Chapter 15

*Joseph awakens with an aching head
and some losses. He takes his leave from Belle, meets
White Moon, earns some money, follows a whim,
receives his lashes, and learns what some of his fortunes
meant.*

A small, white, dirty waif. He had asked me the time. I should have known. To those in the know, "Do you have the time?" or some variant was the alarm that a theft was about to take place. I would always ask, as the London footpads from the age of 5 had learned, for the time to stop my mark and put him at ease. Now American footpads were using the London line. No translation was needed. I had reached for my watch, I remember. That was it. Until I awoke, I remember nothing else. I lay on the same bench with a sore and bloodied head, a newspaper neatly placed like a tent over my face. It took me some minutes to gather my senses. I heard voices around me. When I removed the newspaper, it was a bright morning and there was a couple standing in front of me who spoke, "Times a wastin', lazy bones. Time to get up." Then they giggled as if they were teasing me. They stopped when they saw I'd been bludgeoned. "You're hurt," the woman remarked.

"I'm peachy." I smiled as I sat up. The ache I had was nearly intolerable. The woman asked if I was sure, and I nodded, so they would go. When they did, I gazed into a puddle on the walkway and saw my pitiful swollen face and torn shirt. I tried to straighten up. I had been smart enough to keep my money safe in a pouch near my privates. The footpads had gotten my 'thieves' purse' with three gold crowns and taken my coat, my watch, and a gold ring—and much of my pride. They missed my pouch, my tarnished silver shoe buckles, and my papers.

I went to my lodging and washed, changed my shirt, paid my bill, and left to see Belle. As I walked to the Chinese town, I thought, "Sir, do you have the time," meaning "Give me your watch," and other things. The irony: I, an adept highwayman, robbed by some small thieves—Irish ragamuffins. I knew how my victims must have felt, even though I never laid hands on one in such a violent manner. I had a powder from the hotel keeper, who had cast an inquiring eye at me and my state when I had arrived. I took the powder, drank some willow tea, and my head was somewhat better. I had no broken bones, just the megrim and a two-inch cut on the back of my head.

I wandered back to Pell Street, a little unsteady a'times, and knocked at No. 15. "Joseph, dear boy, what has happened?

Belle looked at the bruise and swelling and tsked the way women do. After I explained, she asked if I had enough money to get home. I told her not all was lost, but now I must find some work to get home, maybe a day or two's pay. She offered from her modest purse, but I could not allow it. She gave me a hat such as sailors wear, and I pulled it on to cover my wound. She then said the rich live in Connecticut and they have plenty of boats. May haps I could find a mechanic's job from some small boat owner. She gave me directions to head north. She forced 8p. upon me for the ferry I must take. We spent most of the morning resuming our lives. I took my leave, telling my mother that she should expect to hear from me by mid-month, after I had asked Essie.

I set out on foot, but as fate would have it, a waggoneer going to New Haven said he'd give me a ride if I helped him load some bags of horse feed. So not all was wrong with the world. I took his offer. His name was Wicket. Wicket and Mountain, horse feed purveyors, we called ourselves after riding for several hours and drinking hard cider. Wicket was a puzzle, as he had said nothing of my race since we had met and treated me as an equal. He talked of the war; I, of the sea, and later of loves gained and lost. Wicket and I stopped, to sleep the night in and under the wagon and rest. I was beginning to feel happy about my mother, about Essie, and life in America. I slept under the wagon.

We reached New Haven the next day, where I took my leave of Wicket, wishing him Godspeed and thanking him after we unloaded some of his wagon. As Belle had said, the harbor was chock full of sallops and smaller boats, some sloops and frigates and a few large cargo boats lading or discharging cargo. It would be easy to find work. The day had been long, however, and I was fatigued, so I found a secluded copse and slept that night under the Creator's star-dotted sky. I wanted to stay away from prying questions. I was fortunate I had my papers, for my wounds made me look like an escaped transported prisoner or convict or slave—not a gentleman *gens* from Pennsylvania.

Along the Connecticut River was beautiful country, verdant and arable. Folk avoided me, no doubt, for it took several days before I looked presentable enough to ask for work. So little of my wealth was left, I was now miserly; and, and, and let me be forgiven my oath and pilched food from small gardens and fruit from orchards to heal. I suppose my past sins were enough to make me deserve this. I had been so frivolous with the feelings of others, and selfish. I still would atone. When I had rid myself of my megrim and aches, I bathed in the river and clothed myself well enough to seek work.

I went to the port and found a ship that had arrived from Ste. Dominiquè with molasses for a New England rum distiller. They were unloading barrels without end. I had heard the New Englanders were the biggest distillers of rum but did not imagine they had such a thirst. Molasses was in big demand. While they worked, one of their winches had given way off-loading a barrel, and the men around were scratching their heads as if they were ignorant dolts, staring at the barrel and pulleys, agape. Their second mate was cursing so much, even I, who had heard much before, was embarrassed for them. I stepped forward and asked them to let me look at it. I guess I was being uppity. They jeered me. A thrill of anger went through me when I heard one of them say, "Blackies don't know nuthin' 'ceptin bein' nosy monkees." Still, I decided I would not react. It was easier to mime some miserable slave, so I said, "But, massa, I done fix sum o' dis' befor'," like the poor blacks I had met. I knew they had spooled the rope wrong through the winch.

The mate said, "Let him try." And I fixed it in five minutes. Then I bowed my head and subserviently stepped away. The mate stepped in, clapped me on the back and thanked me. I said I had been a mechanic, and did he have work in port. He asked my name and read my manumission. With that, I got a three-day job rerigging the jib and respooling their winches. I was offered more, but I said I had to return to Philadelphia. I was paid in gold Reals. No one bothered me. I still had outdoor lodging, but I could eat. When I left the ship, I set out walking away from the river, mistaking my direction for one toward the sea. Before long, I realized my error.

Walking along the river, enjoying the Creator's work, I saw a bald man idling near the water. As I approached, Nanny's-niece's words tolled in my mind: "You will see a white white man, feel the lash many times. . . ." I had not felt the lash, but now I saw an albino Mohegan so white as to make one's hairs prickle. A white not quite pure, with a shimmering undertone like nacre. I waved to him and spoke kindly, so he would know I meant no harm. He greeted me with a grunt. "Do you speak English? Parlez Françaisé?"

"I speak both."

We found a shady space to pass the time together. I shared what food I had, and he, his. And we told our tales. He was named White Moon, and his condition made him a distrusted outcast. The tribal sachem said he was an evil that would infect the tribe like the white's disease (this I took to be the pox). Thus, now neither white nor Mohegan, he was exiled merely by his color. I told him of Thomas Wilson and how easy it was for me to distrust him for the same reasons. We talked about the colonists' treatment of the Indian tribes and the whites' treatment of my race. We wondered aloud about why human beings can be so easily persuaded in ignorance. He warned me that the colonists here were apt to judge on caprice rather than reason. He had no home, no tribe. I took his advice to heart and parted, wishing him better fortune.

After several hours' walk, I found a glade and rested, drifting into sleep with thoughts still too large for my understanding.

The next day, as I walked down the river—this time in the correct direction—near some of the gentry's beautiful boats, admiring them as evening fell, some strange whim came upon me. On a richly teaked sloop, its fittings of brass polished in high luster, I saw a bowl of apples and beside it two Spanish pieces of eight. For some warrantless reason, I took an apple and the Reals. I needed neither the apple nor the money. I knew I was wrong as I did it. It was as if some mischievous imp had dared me. I was immediately apprehended.

A young lad on the opposite shore cried: 'Nigger! Thief!' pointing at me like a child in a schoolyard scolding some dirty man. My shore soon filled with men. I was in trouble, I knew, for the attitude toward blacks in Connecticut was malevolent, and I had been stupid. They talked a righteous talk on the surface, but deep down they thought I and others of my color were no better than savage apes. I had seen it with the child's cry, and in the port when I tried to help. White Moon had warned me.

I was restrained as I tried to run by two men who were like giants, bound with a sheet from one of the boats, and carried thence a short distance to stand before George Pitkin, Esq., the local constable. He took little time telling me I had no defense, and after many words and pointy, arrow-like fingers by those gathering for a show, I was adjudged to be whipped ten stripes. I could say nothing. I knew I was guilty.

But now I realized the punishment I was to receive was one specially laid upon blacks on land and miscreants at sea. I had seen the scars on the backs of men from such justice, and aboard ship I had examined the cat with its leather thongs studded with iron brads. I was soon to learn its bite. And my pleas nor my manumission made not a whit. Echoes of smoke, herbs, mystery and Tarot. Janine, Ogé, Nanny, and Sibyl had spoken to me.

I was taken to a clearing, my hands tied around a tree while I stood upright, and my shirt torn off. A crowd like those at Tyburn hangings in England had gathered, sharing opinions, and crying out righteously at the 'bad Afreek nigger man'. I did not find this odd. There is something in humans that fascinates them by the execution and judgement of those they feel superior to for not having 'sinned'. I was also guilty, I realize now, of the same thing when I went to rattings, and bear and badger baiting. We all love blood sports in a way.

The sentence was executed forthwith. The first lash was so sudden and so painful that I was surprised that such pain could exist. Then there were nine more, each seemingly worse than the previous. Ten stripes laid on with vigor by a strong man. In my pain for penance, I was left there and dismissed. This was the first time I was ever arraigned before any court. No event in my antecedent life produced such mortification as this; that a highway-man of the first eminence, who had robbed in most of the capital cities in Europe, who had attacked gentlemen of the first distinction with success; who had escaped King's-bench prison and Old-Bailey, avoided gaol and the gibbet; that he should be punished for such a petty offence, in such an obscure part of the world, was truly humiliating. It was humiliating most because I was called and punished like a slave with no value. When I spoke, my words carried no weight. To my fortune, they only took my blood and pride, for they did not search me, and the heat of their ire and haste to punish a black man made them forget the mite and the apple I had filched. I was still able to travel. It took me some time to recover as I rested there. They had thrown saltwater on my wounds and a bucket of fresh, and left me unbound. I retraced my steps back toward New-Haven.

As I travelled that day, White Moon was no longer where I had met him. But I met him later as I purchased a new shirt for a quarter the value of a Real. Along the road we both begged for crumbs and drops, little of which came, for I had heard that the Nutmegs, which they called themselves, thought slavery just; that black-skinned people were apes, that we were fearsome brutes, that they were...well, much different than white humans, and they treated natives even worse. This was a surprising difference from Louisiana or Boston.

I yearned for Essie and would find a way home. When I reached the town, I went to market for some bread and cider. I wrote a paper sign with 'Philadelphia' on't and stood in the market, with prayers for a wagon ride or such, with little luck. I found a place to sleep and rested. My wounds on my back were still bleeding, and t'other shirt I had, I needed to save for when I healed.

The next morning, I returned whence I came, ate some apples from the market, and some dried meat 'jerky' which White Moon shared. We sat in the shade of a maple that had just started to don its spring finery, red and russet. My pain had subsided. I felt again peaceful, sanguine. I watched the crowd; there were a few maids or cooks making purchases from the local farmers, some young boys rolling at hoops, two teenage girls who could almost be twins or sisters teasing some young swains. It was almost idyllic. White Moon started when he saw the young girls. I asked whereof his alarm.

Then I noticed young lads—courtiers—pointing at me and the Mohegon and saying things to the girls, who laughed and reddened. I focused on the market wagons to avoid their looks. I noticed the one girl with the freckles rise and dust off her frock, and then her sister. The older boy whispered in the freckled girl's ear, and she laughed and blushed. Something naughty. He and the other left for a moment, and returned shortly after dressed in white with feathers in his cap. An obvious insult to White Moon. They then left the laughing girls. I was relieved

I told White Moon to ignore their insults, but he still angered. We decided to start on the road south, thinking perhaps that a waggoneer might pick us up. I had freshened and the heat increased our thirst, so we drank our water and cider and purchased another jug. White Moon told me that the same girls had come near the village the day he was banished and joined in the curses of his people, that they and the men who only just mocked him were there, and called him a thief. Then one girl pulled her garment down to show her breast and said a white freak would never be able to have its pleasure. He was mortified. At the road to West Haven, we parted, I much saddened that such cruelty existed.

It was warm, and so I drank my cider, walking for New-York. At the distance of one mile, I met the unhappy girl whom, she says, I had so wantonly injured. I recognized her as one of the freckled girls from the market. She was in company with her sister in a wagon and going into New-Haven. 'Yo, blackie, where's your whitey Indian friend?' she shouted from her driver's seat. "He's gone. You should be nice to him. He has a sad life." "Pshaw, he's jes' a freak, and you is prolly escaped or sumptin bad." I began a conversation with them, and attempted by persuasion to have them carry me in their wagon. I said I was trying to get home to see my mother in New York. Still injured from the cat, and having had the cider, my words were slurred. The young girls were terrified at my conduct and endeavoured to avoid me. I offered them a Real if they only took me on the wagon. Upon this, when I reached out to the eldest girl with the coin I proffered, she struggled from me. I then caught the younger, and in tripping, by a mere chance consequently fell with her on the ground.

Something was wrong. I offered money for a ride, but again some impish fate tripped me up. I have uniformly thought that the witnesses were mistaken in swearing to the commission of a rape, which was the cry she made. We fell. She fell. I fell on her. That I abused her in a most brutal and savage manner—that her tender years and pitiable shrieks were unavailing—and that no exertion was wanting to ruin her, I frankly confessed to the court, though I know that I was merely serving those of the crowd who had put up the fierce cries by saying this. I tried to untangle and stand.

There was no reason to hurt her, and I did not. However, I may attempt to palliate this transaction, there can be no excuse given for me; unless intoxication may be plead in mitigation of an offence. But having had less than a tankard of cider, that hardly could be my plea, though it had been potent enough to enfeeble me.

They say it was a most cruel attack upon an innocent girl, whose years, whose entreaties must have softened a heart not callous to every tender feeling. When her cries had brought to her assistance some neighbouring people, they said I continued my barbarity by insulting her in her distress, denying an attack and pleading my boasting rights. I did. I meant no harm and showed the Real as proof. And I again saw the two boys who had been at the market with them. This was taken as glorying in my iniquity. Upon reflection, I am often surprised that I did not attempt my escape, I being the only *gens de coleur* among that white throng; I had no opportunity to effect it.

Alas, I was apprehended, chuffed and beaten about the head and body. Yet, by some unaccountable fatality, I loitered unconcerned, as tho' my conduct would bear the strictest scrutiny. Benumbed. Pride maketh the fool. I had come to believe my own dream of fairplay and absence of bias. The counsel of heaven determined that such a prodigy in vice should no longer infest society that screamed at me with foul and hateful epithets worse than "Nigger" "Monkey" "Rapist". All those words I had heard before, save the last. They disparaged me, my folk, my mother. That my accent was British cast more hatred on me.

As the men on the river had done two day's past, I was bound, this time so tightly the ropes bore into my wounds, and I cried out. This was to no avail. I was roughly dragged to the local gaol and imprisoned. My bonds were loosened. The keeper, seeing the blood on my shirt, took mercy on me and brought rags and fresh water. A large Negro in my cell helped me sit and removed my shirt and washed my back. I was so fatigued, I slept. I was awakened by the Negro, who said his name was Daniel Smart. I thanked him for his kindness. Then like a child I started to defend myself, saying, "I tripped trying to help her. I meant no harm. I was a bit unsteady from the cider. I am innocent. I only want to return to my Essie and home." Daniel sat and looked at me sadly. "How old are you, Joseph?"

"Thirty-two."

"I believe you know by now that the worl' in'n't fair. These mens will suit themselves, and you will be swept away. No matter what you meant or did or say. They 'ready make up their minds. Are you religious?"

"I am a Friend."

"As am I. Seek in silence. He will speak to you." And just then the keeper came, shackled me, and led me to the Justice's chambers. There was haste in the very air.

At four o'clock I was brought before Mister Justice Daggett for examination. The testimony was so pointed that I was ordered into immediate confinement, to await the approaching session of the Superior Court. I had no chance to prepare or speak in my behalf, 'though many times I interrupted to try to plead my innocence. I was returned to my cell. The prison was a fetid nourishment to my conscience, which now overwhelmed me like some great whale crashing down on me with the weight of my past sins.

On the 5th of August, last, I was arraigned before the Bar of the Superior Court. My trial was far more favourable than I expected. The white judgers and the black gibbering monkey. They would not let me speak, except as an answerer to the charges. There was every indulgence granted me which I could have wished; and the court, jurors, and spectators appeared very differently from those I have seen in Old-Bailey or in the crowd that witnessed 'the crime'. The jury had little hesitation, though; they pronounced me 'Guilty'. As I stood shackled with chains around my waist and legs, I was stunned. I beheld with astonishment that in a country where such a sacred regard it held to the liberty of the subject, no man's life can be unjustly taken from him. So, I waited sentence, for I knew I had done no harm and that despite vicissitudes of politics and anger aside, I would someday be released.

I would be justly freed. In the few days that intervened, I befriended Friend Daniel and told him of my plans to return to Philadelphia from New York, build a life with Essie, rescue Belle from her straits, and become a good citizen of the American States. I told him some of this book, of Mistress Sarah and Mister Thomas; of Fling, poor man. He had lived in Germantown and knew the city. We would meet some time. He told me he was only serving a month and would soon be released.

On the Tuesday following, the Chief Justice pronounced Sentence of Death against me.

Death.

I thought myself less moved with this pathetic address than either of the court, or any spectator; and yet, I confess, I was more affected by it than by anything which had previously happened in my life. I was stunned. Eyes closed, gippy, asea. My thoughts in Jamaica with the Maroons, 'a road like a long rope'. I was at its end. Just as paradise in New York had been shown to me, it had now been snatched away. Fortune with her legerdemain had substituted hellfire.

On the next Sabbath, I attended meeting with Daniel. Being older by some twenty years, he gave me support. The address was by the Rev. Dr. Dana on that day, and the subsequent advice and admonitions which I have received from the Clergy of this and other places were calculated to awaken every feeling of my heart. They were self-serving. My heart had been awakened on the *Lethe.* They said much gratitude is due from me to those gentlemen who have exhibited such a tender concern for my immortal interest. Immortality is ineffable but unknown, and I now faced what every man will know: mortality. They only cared for their apparent public piety.

As I sit awaiting my sentence, I realize that it will be centuries before my dream could begin to come true. I have heard when someone asked Daggett if I could defend myself, he said, "He is a black creature, what could he know?" Human beings have great gifts; few use them as the Creator meant. I have been asked to write an account of my life of sin so that Justice Daggett may publish it and gain monies for the 'poor, desolate creature' I so vilely harmed. I have given him an account—one that will serve *his* purpose. This account which

I have written, though, I am giving to Daniel Smart, who is being released tomorrow, along with Essie's address in Philadelphia, Belle Lee's address in New York, the few Reals I had left, my tarnished silver buckles, and my Book of Prayer. I have tried to be a good man, and a good Quaker, since the epiphany I had on the *Lethe*. God grant me mercy.

It now remains that I *die* a death justly merited by my crimes. 'The cries of injured innocence have entered the ears of the Lord of Sabaoth and called for vengeance.' If the reader of this story can acquiesce in my fate and view me 'stumbling on the dark mountains of the shadow of death' with composure, he will yet be compassionate to a soul stained with the foulest crimes, just about to appear unembodied before a God of infinite purity.

Joseph Mountain.

Justice Daggett saw Joseph Mountain hanged on October 1790 at 8:16 in the morning. There were only five at the execution, excepting those officials required to kill a man. Two women unknown to the criminal, two sailors visiting the city, and Daniel Smart, who carried a packet containing a Book of Prayer, a pair of tarnished silver shoe buckles, and a chap book in which Joseph had written an account of his life. Joseph's body was placed in a Potter's Field to rest. Friend Daniel read from his Bible two verses over his body:

"Certainly, I will be with you, and this shall be the sign to you that it is I who have sent you: when you have brought the people out of Egypt, you shall worship God at this mountain." and "When you pass through the waters, I will be with you; and when you pass through the rivers, they will not sweep over you. When you walk through the fire, you will not be burned; the flames will not set you ablaze."

And then Friend Daniel left for Philadelphia. If you wish to read Joseph's version of his life writ at Daggett's behest, which proceeds were for the benefit of the 'injured parties', please refer to the following:

Ed. by David Daggett, 1764-1851 Text encoded by Apex Data Services, Inc., Matthew Kern and Elizabeth S. Wright
First edition, 2003
Academic Affairs Library, UNC-CH
University of North Carolina at Chapel Hill, 2003. © This work is the property of the University of North Carolina at Chapel Hill. It may be used freely by individuals for research, teaching and personal use as long as this statement of availability is included in the text.

Author's Note

This a work of fiction, but Joseph Mountain's historical account has lived with me some fifty-odd years. I was a graduate student at Pennsylvania State University sitting in a carrel in Pattee Library, poring through microfilm of *Early American Imprints* for research on another subject, when I first read the account Joseph dictated while awaiting his execution. Joseph's story was immediately interesting. He had been raised a free Negro in the household of Samuel Mifflin, a noted Philadelphian, before, during, and after the Revolutionary War. As a free young man, he was given a stipend to travel to London and left a few weeks after the Battles of Lexington and Concord in early 1775. He had received a reasonable education for the time, was said to be able, well-mannered, and of good character. He was likeable and intelligent. Yet a 17-year-old boy is still a boy. He happened to meet two itinerant entertainers at a grog shop—young men—who performed entertainments by day, but who made their living as highwaymen by night. He was easily swayed to join them in adventure, Grand Tour and learning be damned.

Joseph was quite successful at his new profession, and over fifteen years of robberies and work at sea as a crew member on several ships, a broken marriage, and much travel, I suppose he laid up a decent fortune and a comfortable living, many adventures, and an education of sorts. But one passage stood out: He mentioned that he had crewed on a slave ship.

Now I had to imagine: what was it like to be a black on the vessel holding several hundreds of your own race, suffering unmitigated agonies in their bondage, under that deck? Surely, I thought, there must have been some epiphany in his life then, hearing their moans and anguished cries. He had to do something, merely to be human.

He had never known that agony, had been educated like a white and was treated like a black, merely because of color. And the record shows it was color that killed him. He was hanged, like Nina Simone's "Strange Fruit," for what was then not a capital crime, if a crime had been committed.

Reading more into his return to the new country, I found his punishment, and his account, quite in keeping with the misogynistic society, Puritan ethic, the miscarriage of justice, the over-weaning anti-black, pro-slave attitudes of his countrymen, and several hundreds of similar hangings. He was a free, American, well-educated black who may have been a thief, but was hanged for an alleged crime by a judge who was a devoted *pro-slavery* advocate. So, I formed a fiction of his brief history—my imagined life of what his might have been. His *real* 'History' was certainly written under the eye of Judge Daggett to profit the injured party, in the same way despots have prisoners make a statement that serves them. The fiction lies in those details that flesh out what his life would have been beyond the "sinner's account" in Daggett's document, "The True History of Joseph Mountain."

The eighteenth century was an enlightened hundred years, but mankind has a way of surprising us and disappointing us. Differences among us will always be an excuse for bias and bigotry. I wrote Joseph Mountain's story believing we can learn to ignore those differences.

Robert Kuncio-Raleigh
Wilmington, NC
June 2018

Acknowledgements

My sincere thanks to my wife, Sara, who, through many trials, has read and critically parsed this book. She is a paradigm of patience and love. Appreciation must also go to my fellow writers—Frank Amoroso, Dr. Hedley Mendez, Lee Ewing, Sean Cherwitch, Glen Taylor, and Myrna Brown—for their readings and some helpful suggestions. Lastly, to my editor, Sonya Bateman, for her painstaking reading of the final draft, and the staff at VBW for their advice and guidance, my heart-felt gratitude.

CPSIA information can be obtained
at www.ICGtesting.com
Printed in the USA
FSHW010113050819
60708FS